MW00669158

ACCOLADES

This book is so much fun it should be illegal. The third in the series doesn't disappoint, but delights. The author keeps coming up with fascinating historical Galveston locations to weave into her narrative.

No one can keep her in the corner--not even her Prohibition agent beau, James Burton. Will he finally learn the secret that stokes his jealousy of a rival who isn't really a rival? Will the bad guys gun him down or frame him? You'll have to call up the book to find out.
—*Noreen Marcus, freelance reporter and editor*

This is the best one yet. Lots of action, higher stakes and even more romance. I love all the Jazz Age references...A great mystery read.
—*Leti Del Mar, Author of The Inadvertent Thief*

I loved this. Quite simply, it's a lady's version of the popular T.V. show Boardwalk Empire. GOLD DIGGERS is full of mobsters, shady deals and dirty policemen, and you never fully know who's trustworthy. Jazz is feisty as the protagonist, she's fearless and doesn't give a jot what the chauvinistic men around her think; she's proving Agent James Burton was framed and that's that. She's great!

In all honesty, I don't know a whole lot about the Prohibition era but the author really seems to know her stuff, gently weaving in details without overwhelming or confusing an uninformed reader. The characters all have plenty of 'moxie' and are well thought-out and likeable. There's a constant sense of mystery that keeps you turning the pages, with a pace that's spot-on.
—*Charlotte Foreman, BestChickLit.com Blog (U.K.)*

A hugely enjoyable mystery....The setting is simply marvellous, the characters colourful, the mystery is well-plotted and overall the book is simply great fun.
—*ChristophFischerBooks.com (U.K), Top 500 Amazon Reviewer, Author, Time To Let Go, Sebastian, etc.*

ACCOLADES

Collier is a phenomenal writer who has a knack for making the reader connect on a different level with her characters.. The plot line always keeps me on my toes and I anxiously await the next page, the next chapter and the conclusion....A talented and emerging voice in the historical mystery genre.
—*Kimberlee, "Girl Lost in a Book" Blog*

I'm addicted to the Roaring 20's era, and this third installment in the Jazz Age Mystery series supplies an overabundance of fuel to feed that addiction. In other words, this book is pos-i-lute-ly the cat's meow! Jazz is at her prime this time around, using her wits and sleuthing skills to come to the aid of Sammy and Burton, both of whose lives are at stake.

We also get to witness grisly murders and near-murders, a gangster funeral, and Jazz showing her super-girly side. There is also more romance, but not enough to detract from the storyline. But it was the climax that kept me on the edge of my seat; the author's descriptions made me feel like I was right alongside Jazz in witnessing a definitive moment of the Prohibition era.
—*Kristen Swearingen, Amazon Reader/Reviewer*

This series just gets better and better. The heroine, Jazz, is feisty, fearless, full of moxie, and is a hoot. Journalism is the right profession for her—she's a nosy Nellie! But always with good intentions, and she's a great sleuth. Jazz and the gutsy, principled Prohibition Agent James Burton got closer in this third book in the series, and a little romance adds a spark to the mystery. I enjoyed the sideline with Jazz's Aunt Eva and Sheriff Sanders too.

Collier does such a good job of putting the reader in the 1920s with her attention to detail. I can picture the story as if I'm watching an old black & white movie. So much fun!
—*Amy Metz, Author of the Goose Pimple Junction mystery series*

GOLD DIGGERS, GAMBLERS AND GUNS

A JAZZ AGE MYSTERY (#3)

ELLEN MANSOOR COLLIER

Text Copyright © 2014 by Ellen Mansoor Collier

Photo Cover Design © 2015 by Jeff J. Mansoor and Ellen Mansoor Collier
Back Cover Design and Photo Enhancement: Ghadir Al Jaro

Interior Page Design: Ellen Mansoor Collier and Gary E. Collier

Cover Illustration: George Barbier, "Eventails," c. 1924

Alternate Cover Artwork: Vintage Photos

DECO DAME PRESS

All rights reserved. Published in the United States by Deco Dame Press
www.flapperfinds.com

ISBN: 978-0-9894170-6-8

First Edition

The text of this book is Garamond 12-point

CONTENTS

Read the Complete "Jazz Age Mystery" Series

By Ellen Mansoor Collier:

FLAPPERS, FLASKS And FOUL PLAY
A Jazz Age Mystery #1 (2012)

BATHING BEAUTIES, BOOZE And BULLETS
A Jazz Age Mystery #2 (2013)

VAMPS, VILLAINS And VAUDEVILLE
A Jazz Age Mystery #4 (2015)

PREFACE

By: Ellen Mansoor Collier

Before Las Vegas, Galveston, Texas reigned as the "Sin City of the Southwest"—a magnet for gold diggers, gamblers and gangsters. Inspired by real people and places, **GOLD DIGGERS, GAMBLERS AND GUNS** is set in 1927 Galveston, where businessmen rubbed elbows with bootleggers and real-life rival gangs ruled the Island with greed and graft.

During Prohibition, the Beach Gang and Downtown Gang fought constant turf wars for control over booze, gambling, slot machines, clubs and prostitution. To keep the peace, the gangs tried to compromise by dividing the Island into two halves: Bootleggers Ollie Quinn and Dutch Voight headed the Beach Gang, south of Broadway and on the Seawall. The infamous but long-gone swanky Hollywood Dinner Club on 61st Street and the Turf Club on 23rd Street (which became the gang's headquarters, renamed the Surf Club in the novels) were located in the Beach Gang's territory.

Colorful crime boss Johnny Jack Nounes ran the Downtown Gang, the area north of Broadway. Nounes once partnered with Frank Nitti, Al Capone's legendary enforcer, who tried but failed to muscle in on the local turf.

GOLD DIGGERS, GAMBLERS AND GUNS is loosely based on actual and fabricated events, leading to the Maceos' gradual take-over of both gangs in the late 1920s and early 1930s. Rum Row was an actual location 35-miles southwest of the Island off West Beach where the Beach Gang picked up its booze drops. Ollie Quinn owned the Modern Vending Company and leased slot machines and gambling equipment to other local bar owners and small businesses.

Like many port cities, Galveston greatly profited from Prohibition—bar owners, businessmen and bootleggers alike—until it was nationally repealed in 1933.

PREFACE

Enacted in January, 1920, the Volstead Act prohibited "the manufacture, sale, transport and possession of intoxicating liquor or distilled spirits containing more than 0.5% alcohol for beverage purposes." The Treasury Department employed hundreds of Prohibition agents to enforce the new law, but that proved futile as most local police and the public refused to follow the not-so "Noble Experiment."

The Maceo brothers, Rosario and Sam (Papa Rose and Big Sam), were born in Sicily and immigrated to Louisiana with their family in 1901. After moving to Galveston, they eventually took control of the Island, known as the "Free State of Galveston" for its vice and laissez-faire attitude, for roughly 25 years, from late 1927 on, until their deaths. The Maceo empire faded when Sam Maceo died in 1951 of cancer, and Rose Maceo passed on due to heart disease in 1954.

The **Galveston Gazette** is a fictitious newspaper, but the headlines in the novel are based on actual stories that appeared in **The Galveston Daily News,** the first and oldest newspaper in Texas, founded in 1842 and still in publication. Since many of the gangland crimes and activities went largely unreported and/or under-reported, the main characters and circumstances in the novel are fictitious and not intended to malign or distort actual persons or cases, but are purely the author's imagined version of possible events.

CHAPTER ONE

Saturday

"Champagne?" A tall, young waiter in a penguin suit hovered over us, holding a chilled bottle of Dom Pérignon. "Compliments of Sam Maceo."

"Of course. Just don't tell anyone." I smiled at the handsome youth, nodding my approval as he poured us two glasses of fizzy bubbly, his hands shaking—no doubt uncomfortable serving Champagne to a Prohibition agent in public.

Agent James Burton and I were celebrating at the swanky Hollywood Dinner Club a week after Galveston's annual Bathing Beauty Revue ("The International Pageant of Pulchritude"), pretending all was swell despite the death threat hanging over his head. He'd single-handedly managed to make a fool out of Johnny Jack Nounes, leader of the Downtown Gang—and how! Rumor had it, Nounes once partnered with Frank Nitti, Al Capone's enforcer, learning all the tricks of the gangster trade.

The crowd gasped, ostrich-feather fans quivering with excitement, waiting for Burton's reaction. Who watched us from behind those oversized menus? Gold diggers? Grifters? Goons?

"Yes, ma'am." He set the bottle in a silver ice bucket, blinked at me and scurried away.

Ma'am? At only twenty-one, I was already a ma'am?

"Do I look like a ma'am to you?" I asked Burton, feeling my face flame. After all my primping, did the waiter mistake me for an old maid? I'd dressed to the nines in my silk chiffon gown with a low-cut back and halter neck, long faux pearls and sparkly chandelier earrings. My mother always told me: Who needed money when you had style?

"You're the tiger's stripes," Burton replied, chivalrous as usual. "But I'd rather not be spotted here."

"Why not relax and enjoy the evening?" I smiled at him, sipping Champagne, awed by the lavish surroundings. "This is Sam Maceo's way of thanking you for locking up Johnny Jack. A Beach Gang club is the safest place to be, especially with the Downtown Gang gunning for you."

Who was I fooling? I was so nervous, my knees were knocking.

"I'm more worried about my reputation than Johnny Jack." Burton eyed the glasses. "This may not be such a smart idea. Drinking in public. What if we're seen—again?"

True, the scene was eerily familiar, reminiscent of the Surf Club fiasco, but now circumstances were completely different.

"James, you know drinking is legal if the liquor is on the house. Besides, it's considered rude to refuse a gift from our host." I smiled at him, pointing to the bottle. "As you can see, it's French Champagne and there's no Prohibition in France. When in Rome...or should I say Paris?"

"Galveston isn't exactly Rome or Paris. But I get the telegram." He grinned, taking a sip.

"A votre santé'!" I toasted him, lifting my glass. I wished I could pull out a Bakelite cigarette holder and have him light it for effect, but frankly, smoking made me nauseous.

I took a sip of Champagne, pretending I was a regular at the ritzy Hollywood Dinner Club, the high-class hotspot where everybody came to see and be seen. Lucky for us, the Maceos were on the best of terms with local officials, who liked to frequent the posh bar and casino.

Burton leaned forward. "Do you feel like we're in a zoo, being watched from all angles?"

"I'll say!" I nodded. "Remember, you're a local celebrity now. Getting noticed comes with the job, like it or not."

"How can I do my job when your newshounds are always following me around, trying to take my picture? Can't you do anything?" he complained.

"Me? I'm just a lowly society reporter. They never pay much attention to me."

Not the kind of attention I wanted anyway.

"Well, I may have a word with your editor-in-chief." Burton drummed his fingers on the table. "People are starting to recognize me on the street. They even come up and shake my hand, tell me I'm doing a good job. That's fine and dandy, but I'm not running for public office. How can I raid any speakeasies or stop any booze drops if they see me coming a mile away?"

He was right: With notoriety came a loss of freedom, and privacy. After all, he'd made a name for himself as the new up-and-coming Prohibition agent in town with articles and photos galore in the *Galveston Gazette*. If my social-climbing boss—Mrs. Harper, queen of Galveston gossip—found out we were here, we'd no doubt get a bold-faced mention in her society column.

I prayed none of the *Gazette* staffers had hidden among the guests, waiting for a scoop. Not that we reporters could afford such a ritzy joint, but a few promises at the door never hurt. Truth was, gangsters liked positive press as much as the Old Guard.

As I glanced around the swanky club, outlandish in its tropical safari theme, I noticed the well-heeled couples tittering behind cupped hands. A couple of vamps even had the nerve to make googly eyes at Burton! Did they recognize him from the paper?

The ten-piece band cranked up, playing a soft instrumental jazz medley, covering up our conversation. Swarthy Valentino look-alikes locked limbs with Theda Bara and Gloria Swanson copycats, in a sea of breathless tangos and rumbas. When the band played "Ain't She Sweet?", a swarm of couples rushed out to dance the Charleston and Black Bottom.

I sank into the plush plum leather booth, not in the mood to make a spectacle of myself on the dance floor, and broached the subject we'd avoided all evening: "What will you do when Johnny Jack gets out of jail?"

"Word is, he'll stay behind bars for a while," Burton said, smug attitude in place. "I hear he's got lots of old scores to settle and the cops and councilmen are cashing in—literally."

I stifled a smile. "So the longer Johnny Jack is locked up, the more money they collect? That's one way of making crime pay."

"I'll say. And they're in no hurry to release him and lose their cash cow. Or in this case, steer."

I grinned at the image of Johnny Jack on display like a prize bull at a state fair, leaving a trail of twenty dollar bills. Everyone knew he liked to flash his cash in public, but I bet his pockets were getting lean in prison. Still, I couldn't help but worry.

"Be realistic, James. They're bound to let him out soon."

"Why do you think I'm here? I'd rather be out with you than sitting at home alone, waiting for Johnny Jack to attack. Look at this place. Security is tighter than Fort Knox." He flashed a sly smile. "And this way, we both get a free meal out of the deal."

True, several bodyguards, armed and foreboding, lurked like massive lions stalking the fake jungle. I crumpled up my crisp white napkin. "Can't the police help? Watch your back?"

His mouth turned up. "Those palookas? They'd rather stand in line to get rid of me, right behind Johnny Jack." No secret that the local cops resented his presence on the island, claiming he interfered with their under-the-table shenanigans. So far he'd stuck to his principles *and* his guns. Fact is, he needed a few weapons if he wanted to stand up to Galveston's gangs.

In the background, I heard a scuffle, loud voices, furniture scraping across the floor, an object being thrown. Burton tensed up and turned toward the noise, slate-blue eyes darting around the room.

"What's all the ruckus? A fight?" I stared at the casino, hoping for some excitement. The other diners also shifted in their chairs, whispering and clucking like nosy busybodies. Finally a diversion from the "James and Jazz nightclub act."

"I'll go see what's wrong." Burton stood up just as two bouncers escorted, or rather dragged, a dark, disheveled middle-aged man in a top hat and tuxedo, toward the exit. His swollen face had taken quite a pummeling, resembling raw beefsteak. A bleached blonde floozy wrapped in a feather boa followed him, loudly complaining, "Unhand him, you beasts! That's no way to treat a paying guest. He won fair and square. The Maceos owe us money!"

I gripped Burton's arm, his muscles taut beneath his sleek suit. "James, wait. You're off-duty now. This isn't your department."

"I can't stop being a lawman just because I'm out with my girl."

My girl? When had we made it official?

Holding my breath, I watched as he approached the Maceos' men, asking, "Where are you taking him?" When they refused to answer, he rushed toward the commotion in the back.

How could I blame him? Curious, I leapt out of my chair and pretended to look for the powder room, making eye contact with the gun molls giving me the once-over. Did they think Agent Burton was going to raid the place?

Rows of slot machines and black jack tables sat positioned in full view of the dining room, beckoning diners to try their luck. A few gold diggers decked out in beaded gowns and feathers draped their arms over geezers old enough to be their fathers, if not their grandfathers, betting at the craps tables.

"Want me to blow on your dice, honey?" I heard one gal purr to a fat cat in a top hat. How could he refuse? Some guys in tuxedoes guarded a couple of closed rooms, scowling as I glanced their way.

I imagined the high-rollers were losing their shirts while club owners Ollie Quinn and the Maceos counted their profits like Ebeneezer Scrooge.

In the powder room, the mirrored walls reflected the elegant seating area with its marble wash basin and gold fixtures—real gold or plated?—straight out of a movie set.

"Nice gown." I smiled at a flashy flapper who wore an ice-blue sheath with a big bow on one hip, her plunging neckline dangerously close to revealing all her assets.

"Thanks!" she drawled. "You don't look so bad yourself, sister."

"Any idea what that fight was all about?" I washed my hands, acting nonchalant.

"Who knows?" She rolled her big blue eyes. "Those gamblers are always accusing each other of cheating."

I wanted to ask more questions, but an older Negro attendant handed me a fluffy towel with a frown. I rushed back to the table just as Burton returned with Sam Maceo glued to his side.

"Don't worry, Agent Burton, we've got this little misunderstanding all under control."

With Maceo's help, Burton stiffly sat down, Sam's hand clamped hard on his shoulder, pushing him into place.

Burton raised his brows. "So what happened?"

Maceo's eyes widened before he smiled, ever the gracious host. "Just a friendly game of poker that got out of hand. You know how boys get when they're losing all their jack."

"Who was that man?" Burton pressed. "The one with his nose out of joint."

"Some wiseguys got hot under the collar, that's all. Accused this city slicker of cheating. So Rose took care of the situation on the spot." Maceo shrugged it off, knowing his brother Rosario provided ample muscle and protection. "We call it cleaning house."

"Does this city slicker have a name?" Burton asked.

"I'm sure he does." Maceo gave him a pointed look, then turned his full charm on me. "Wouldn't you rather be enjoying the company of this lovely lady?" He took my hand and kissed it in an Old-World manner. I was dying to ask questions, but his courtly gesture caught me off-guard. "You write all those love stories for the *Gazette*, right?" His dark eyes pierced mine.

"I wouldn't call them love stories..." I sputtered. "You mean weddings, engagements, charity balls, that sort of thing."

"Well, keep up the good work, doll. I hope you two lovebirds enjoy your evening."

Lovebirds? I squirmed in the plush booth and stole a glance at Burton to see his reaction. But he seemed distracted, probably focused on the poor saps at the poker game.

Maceo patted my back, his hand warm against my bare skin, and disappeared into the crowd. I shivered, not only because I was freezing. The Maceos kept the temperature low to prove to patrons that the Hollywood Dinner Club was indeed fully air-conditioned— the first nightclub in the country to provide cool climate-controlled comfort.

"He wasn't very forthcoming, was he?" I said to Burton. "Did you see anything fishy?"

"A bunch of stuffed shirts sitting around a table playing poker. Seems a few goons ganged up on this joker, beat him to a pulp. Wonder if he really tried to cheat them?"

"Did you recognize anyone?" I asked. "Any bigwigs?"

"Not off-hand. I think the victim is from out of town, maybe a card shark. I wonder what they plan to do next. Take him for a ride?" Burton suddenly stood up, put on his new Stetson and held out his hand. "Let's go. Maybe we can follow them?"

Flustered, I grabbed my mesh bag, nervous yet excited at the thought of going on an actual police chase. "If you don't mind, I'll take the Champagne." I shoved in the cork and picked up the bottle. "Hate to let all this fine bubbly go to waste."

All heads turned as we made our exit, the staff gallantly opening the wide double doors. Outside, the humidity hit me like a slap and my carefree curls began to droop.

"It's a 1925 Packard convertible," Burton told the valet, scanning the area for signs of the men. "Say, did you see the last car that just left? Any idea where it was going?"

"Beats me," the youth said with a shrug. "But they were in some kind of hurry."

As Burton stepped off the walkway, following the valet into the parking lot, an old Ford swerved around the corner, brakes and tires screeching, headed right at Burton.

"Look out!" I screamed, dropping the bottle of Champagne, hearing it shatter on the pavement, spraying liquid and tiny specks of glass. Everything seemed to happen in slow motion: I saw a flash of light and heard loud, popping noises, covering my head as shots rang out, staring in shock when Burton collapsed on the lot.

CHAPTER TWO

I stood there in stunned silence, my hands over my mouth, my heart racing. Numb, I wanted to scream but no sound came out. In a trance, I raced over to see Agent Burton, staring at his crumpled form lying still on the lot. Surely this was all a mistake, a bad dream.

The valet leaned over, shaking his shoulder, saying, "Are you OK, mister?" But Burton didn't answer.

"Get his car! I'm taking him to the hospital!" I commanded the valet, then squatted down by James to see if he'd been seriously hurt.

"James, can you hear me?" I blinked back tears as I stroked his arm, looking for signs of life, but his body remained still. Damn it!

If I hadn't insisted that he accept Maceo's invitation tonight, then he'd still be alive and well. Why did this have to happen?

I bent down to check his breathing, then jumped when I heard: "Are they all gone?"

"James! You're OK!" I wanted to kiss him, but a small crowd gathered and I didn't want to create an even bigger scene.

"Let's make this look good," he said, reaching for my hand and scrambling to his feet. "Pretend they got in a shot." He clutched his side and began to moan, arm draped heavily across my shoulders, limping toward his Packard Roadster.

Sam Maceo rushed outside, clenching his hands, pacing the parking lot. Of course he didn't want it to get around that thugs were taking crazy potshots at the lone Galveston Prohibition agent.

"Did you see anyone? I know it wasn't one of my guys!" Maceo wasn't looking directly at Burton, and I had a sneaking suspicion he was more concerned about his fancy club and fine reputation than Burton's well-being. "Is there anything we can do? Those dirty bastards. I'll find out who did this to you and make them pay."

Burton attempted a weak smile. "Don't worry, I'll be fine."

"Sure?" Maceo patted his shoulder. "Send your hospital bills to me. I'll take care of it."

"That won't be necessary." Burton winced. "Too bad we have to leave so soon."

"Sorry this happened, Agent Burton. Come back anytime. Tab is on me." Big Sam forced a smile before turning toward the club, two goons on his heels.

"We'll take a rain check," Burton called out. "Thanks for the evening."

After Maceo and his entourage retreated, I told Burton, "Are you nuts? Why did you thank him for almost getting you killed?"

"Killed?" He observed the small group of gawkers gathered around the lot. "Who knows? I may not have even been the target."

"Oh really?" Shaken, I bent over and picked up his new Stetson cowboy hat, the one I convinced him to buy so he'd "blend in" with the locals, and held it up for his inspection. A clean bullet hole had been shot right through the crown. "Looks like they were aiming right for your head." I shuddered at the thought. Sure, I knew Galveston could be a dangerous town, especially at night, but I'd never personally witnessed any type of violence, let alone an attempted murder, while it was happening. Until tonight.

"They must think you're all hat and no cattle," I razzed him, hiding my anxiety.

"What in hell does that mean?" Burton frowned. "Remember, I'm a Yankee."

"All talk, no action. Big head, full of hot air." Clichés, I know, but it was the best way to explain our Southern sayings.

"I get it. Well, we'll see about that." He gave me a smirk while he studied the bullet hole, then put the hat on. "I'll wear it as a badge of honor. Damn thing may have saved my life."

"Worth every penny." At Eiband's, he'd grumbled about having to fork over ten bucks for the "damn thing," but now I bet he was glad he had.

As he slid behind the wheel of his car, I asked, "Want me to drive? Don't you want this to look convincing?"

"Hell, no." Burton made a face. "Then I'll *really* be in danger."

"You slay me." Glad to see he hadn't lost his head or his wit—if you call insults witty.

As we drove off, I could see that, despite his cool demeanor, Agent Burton seemed rattled, his hands not quite steady on the wheel. "Well, that put a damper on the evening. Let's hope Maceo can help me find these goons."

"Maybe the Maceos were in on it. This could all be for show."

"I don't think Big Sam condones that kind of violence."

"What about his brother Rose? The thugs he calls the Night Raiders? I've heard he's got a reputation for using force to keep folks in line, even people on his payroll."

Rose Maceo ran a secret group of goons who literally took the law into their own hands, sometimes lethal but always effective. Trouble was, the Maceos' form of justice usually favored the gangsters' so-called code of ethics.

Burton turned to study me. "I'll keep it in mind. But I think you'd better stick to your society stories, and leave the law enforcement to me."

"Gee, thanks." He sounded a lot like my editors, not to mention Mack, our cranky star senior reporter, and the rest of the *Gazette* staff, trying to keep the little woman in her place.

He turned on Beach Boulevard , heading east along the Seawall, away from the hustle and bustle of the tourist traps and hotels. Before they broke ground, Ollie Quinn and Dutch Voight had planned to build the Hollywood in a remote area of Galveston, far from cops' and clergymen's prying eyes. Still, with Sam Maceo's knack for publicity and fanfare, the Hollywood Club was *the* destination for celebrities and vacationers looking for some excitement and not-so-cheap thrills.

"Where are we going?" I asked. "Big Red is across town."

"Who said anything about a hospital?" Burton frowned. "I'm not hurt. Thought we'd drive around, see if we can find anything, or anyone."

"Don't you want to get checked out first? Make sure you're OK? That was a nasty spill you took on the pavement." I studied him in the dark, but all I could see was a scrape on his cheek.

"I have a feeling they might come looking for me there, and try to finish the job." Burton scowled. "Hey, I'm a trained Federal agent. I know when to duck. That fall was for their sakes, to make those goons think they got in a shot."

"Smart move." I recalled how my heart stopped when I saw him collapse. "But you almost gave me heart failure."

"You don't say." He gave me a sly grin, illuminated under the half-moon. "Does that mean you're worried about me?"

"Of course I'm worried! When someone takes a shot at one of my friends, it's serious."

"Oh, we're back to being friends now?" He set his jaw, his grin disappearing. "Maybe it's time I took you home."

"Where will you go?" I had no idea where he lived, but I knew it wasn't safe after tonight.

"Not straight home. Why do you think I'm driving around in circles?" His eyes narrowed and he checked the mirrors. "I want to make sure we're not being followed."

"Followed?" I hadn't considered that possibility, assuming, hoping, the shot was a random, one-time act—more of a warning than a sneak attack.

"Let's just say we're taking the scenic route. Will that help?"

I knew he was downplaying the severity of the situation. Normally I'd enjoy the drive, take in the serenity of the beach, the calm consistency of the waves hitting the shore. But tonight the darkness seemed flat, lifeless—and dangerous. I kept turning around in my seat, staring out the windows, behind us, in front of us, doing a 180-circle. At any moment, a shot could ring out again, and hit its intended target.

I had a brainstorm, but didn't want Burton to get the wrong idea. "Say, why don't you stay at Aunt Eva's boarding house for a night or two? We just had a boarder move to Houston so there's plenty of room. I know Eva would love to have you as our guest."

It was obvious that my spinster aunt had a little crush on the tall, handsome agent. Perhaps he reminded her of her fiancé, who died fighting in the Great War.

"What about you?" Burton eyed me, his expression softening. "Thanks for the offer, Jazz, but I don't want to put you or anyone else in possible danger."

"We won't be in any danger. Frankly, I'd feel safer if you were there." I didn't want to admit that I'd probably lie awake all night worrying about him, either way.

"I don't want to take that chance." His face grim, he checked the rearview mirror, and suddenly turned the car around. "So far, the coast looks clear."

"Any idea who'd want to shoot you?" I couldn't bear to use the word kill.

"Besides Johnny Jack? I'll bet there are a few bullets with my name on them. Last week I busted a small operation based in Houston. They were unloading their stock on the beach here and storing their stuff at some abandoned warehouse in east Galveston, then taking it to the bars along Harrisburg." Burton slowed down to pass a horse and carriage, the couple dressed in their evening finery. Had they seen us at the Hollywood? "They may not be too happy with me."

This could take all night. "So you have a long list of enemies."

"Ten miles long," he said with a nod. "Occupational hazard."

As we drove along the beach, I racked my brain trying to think of ways to keep James safe. He couldn't very well leave town, and admit defeat. And I doubted the cops cared enough to watch his back. "So what are you going to do?"

Burton shrugged. "What can I do? Hire a bodyguard? A hit man? Hide behind a human tank like Dino?"

Dino acted as my brother Sammy's right-hand man and personal watchdog at his bar, the Oasis. "Why not? Might be a good idea. It's only temporary."

"That's not my style. Even if I wanted to, I don't have the dough to get round-the-clock protection."

"It was just an idea." I let out a sigh. "Better safe than sorry."

When we neared the boarding house, he cut the headlights and slowed to a stop two houses down. "Sorry I can't walk you to the door tonight. Like you said, I need to be careful."

He reached over and gave me a hug, barely brushing my cheek, in lieu of a real kiss. I didn't blame him. I wasn't in the mood either.

"Sure you won't come inside? You could park your car in the alley across the street, sleep in the parlor if you want." I couldn't believe I was practically begging James to spend the night with me, sort of. A month ago, I wouldn't even have welcomed a kiss.

He shook his head and I saw uncertainty behind his steady slate-blue eyes. "Wish I could, but I'll have to figure this out on my own."

CHAPTER THREE

My heart heavy, I waved good-bye to Agent Burton as he drove off down the street, praying it wasn't the last time I'd see him. Who knew what Johnny Jack's goons had in store for the token Probie in town? Head down, I trudged up the brick walk, trying not to assume the worst, hoping the gunshot had been a fluke, a case of mistaken identity. Didn't half the men in Texas wear cowboy hats out to dinner? In the South, a Stetson was considered as dressy as a top hat.

Eva rushed to open the door, a look of excited anticipation on her face. I hated to sour her mood, so I averted my eyes and feigned exhaustion. My aunt wasn't fooled and reached over to rub my shoulders. "What's wrong, Jasmine? You look upset. Did you and James break up?"

So much for my poker face. "No, nothing like that...It's just his job can be very unpredictable. And dangerous."

"What happened?" She stopped, her eyes widening in alarm. "Didn't I warn you about those high-falutin' spots like the Hollywood Dinner Club? The only people who go there are gangsters and ladies of the night!"

"Don't forget, the kick-off dance performance for the Bathing Girl Revue was held there just over a week ago," I reminded her. "The Sealys, Moodys and Mayor Hodgkins aren't exactly gangsters."

"Well, who knows what they do behind closed doors?" Eva huffed. "If you consort with goons and gold diggers, then...as they say, birds of a feather..."

She had a point. Sure, behind the façade of glitz and glamour, the Hollywood Dinner Club was in reality a fancy casino and speakeasy. How else could the Maceos pay their bills and attract such famous performers as Ray Noble, Sophie Tucker and the Ritz Brothers? Still, I didn't feel like defending the Maceos or their club, no matter how exclusive, not after tonight.

In a way, I wanted to confide in her, but wasn't willing to hear another lecture on the evils of Galveston in general and speakeasies in particular. After all, the Oasis was practically the only place where I could visit my half-brother Sammy Cook, since he wasn't a welcome visitor at the boarding house. Our well-meaning father had driven a wide wedge in our family when my mother found out Sammy was his illegitimate son—no matter that he was born years before they got married. What really upset her was the fact that my dad had left half his estate to his bastard boy. Surprise!

Sadly, my mother could hold a grudge forever and rather than face the truth, she'd left to spend the summer in Europe with her family. Somehow I predicted she'd remain there for a year or longer—to save face, and perhaps a little money.

"Jasmine, you know I'm here if you ever want to talk," Eva said softly. "You're my responsibility while your mother is away. I don't want you to make the same mistakes I did, and end up...alone." Her eyes misted and before I could reply, she returned to the kitchen to commence banging pots and pans around.

"Thanks, Eva," I called out but I doubt she heard me over the racket. Slowly I climbed up the stairs, wondering where James was at that moment. Was he going home or making the rounds at area speakeasies, looking for the get-away car and the shooter? What did he mean by: I need to figure this out on my own? What was he planning to do?

I needed to talk to someone who understood the dangers Burton faced, who knew Johnny Jack and the gangster's life—my half-brother Sammy. He was all-too-familiar with gang rivalries and revenge and turf wars. I couldn't risk calling him with Eva in the next room, and those Nosy Nellie's eavesdropping over the phone lines at the switchboard. Something this important had to be discussed in person. But now it was after ten o'clock and I doubted Aunt Eva would even allow me to leave the house, much less go to Sammy's bar alone so late at night.

Still dazed, I sat on my bed, staring at my floral hook rug, wondering what to do, worried to death about James. Were we being followed? How had the sniper timed the shot so perfectly? Did he deliberately miss or was it just a warning? Then a thought came to me: What if the hit man was hiding in the parking lot all evening, waiting for his chance? Maybe the valet tipped him off for a small bribe? These troubling thoughts raced through my brain while I paced my tiny bedroom, trying to think of a solution: Should he leave town? Go into hiding? Quit his job?

With a sigh, I took off my gown, watching the beads and sequins sparkle in the warm glow of my new geisha girl perfume lamp. Would my treasured gown always remind me of this terrifying night? I tried to get ready for bed but my mind and body wouldn't cooperate. How would I ever get any sleep tonight?

When I heard steps on the stairs, I rushed outside to see Amanda, finally back from working a late shift at the Star Drugstore diner. Who better to accompany me to the Oasis on such short notice, especially since she and Sammy were sweethearts. At least I hoped their tumultuous relationship was still on, not off. For my own peace of mind, I tried my best to stay out of their roller-coaster ride of a romance.

"Amanda!" I whispered, signaling to her in the hall, and pulling her into my room. "Put on a change of clothes and come with me to the Oasis. Please?"

"Now? What's the rush?" She frowned, and unpinned her blond hair from its tight bun, long ringlets spilling over her uniform. "At least give me a chance to bathe first. I smell like burgers and fries."

"There's no time," I pleaded with her. "Just spritz on a little Orange Blossom perfume and shake baby powder in your hair. No one will notice the difference."

"Sammy will notice," she pouted, taking a whiff of her long locks. "I don't want to smell like a greasy spoon."

"The Oasis doesn't resemble a rose garden. More like a smoky beer hall."

Amanda stared at me. "So what's wrong? You act like it's a matter of life and death."

"James' life may be at stake." I nodded. "Come on, time's wasting. Let's shake a leg."

She didn't need much excuse to see Sammy, but I had to commend her for going out on such short notice. With her long blond hair and blue eyes, Amanda was a knock-out and she knew it, and naturally she preferred to always look her best.

After changing into our glad rags, Amanda and I tiptoed down the stairs. Luckily Aunt Eva's bedroom door was closed and her lights were out. A good sign, since she liked to read late at night. Then we snuck out the back, hoping the Sheltie next door wouldn't bark and alert our neighbors to our nocturnal departure.

Fortunately the trolleys ran late Saturday nights. We got some curious looks when we boarded the car and sat in the back, trying to fade into the woodwork. In our ruffled frocks, we were a sharp contrast to the seats full of half-baked rummies and shop girls and housemaids returning home. Half an hour later, we arrived on Market Street, not far from the Oasis.

As we walked down speakeasy row, the street filled with laughing couples and a few blind-drunk bums, I had a chance to tell Amanda the story in as much detail as possible, considering I had no idea what really happened.

"Do you think Johnny Jack put the hit out on James?" Her face glowed under the tall Victorian street lamps.

"Probably. I wouldn't be surprised if the Downtown Gang is behind the whole thing. Maybe they set up a plant at the card game, and they found out and kicked him out?"

"Isn't Johnny Jack still in prison? Why shoot at a Fed agent in such a public place?"

"Payback," I explained. "Johnny Jack is furious that Burton threw him in jail, instead of Sam Maceo. So he's trying to discredit the Maceos, and ruin their good reputation as well as their business."

"Two birds with one stone...or should I say bullet? I hope Burton takes it seriously. A shot to the head means business."

"You said it. What's strange is, the shooter's car was close enough to hit Burton. A few inches lower and..." I shivered, despite the muggy night air, recalling the shock I felt when I saw the crisp bullet hole in his Stetson. "I still have the shakes. The car appeared out of nowhere, and deliberately tried to run him down."

"Those bastards. Glad Burton is OK." She seemed sympathetic.

I slowed down to survey the area as we neared the Oasis, glancing around for any shady characters in the crowd, jerking back when a wayward Model T hit a nearby curb. Luckily we managed to get to the front of the line in minutes.

After we knocked a code on the heavy door, I realized I was too rattled to recall this week's password, or rather phrase, that Sammy changed each week as a precaution.

"Don't worry," Amanda said. "Once they see us..."

The glass window slid open and Sammy's olive eyes peered out the opening.

"Sammy?" I said, surprised. "What's wrong? Where's Dino?"

Dino usually stood guard at the Oasis entrance blocking the door, his burly frame big as an armoire, inspecting and intimidating the would-be revelers.

Sammy ignored the question, avoiding our gaze. "What a treat. What are you two lovely ladies doing here so late? It may not be a good idea to stick around tonight."

"I need to talk to you." I widened my eyes. "It's urgent."

He winked at Amanda before opening the wooden door with the flourish of a trained bellman. The door resembled the gates of a castle fortress with its heavy brass hardware and bolted lock inside— thick enough to ward off the axes and bullet holes from ambitious Texas Rangers and perhaps one lone Prohibition agent.

"Say, toots. I've missed you," he told Amanda when she entered, squeezing her hand. She blushed, turning into a mute bed doll before my eyes. Sure, she might seem like a delicate Southern belle on the outside, but the real Amanda was a smart, feisty flapper, fearless as a bobcat. Why did otherwise strong women seem to melt in Sammy's presence?

"Is everything jake?" I asked Sammy. "Why are you manning the entrance, not Dino?"

"I'm waiting for a special guest," he said sarcastically. "He's supposed to be here later tonight."

"You don't say. And who's this guest of honor?"

"You haven't heard?" Sammy's handsome features creased with worry. "Guess who got sprung from jail tonight? Our favorite mob boss, Johnny Jack Nounes."

CHAPTER FOUR

"Johnny Jack is coming here tonight?" I sucked in my breath. "Why? What does he want?"

Sammy wasn't in any position to turn away the leader of the Downtown Gang, especially since the Oasis was located on Market Street, in the heart of their turf.

"Take a wild guess." His olive eyes went flat. "He blames me for getting arrested and thrown in jail, instead of the Maceos. He'll find a way to make me pay for Burton's screw-up."

He stuck his head out the door and looked up and down the street before shutting it tight.

"Damn. Speaking of Burton, I want to tell you some news. We'd just left the Hollywood Club when some thug tried to take a potshot at him in the parking lot. Nearly hit him too. Luckily they only knocked off his hat."

"Glad you're OK." Sammy scowled. "That's dirty business, going after a Fed agent."

"I'll say." I lowered my voice. "Do you think Johnny Jack is behind the shooting? Maybe he ordered a hit on Burton?"

"I doubt he'd be so conspicuous, ordering a hit on Burton the same night he leaves jail. Maybe one of his goons jumped the gun, tried to impress his boss." He snorted. "Sort of a homecoming gift."

"That makes sense. But Burton has lots of enemies. Any barkeep up or down the coast might have wanted him dead. He recently shut down a small operation based out of Houston."

"Jazz, I don't want to lecture you, but maybe you shouldn't see Burton for a while." Sammy's mouth twisted, and he ran his fingers through his wavy dark hair. "I know he's on the level and he's done us some favors, but until this mess clears up...I'd stay away and out of sight."

"I was thinking the same thing," Amanda piped up. "Friend or beau, it's too dangerous to be seen with him now."

I hated to admit, they might be right. I didn't want to abandon James, leaving him to fend for himself. But what could I do to help? I doubted he had much local support on either side of the law since both the cops and criminals considered him a thorn in their side—or to put it bluntly, a pain in the ass.

Rumor had it half the cops on the Galveston force were on the gangs' payroll and no one could tell who was on the make or who was on the up and up. When cops and crooks shared beers at bars, you never knew who to trust or who would take advantage of privileged information.

A couple of sots walked up to the door, and Sammy motioned for us to go downstairs.

"Think we should leave now?" Amanda asked, looking worried.

"Not yet. I'd hate to come face to face with Johnny Jack tonight, but I wonder what he wants. I still think he put out the hit, no matter what Sammy says. It's too much of a coincidence."

"I doubt he'll stop by soon," Amanda said. "Let's stay awhile, have a cocktail or two."

I didn't want to spoil her fun, but I'd come here for Sammy's help, not to advance their romance. The two middle-aged jokers barged in, eyeing us up and down, whistling at us like we were bathing beauties on public display. Sure, if they looked like Valentino, I might have taken it as a compliment, but not coming from these portly, balding milquetoasts.

Amanda turned to watch Sammy's reaction, but he was cool as usual, giving the guys a slight push toward the stairs.

"Party starts down there, fellas," he said gruffly. "Up here, we keep it private."

After they stumbled downstairs, Sammy said, "Maybe it's time you gals went home."

"We just got here." Amanda's face fell. "I'm not ready to leave."

"What should I tell Burton?" I asked. "I doubt he knows Johnny Jack's been released."

"My advice? Tell him to lay low, not stick his neck out too far. He should stay away from the Downtown Gang's turf for a while, and out of their bars." Sammy shook his finger. "He's better off raiding places like small mom-and-pop shops, grocers and diners, even cathouses."

"Sammy!" I blushed. "Why would I encourage him to raid bordellos?" Then I recalled Mrs. Templeton's house of ill repute, adding, "He'll only go if it's absolutely necessary."

"Just testing you. I figured you were sweet on him. Why else would you risk Eva's curfew and come see me at this hour?"

Sammy and Amanda exchanged knowing glances.

"Can you blame me for being upset? Any idea what Johnny Jack might do next?"

"I don't know if I should get involved. I'm already in hot water 'cause of Burton."

"After all that Burton has done for you? I know you're not best buddies, but...can you help him out, for my sake?"

"What do you expect me to do?" Sammy shrugged. "Say, why don't you get Dino up here? Grab a soda and wait in my office."

Suddenly his tone changed and he stared at us wild-eyed, his voice a deep rasp. "Girls, get out of sight. I see Johnny Jack's Bentley out front and he doesn't look happy. I'll try to distract him while you two go downstairs."

I was tempted to face the monster I suspected was behind Burton's hit tonight, but frankly, I was terrified. What if Johnny Jack and his gang *had* tried to shoot Burton? He could identify me as his date, and possibly take matters into his own hands.

Still, if I couldn't confront Johnny Jack directly, at least I could spy on him. Amanda tugged on my arm and headed for the stairs, but I motioned for her to sit by me near the entrance. Nervously, she crouched beside me, our backs flat against the wall.

Sammy glared at us before he opened the door, spreading his arms wide as he walked outside, declaring, "Johnny Jack, you're a sight for sore eyes! You look like you were in Hot Springs, not laid up in the Big House. Welcome home, pal."

Pal? What bull! I shoved an empty beer can in the doorjamb, keeping it open just wide enough for me to eavesdrop, if you call yelling in Sammy's face an actual conversation.

"Oh yeah? What in hell did you say to that damn Fed agent, you son-of-a-bitch?" Johnny Jack sputtered. "Where'd he get the idea to arrest me, to shut down my place of business, instead of those assholes, the Maceos?"

I tensed up, my heart racing, wishing I could watch the two men face off. Hiking up my frock, I started to crawl across the rough wood floor, but Amanda grabbed my ankle. I yanked loose from her tight grip, and squatted down by the door opening, ready to watch the fireworks.

Always dapper, Johnny Jack wore a ten-gallon cowboy hat so big it made Burton's Stetson look like a baseball cap. Two burly men in black undertaker suits and matching fedoras flanked him, arms crossed over their massive chests. If those hoods so much as touched Sammy, I'd scream bloody murder and attack them with everything I had, which admittedly wasn't much. A Mandalian mesh bag didn't quite qualify as a lethal weapon.

"Amanda, go get Dino," I whispered. "Just in case."

"What do you see? Are they fighting?" She tried to peer out over my shoulder.

"Not yet. Please, find Dino or Frank. Tell them to bring a gun—or two."

Sammy remained calm, refusing to get riled up, no doubt because he was outnumbered by the Downtown Gang's goons.

"As I told you, I have no sway with the local Fed. What kind of dumb palooka do you take me for? I know better than to get chummy with a Prohibition agent. I stay out of his way, and he stays out of mine, that's all." He shrugged. "Sounds like he's trying to show off to those muckety-mucks in Washington, prove he can land a big fish like you. You're hard-boiled, you can handle it. So what's a little time in the pen? We've all been there."

Johnny Jack stood there, fury etched all over his face, clenching and unclenching his fists. I had to hand it to Sammy, he could smooth-talk his way out of almost anything.

"I gotta make up for lost profits," Johnny Jack roared. "You know those new slot machines Dutch and Ollie are putting in their shops and bars? I figured, why should the Beach Gang make all the dough? We started installing them this week while I was behind bars. Your joint will get a machine tomorrow."

Sammy pasted on a smile, no doubt grateful that Johnny Jack had let him off the hook so easily. "Good idea. I hear those one-armed bandits are a big hit all over town. Glad to help raise some cash for the gang."

"You can thank your Fed agent friend," he scowled. "Since you blew your last assignment, I've got a special job for you." Johnny Jack lit a cigarette, facing Sammy, daring him to disobey. "Guess who's gonna be our new bag boy? I expect you to go door to door, collecting our weekly take from every place on our turf. Rent, slots, poker games, the works. Think you're up to it? If they refuse or come up short, you know what to do."

Even in the dark, I could see the blood drain from Sammy's face. "Whatever you say, Johnny." He forced a smile. "I'm your guy."

What? Did Sammy actually agree to act as Johnny Jack's enforcer and personal collection agency? No one wanted to be put in that position—bullying your buddies for money, the gang leader breathing down your neck, and for what? I knew that the collection biz was a never-ending cycle, a senseless game of give and take and greed. He might as well be a snitch, working for Agent Burton. Either way, he was a goner.

The stairs groaned, and Dino's big bald head appeared, beads of sweat covering his face, holding a pistol. "Where is Johnny Jack? Wait till I get my hands on that bastard!"

If Dino went off half-cocked, he'd blow our cover and possibly put Sammy, all of us, in more danger. "Calm down, big guy," I told him, finger to my lips. "They're walking out to the Bentley. He's ready to leave, thank goodness. Can't hear a thing now."

"Is Sammy OK?" Amanda whispered.

"Sounds like Johnny Jack gave Sammy a new job." I chose my words carefully.

"What do you mean? What kind of job?"

"Let Sammy tell us the whole story. He's coming back now."

I took a final peek and scurried out of the way, standing up before Sammy opened the heavy door.

"What did I say to you gals? You could've gotten in a lot of trouble, hiding here. I thought I told you to go downstairs," he snapped, glancing at our anxious faces, but I saw real fear, not anger, in his eyes.

"What happened?" Amanda asked, wringing her hands. "What did he want?"

"Just a small favor. Nothing I can't handle." Sammy looked away and shrugged.

"Hogwash! Tell us the truth. Aren't you his personal bag man now?" I didn't mean to sound so harsh, but I wanted Amanda and Dino to know what Sammy was getting himself into.

He glared at me, eyes blazing, but I knew his anger wasn't aimed at me. "Were you listening to our private conversation?"

"Private? You were standing out in front, arguing in plain sight," I pointed out, hands on my hips. "I got worried. I wanted to keep an eye on you, just in case."

"Sorry, Jazz." He looked downcast, pulling up his shirt collar. "You know I didn't mean to take it out on you. How can I say no to Nounes? He's got me by the balls."

"What do you mean? What did he want?" Amanda reached over and squeezed his arm.

"Let's just say I'm Johnny Jack's new errand boy." His expression turned to stone. "He expects me to go around the Downtown Gang's turf, collecting his take."

"That's not so bad. You just go from place to place, picking up money, right?" Amanda made it sound so easy. Was she playing dumb for his benefit?

"Let me do it," Dino volunteered. "I know how to get jack out of these tightwads."

"There's a lot more to it than collecting cash." Sammy shook his head. "I'm not exactly Robin Hood, more like an enforcer. If these shopkeepers don't pay up, then he expects me to use any means necessary, even if it gets violent. Those guys don't like to be pushed around by anyone. As far as I'm concerned, Johnny Jack just handed me a death sentence."

CHAPTER FIVE

"Violence isn't your style," I told Sammy, taking deep breaths to calm down. "You're more likely to pay off people's debts out of your own pocket."

"Right, and Johnny Jack knows it. He's trying to create problems between me and the barkeeps, turn them against me. He wants to make me his patsy. If anything goes wrong, he can pin it on me and the Downtown Gang will back him up."

That sounded familiar. I felt for Sammy. Would he ever get out from under Johnny Jack's control?

"Sammy, if anyone can figure out a way to keep the peace, it's you." I tried to sound reassuring. "Your pals won't blame you. They know Johnny Jack backed you into a corner."

"I hope you're right." He turned to Dino, his shoulders slumped. "Go ahead and watch the front, will ya? I'm taking these ladies home."

We followed him to the alley in back, and climbed into his roadster, Amanda claiming the passenger seat next to Sammy.

He eyed me in the rearview mirror as he drove. "So did you or Burton get a good look at the shooter? The car?"

"All I saw was a plain old Model T race out and heard a gunshot. I almost fainted when James fell on the ground, but he wanted them to think he'd been hit."

"Wonder how long it'll take them to find out he was playing opossum, and come finish the job?" Sammy frowned. "Looks like Burton and I are in the same boat, for once."

"Can you do me a favor? Can you find out if Johnny Jack or one of his goons was involved? Ask around, see what you can dig up."

"Sure, I'll try, but I don't want to make anyone suspicious."

"Thanks, Sammy. I know you've got your own problems."

Amanda's face fell. "If anything happened to you..."

"Don't worry about me, toots. I'll find a way to make it work. Just gotta get Johnny Jack off my back." Sammy forced a smile. "Hey, I'm a poet now."

At the boarding house, he gave Amanda a quick peck on the cheek. "Wish I could walk you to the door, ladies, but I don't trust Dino alone at my bar." He turned toward me. "Sorry about Burton. I'll let you know if I find out anything. Say, where is he, by the way?"

"Wish I knew. Someplace safe, I hope." I patted his shoulder, then got out of his roadster. "Same goes for you, Sammy. Watch your back. Good luck."

"Thanks, Jazz. I'll need it." His olive eyes looked dull, lifeless, as if the fire had gone dark.

After Amanda and I snuck back into the boarding house, we stayed up late, talking into the night. Luckily, my aunt Eva appeared to have slept through the whole thing.

"What a jam!" Amanda said, shaking her head. "I wish they'd find a way to get rid of Johnny Jack once and for all."

"Fat chance. He's got more tricks up his sleeve than Houdini."

"You said it, sister. Wish we could help both our fellas." She tilted her head, tracing a pattern on my old quilt bedspread. "So what's the story with you and Burton? Are you two getting closer? You were so upset tonight."

"I'm all balled up. Sure, I like Burton, but what if he finds out Sammy is my brother? He may get mad at me for covering it up or see it as a conflict of interest." I sighed. "Suppose he wants me to be a go-between, or ask Sammy to do favors, to get information on Johnny Jack."

She frowned. "Burton seems to be a stand-up guy. I doubt he'd ask you to spy for him."

"What if he changes his mind?" I shook my head. "Too many risks involved. Say Burton lets it slip to his cop buddies by accident and they use that fact as leverage. The gangs may accuse Sammy of being a snitch—or worse. Remember what happened last time? Sammy wound up in jail!"

"That was the gang's fault. They set Sammy up," Amanda pointed out. "Maybe Burton thinks you're using *him* to get story ideas or an inside scoop. Don't forget, it works both ways."

"True, but until I feel I can completely trust him, I still have to keep him at arm's length. And he may not want to wait around while I make up my mind."

Amanda gave me a sad, defeated smile before slipping out the door. "Good night, Jazz. Sweet dreams—if possible."

The smell of orange blossoms wafted through my room, lulling me to sleep. I climbed into bed and turned off my boudoir lights, keeping my perfume lamp on for a while, comforting as a down quilt. Surprisingly, I fell fast asleep, too exhausted to keep worrying.

Sunday

The next morning, I woke up early and decided to go into the *Gazette* to get some work done and escape Eva's daily grilling for gossip. Clearly nosiness ran in my family. But Eva managed to lure me to the kitchen table with a batch of her wonderful pecan waffles. The boarders were still asleep so Eva sat with me at the small enamel table while we ate breakfast.

"Is everything fine with you and James?" she asked.

"Sure, I just worry about him sometimes. His job can be so unpredictable."

"True, but it's a noble profession. He's upholding the law, keeping people safe from bootleggers and criminals." She eyed me over her waffles. "Despite its flaws, the public has to respect the rules of Prohibition."

"Even James questions the Volstead Act. He thinks it's making crime worse. Rum-runners get rich while the public pays the price."

Eva seemed upset, so I decided to change the subject. Still, I'd rather talk politics than bring up James or Sammy and their misadventures. So far, she didn't seem to realize we'd snuck out late last night to the Oasis, and I hoped Amanda wouldn't spill the beans.

"So how's your gentleman friend?" I asked. When she looked puzzled, I added, "The one who took you to the bathing beauty pageant? Will you see him at church today?"

Eva blushed crimson and dotted her mouth with a linen napkin. "We're just friends. Coffee?" She jumped up and grabbed a fresh pot. Why was she avoiding the subject?

"Sure, I'll have a cup. Beats that pile of mud they serve at the *Gazette*." I added lots of cream and sugar, savoring the chicory taste. "I need to work for a while today, then I'll be home for supper, in time to help you do the dishes." That cheered her up, and half an hour later, I was bumping along on the trolley, on my way to the paper, glad for a change of scene.

Normally I tried to help out on weekends for a few hours, but today I had an ulterior motive. With the office mostly empty, I hoped to catch Mack or Nathan and find out what, if anything, they knew about the near-miss attack on Burton and Johnny Jack's release.

Finn, our resident newsie, sat on the front steps, a stack of newspapers by his side, looking glum. "Slow day?" I teased him, tousling his sandy hair. "No headlines today?"

"Everyone's in church," he complained. "Gotta wait till they're done praying."

"Where's Golly?" I looked around for our pet stray black cat, but she wasn't around.

"She took off after I fed her some tuna. Now there's no one to talk to."

Finn looked so downcast, I couldn't help but smile at his freckled face, smeared with soot and ink from the paper. Poor kid probably used the papers as a pillow. Where did he go to sleep at night, I wondered? Who watched out for the little tyke?

"Say, Finn, why don't you try the Baptist church down the street? It's almost noon. I bet they're in the mood for the Sunday funnies after a dull sermon."

He brightened, and grabbed a stack. "Sure it's OK? Won't Mr. Thomas mind?"

"Go ahead," I told him, knowing our editor-in-chief had a soft spot for the energetic orphan. "A guy's gotta make a living."

"Thanks, Jazz. Watch my stack, will ya? If I sell out, I'll be back for the rest." He raced down the street as fast as his little legs could go, waving as he ran off.

Apparently everyone had problems, big, small and in-between.

The office seemed quieter than usual, with only a couple of reporters scattered around the newsroom. No surprise. Our newshounds liked to spend Saturday nights catching up on their drinking and carousing, all under the guise of investigative journalism—if you call chasing skirts and boozing all night much of an investigation.

Where was Mack? Nathan? No one seemed to notice as I settled in at my desk, since they were too busy at their typewriters or on the phone. I shuffled through my papers, trying to focus, but I kept picturing the Model T careening around the corner, James collapsing in the parking lot.

Then I saw Johnny Jack's angry face, heard his menacing tone, recalling the dread in Sammy's eyes. How could I concentrate on editing Mrs. Harper's gossip column? Did people really care about debutante balls and charity fund-raisers?

Finally I found a news item that seemed interesting, about a young widow with two small children, who started her own home-business making scented candles. Now the nicest stores in town featured her sweet-smelling candles. Good for her, I thought, trying to pay her own bills and creating work for herself, not asking for help or hand-outs. Perhaps I could interview her, turn it into a short feature instead of a two-graph tidbit?

I was making notes when Mack walked in, looking even scruffier than usual, and made a beeline for my desk. "Surprised to see you here after last night, Jazz. I thought you'd be playing nursemaid with your Fed agent fella."

My face felt hot, and my jaw dropped open. Very professional. "How did you know?"

"Don't look so shocked. When some hood takes a potshot at a Prohibition agent, that's news. Since he didn't show up at John Sealy Hospital, I take it he's fine?"

Was he baiting me, pretending to know more than he let on, to get me to talk? "He's OK, thank God." I forced a smile. "Boy, your sources are everywhere. Or should I call them spies?"

"Whatever you call them, that's how I do my job." His eyes narrowed. "So where is he now? Can you get me an interview today? News gets old fast."

"Wish I knew," I shrugged. "Hope he's somewhere safe."

"Well, keep me posted. I'll try the police station, see if he's working today."

Mack turned to go, but I tugged on his sleeve. "Any idea who might have done it? We didn't see much in the dark."

"You think it's just a coincidence that Johnny Jack was released yesterday? He's had a while to plot his revenge against your beau."

"Isn't that a little obvious, even for Johnny Jack?" I frowned. "Would he incriminate himself so soon after he got out of prison?"

"That's Johnny Jack for you, flashy son of a gun. Lots of guts, not many smarts." Mack studied me, plugging a cigar in his face. "Why? What have you heard?"

"Not much." If I admitted to Mack I'd seen Johnny Jack up close at the Oasis last night, he'd start asking too many questions. "Say, are you going to write up the story about Agent Burton?"

"Sure, why not? It's news, isn't it?" He scowled before ambling to his desk.

Damn it! I knew he was right, but what could I say to stop him? "Won't that make things worse?" I argued. "If the gangs find him, he's a sitting duck."

The phone rang on Mack's desk, and I listened as he answered. "You don't say. When? Where? Got a name?" He jotted down a few notes. "OK, I'll be right there."

Without a word, he gathered up his things, his back to me, knocking papers off his desk, not bothering to pick them up.

"What is it, Mack? What happened?" I asked, alarmed.

"You're in luck, kid. I'll hold off on writing about your Fed fella until I check out this lead." He frowned, irritated. "Any idea where Nathan is today?"

"I think his equipment is all here, so he may be home. I'll try to reach him there." I went over to Mrs. Harper's desk and asked the operator to connect me. "What's the message?"

"Tell him to meet me on the corner of Market and Twenty-third Street and pronto," he barked. "Some poor sap was murdered last night. They found him by a slot machine, clutching some tokens."

CHAPTER SIX

My heart seized, my mind raced—the murder had taken place near Sammy's bar. No, Sammy couldn't be involved, could he? Johnny Jack had just anointed him as bag boy last night, so it was too soon to start his collections route.

"It's not the Oasis, is it?" I asked. "Did they ID the victim yet?"

"Your pal's place? No, this bar's called the Rusty Bucket." Mack's dark brown eyes narrowed. "I think it was the owner. Maybe a robbery gone wrong."

What a relief. "Wait, I'm coming with you," I told him. I needed to find out what happened before Sammy heard the news.

"Like hell you are," he frowned. "Men cover murders. You gals should stick to your fluffy puff pieces."

"Says you." He acted as if I'd never seen a crime scene before. "Well, then I'll catch a ride with Nathan. Or I'll take the trolley and walk!" I jerked out of my chair, breathing hard.

"Suit yourself." Mack shook his head, adding, "Sorry, Jazz, but if I had a daughter, I'd never allow her near a murder scene. You never know what to expect. Evil can appear in the most innocent places, in the most hideous of ways. Why do you even want to be exposed to those kinds of things?"

I was about to give Mack an earful when he put on his hat and rushed out the front door.

Clearly, Mack still lived in the Dark Ages when women were locked away in their own homes like prisoners, tending to their families, husbands and children. Did he really expect female reporters to be satisfied writing only about weddings and birth announcements and costume balls?

Thank goodness my open-minded father had always encouraged my education and ambition, even if my mother didn't quite approve. Yes, she admired the fact that I held down a good job, but she'd be much happier if I had a husband and two or three children to round out the rosy picture.

Finn appeared on the front steps, beaming like a jack o' lantern with his missing teeth. He waved and stuck his head in the door. "Good news, Jazz! The papers sold like hotcakes. Now I'm going to Saint Mary's Catholic church. It gets out in ten minutes. Thanks!"

"Attaboy!" I told him, feeling guilty for not watching his papers, but murders came first.

When the operator connected me to Nathan, I told him about the Rusty Bucket murder. "It's about time we had some exciting news," he said. "I'll stop by to pick up my camera."

"Murder is an act of desperation," I replied. To a hard-boiled cop or reporter, a dead body was exciting as long as you didn't know the victim, or the killer.

"I'll say. But photos of happy people don't make headlines."

I knew how he felt. Personally, I wasn't interested in the actual crime scene as much as the motive behind the murder, the mental state of the killer as well as the victim at the time of death. What led to the killing? Was it premeditated or accidental? Morbid, true, but it beat describing the latest Junior League bride's wedding bouquet.

I picked up Nathan's camera equipment and put it on my desk, holding them hostage, in a way. As the minutes ticked by, I was tempted to call Sammy at the Oasis to ask him about the murder, but was worried the operators might spread the news. Those Nosie Nellies knew as much, if not more, than our news hounds. I paced around the newsroom until Nathan arrived, eager and breathless.

"Here's your camera." I thrust the equipment in his arms. "Now let's hit the road."

"Jazz." He gave me a stern look. "Sure you want to go?"

"Hey, we're a team, aren't we? If you recall, I let you tag along on my last story, and all you did was ogle the bathing beauties."

"True." Nathan grinned at the memory. "Don't say I didn't warn you." He shrugged the equipment over his shoulder and held out the flash. "Give me a hand, will ya? Come on. I'm parked in front."

On the ride over, I steeled myself, wondering what led to the murder. Was it a botched robbery? A fight over a card game or a dame? Was Johnny Jack behind this hit, too?

"What's wrong, Jazz? You're all wound up like a top." Nathan studied me as he drove with one hand. "Do you know anything about this case?"

"All I know is after Johnny Jack got out of jail, all hell broke loose." I turned to face Nathan, counting on my fingers. "First, some sniper takes a shot at Agent Burton last night at the Hollywood. Then Johnny Jack shows up at the Oasis later that night and threatens Sammy. Next thing you know, some poor barkeep turns up dead on Market Street. There's got to be a connection, and it all leads to Johnny Jack."

Nathan let out a whistle. "Is Burton OK? He's not hurt, right?"

"He dodged a bullet, literally. But I haven't talked to him since last night. I just hope he's someplace safe."

"Close call. So how did Johnny Jack threaten Sammy? What happened?"

"He blames him for Burton's raid on the Grotto—and his arrest." I let out a frustrated breath of air. "Johnny Jack appointed Sammy as the Downtown Gang's new bag man. Now he'll be collecting back rent on barkeeps and shop owners who can't pay."

"Poor guy. Not a fun line of work." Nathan shot me a sympathetic look. "Say, how do you know all this?"

"I was at the Oasis with Amanda last night. Eavesdropping, of course." Who knows what else Sammy and Johnny Jack discussed by the Bentley, out of earshot?

"I wouldn't expect anything less from you." Nathan smiled. "But if Johnny Jack caught you snooping...it may be very dangerous." He slowed down to let a family cross the street, the distracted mother surrounded by young children who seemed oblivious to the traffic.

"Johnny Jack will try to find a way to pin this murder on Sammy," I fumed. "He doesn't trust Sammy 'cause he's friends with the Maceos. Frankly, I think Johnny Jack is jealous since they own the ritzy Hollywood Dinner Club and his bars are just honky-tonks."

"You may be right." Nathan nodded. "Boy, I'd hate to be in Sammy's shoes, caught between two gangs. You don't think Sammy's involved, do you?"

"No, why would he be?" I felt defensive, though I'd been wondering that same thing. "By the way, the victim was found holding some tokens next to a slot machine. Mack thinks it was a burglary in progress that the owner tried to stop."

"What a way to go. I doubt the amount was worth his life."

"I wonder if it was the same type of slot machine the Beach Gang put in? Their shops and bars may be getting robbed, too."

"Haven't heard anything. Word is, this whole racket is making Ollie Quinn a rich man. He not only manufactures the machines, he makes the Beach Gang pay for the slots out of their own pockets." Nathan raised his brows. "He's supposed to split the take fifty-fifty, but I hear he keeps most of the profits and gives the poor suckers the rest. Chump change, if you ask me."

I let out a sigh. "Knowing Johnny Jack and his greedy goons, his vendors will be lucky to get ten percent. I doubt they'll be willing to turn over so much cash to Sammy without a fight."

"A fight is right." Nathan pulled up on Market Street, parked behind a cop car and grabbed his camera equipment. Would Sammy or Dino be there, I wondered?

At the Rusty Bucket, I followed close behind, pretending I was a real crime reporter, looking straight ahead so the police and newshounds wouldn't try to shut me out.

Sure enough, a couple of cops tried to block my way but I simply replied, "I'm with the *Gazette*," as if that explained everything. When we entered the bar, I noticed obvious signs of a struggle: tables and chairs knocked over, broken glasses, papers strewn about. Right by the front door, in all its gleaming glory, sat a brand-new nickel slot machine, a one-armed bandit displaying diamonds, spades, hearts, horseshoes and a cracked Liberty bell.

A huddle of newshawks stared at the floor and I saw the figure of a man, lying by the new machine, arms at odd angles, but I was too far away to determine his cause of death.

"Coming through," Nathan said, forcing his way into the circle. Edging closer, I could barely make out the victim's face—a plain man in his mid-forties, sandy hair, freckled skin.

As I changed positions, I saw a huge gaping hole in his skull, hair caked with blood and bone. My stomach lurched and I covered my mouth with both hands, trying not to upchuck.

By the man's side lay a bloodied baseball bat—the weapon of choice for thugs and cowards and enforcers who liked to use threats and intimidation to make their point. Why would the killers leave the bloody baseball bat in plain sight, next to the victim?

Across the room, Mack stared at me, stone-faced, with an angry "I told you so" glare. Feeling dizzy, I made my way across the room and sat down at a small table by the piano. No one seemed to notice as I went behind the counter, searching the ice-box for water. Hands trembling, I gulped it down, then pressed the frosty glass against my perspiring face, enjoying the cool sensation.

Still shaky, I sat down at the table, observing the crime scene from a safe distance: the reporters taking notes, badgering the sheriff for information, an M.E. squatting by the body, taking samples of hair and blood. That's when I saw it, half-hidden under the player piano bench: An almost-new Stetson, slightly scuffed, with a clean bullet hole in the crown.

CHAPTER SEVEN

Was I hallucinating or was that Agent Burton's Stetson under the player piano? And what in hell was it doing at this murder scene?

My heart thudded so hard, I placed my hands over my chest to quiet it down, afraid they'd hear it beating, loud as in Poe's *"The Telltale Heart."* I swear, if I wasn't sitting down, I probably would've fainted and upchucked all at once. Not a pretty picture.

Did Burton see the shooter's car and follow him to this bar? Was he snooping around and got into a fight with the bar owner? Worse, what if Burton witnessed a robbery in progress and the killers tried to shut him up? So where in the world was he?

I started breathing heavily, trying to rationalize, while these muddled thoughts raced through my mind. Even if Burton acted in self-defense, he'd never use anything as heavy-handed as a baseball bat—that was more of a mobster's approach. A lawman like Burton wouldn't have been so careless as to leave his hat behind, especially next to a murder victim.

I could keep playing out different scenarios in my head, but now I had to do something about the hat—and fast. Seems no one else had spotted the Stetson, yet. I was afraid that as soon as the body was taken away, there it would be like a flashing neon sign, announcing: "I'm your guy!"

Slowly I headed for the player piano and sat down on the bench, watching Nathan take photos of the corpse. As the bulb flashed, emitting a burst of powder, I squeezed my eyes shut, temporarily blinded by the light. I was working up my nerve when I heard a woman's voice cry out, "Oh my God! Not poor Charlie!"

I looked up to see an attractive young flapper in church clothes burst into tears and run out the door. Was she the victim's wife or girlfriend? Still, she was just the distraction I needed. As the men gaped, I gave the Stetson a quick kick and shoved it behind the piano, out of sight. I hoped that would stall the detectives—for now.

"Who's the doll?" I heard Mack ask the group of newsmen. "Parker's girl?"

"Charlie's got a ball and chain," a guy with a plaid cap replied. "Flo's dating one of his friends. Probably heard the news and had to see Charlie for herself. What a looker. Lucky guy."

"You mean the friend," Mack cracked. "Charlie's out of whack."

While the men laughed and shot the breeze, I began to panic: Would hiding the Stetson make things worse? Should I return the hat to its former place?

Too late. Nathan approached me, all laden down with camera equipment. "I've got to pick up more rolls in my car."

"I'll go with you. Too stuffy in here anyway." Outside, the heat felt like a sauna. A small crowd had gathered, gossiping in whispers, the women fanning themselves with Sunday bonnets. Obviously word had spread about the murder, and the church crowd wanted to pray for the sinners, or at least get a close-up view.

"I feel sorry for that poor gal," I told Nathan, holding his car door open. "I wonder if she knows anything?"

"I doubt it. Did you see her reaction? She couldn't even stomach the sight."

"That makes two of us. What a shock to see someone you know beaten to death." I nodded in sympathy. "Who was the victim?"

"They ID'd him as the bar owner, Charlie Parker. Either someone was trying to rob the guy or Johnny Jack's goons came to collect, and he put up a good fight." Nathan shrugged. "Well, not good enough. Can you imagine losing your life for a few bucks?"

Thinking of Sammy, my stomach tightened. "Did the sheriff or cops say anything? Any clues or leads?"

"Not much, but I'm sure Mack will find a way to weasel some dirt out of them."

"Maybe there was more to it than a robbery," I mused.

"Where'd you get that idea?" Nathan studied me.

I shook my head. "Just thinking out loud, considering all angles." I glanced at the crowd, wondering if the killer was among them, waiting and watching, observing the scene.

With a start, I realized Sammy was standing out on the sidewalk in front of the Oasis. What had he heard? "Excuse me, Nathan. I'm going to talk to Sammy, see if he knows anything. Come by the Oasis when you're done. I've seen enough murder victims for one day."

"Good idea. I could use a stiff drink after this mess. Let me know what you find out."

Damn, why did I tell him Sammy was Johnny Jack's new *collection agent*? That tidbit might show up in Mack's next front-page story and make Sammy an immediate suspect, along with Burton. I gave him a slight wave, but he stepped back, as if afraid he'd be spotted.

"What's the rumpus?" Sammy shoved his hands in his jeans pockets, cocking his head down the street. "What are all the cops doing here? Why are *you* here?"

Was he playing dumb? "Didn't you hear the news? The owner of the Rusty Bucket got his brains bashed in with a baseball bat. I hoped you might know something about the murder."

His olive skin turned pale, his hazel eyes flashed in panic. "Charlie? He got whacked? Why would I know anything? Unless..."

"Unless what?"

"Unless they're trying to frame me."

"Frame you? Is that why Johnny Jack came by last night?"

"Sure explains why he made a big scene in front of my place. So there'd be witnesses." Sammy snorted. "Everyone on Market Street knows Charlie owes back rent on his bar. That's why the Bucket was the first joint to get the new slot machine, so Johnny Jack could squeeze every last dime out of him." He stared down the street. "Poor Charlie. He was a real nice fella."

"So why would anyone blame *you*? You haven't even officially started collecting payments yet."

"Johnny Jack said Charlie was at the top of my list. I was going to give him a few days to make his payments. Seems Nounes beat me to the punch." He shuffled his feet and started pacing in front of the Oasis. "Damn that asshole. That's why he rushed over here last night, to officially crown me his bag man—and to give me a motive for murder."

I hated to see Sammy keep torturing himself, so I had to speak up. "Sammy, you're all wet. I don't think they're framing you at all. They're trying to set up Agent Burton."

"Burton?" Sammy did a double-take. "He's so squeaky clean, he'd never get his hands dirty. Why do you think he's being framed?"

I leaned in, keeping my voice low. "I saw his Stetson at the crime scene. The one with the bullet hole. I...uh...I tried to hide it so the cops wouldn't find it, at least for a while."

"You did what? Jazz, you should know that's a serious offense— tampering with a crime scene." Despite his gruff tone, his face lifted. "Where in hell can you hide a cowboy hat?"

"Behind the piano. Don't worry, I don't think anyone saw me."

"Are you sure Burton didn't do it? He's certainly capable."

"Bunk!" I made a face. "Unless he acted in self-defense."

"Either way, you need to warn him," Sammy said. "If they find out it's Burton's hat, he could be their number one suspect."

"Trouble is, I have no idea where he is or if he's even OK. For all I know, the killer beat the crap out of him too." I let out a sigh. "If only Burton had stayed with us at the boarding house last night, this wouldn't have happened."

"Jazz, it's not your fault. Burton knows how to handle himself."

Strange, Burton had once said the same thing about Sammy. "At least I can be his alibi for last night."

"Jazz, I'm warning you. Don't stick out your neck for Burton." He shook a finger at me. "Wait a while, see what the cops dig up. If he's smart, he'll stay out of sight."

"I hope so." I glanced down the street to see if the police cars had left. "Let me know if you hear anything."

"Thanks for the update. Gets me in the clear, for now." He gave me a sympathetic smile. "Sorry about Burton. He's a good egg, even for a Fed. And a Yankee. But be careful, Jazz. If the Downtown Gang suspects you're mixed up with Burton, you could be next on their hit list."

Me—on a hit list? Just peachy. "The same goes for you, Sammy. Stay out of trouble." I shuddered, motioning toward the Rusty Bucket, where the crowd in front was finally thinning out. "I saw what they did to your poor friend Charlie."

Since Nathan hadn't shown up at the Oasis, I reluctantly returned to the crime scene—just as the medics carried the body out on a stretcher, thank goodness. So far I'd managed not to upchuck in public, yet. Still, this gave me time to examine the bar, look for any clues. I took note of the scratched and worn tables and chairs, the stained curtains, the wood counter, carved with initials—not exactly the Ritz. But I wasn't the only one scouring the area, naturally. Mack and the newshawks leaned against the bar counter, comparing notes, guarding their space.

I stared at the chalk outline of the victim, looking for evidence of blood or hair on the worn wood floor or any other damage to the bar. A few faded photos of racehorses and greyhounds adorned the walls. What happened to the tokens in his hands? For a crime scene, the area seemed fairly clean. Was it wiped off after Parker was bludgeoned to death?

Trying to blend into the woodwork, I casually wandered across the room and glanced behind the player piano: The hat was gone.

Just then, the burly sheriff waved the Stetson over his head, his loud voice booming across the room: "Does anyone know who this hat belongs to? Lucky bastard. That bullet sure came close. If we find the owner, we might find our killer."

CHAPTER EIGHT

I sucked in my breath. So much for my clever sleight-of-hat.

"Good thing the guy didn't lose his head, too," one cop cracked while the men snickered.

"Not like poor Charlie," a reporter snorted. "Sorry, Charlie."

Hilarious. Figured those lushes were on a first-name basis with the bar owner.

"How do you know the hat belonged to the killer?" I piped up. "I didn't see any blood stains or damage. Maybe the guy was just a witness to the beating."

All eyes turned to me and a hush fell over the bar. The sheriff moseyed over and planted his black boots in front of me.

"How do you know so much about this hat?" He gave me the once-over. "What are you doing here anyway? Did you know the victim, or perhaps the killer?"

"Not at all. It was only an observation." Why couldn't I learn to keep my trap shut?

"Oh yeah? You sure must have eagle eyes to notice all those minor details from way over there." The sheriff yanked up his pants over his prominent belly. "What's your name, little lady?"

Little lady? "Back off, Sanders." Mack called out. "She's one of us." One of us? I swelled with pride.

Then the sheriff replied, "Well, you newshounds need to keep her on a tighter leash. Murder scenes ain't no place for young girls."

"You said it, Sanders!" I heard Mack and the newsboys chuckling in the background.

"Excuse me?" I crossed my arms and glared at the sheriff. "Did you say a *leash*?"

I was about to give him a piece of my mind, and possibly my freedom, when Nathan yanked me by my elbow. "We were just leaving, Sheriff Sanders."

Gee, thanks for defending me, fellas. Fuming, I followed Nathan to the door, trying to hold my tongue. No, it wouldn't help Burton's case any if I blew my top.

"Good luck!" I couldn't resist calling out, glaring at the men, ignoring their collective grins. At least that small scene took their minds off the murder, and Burton's hat, for now.

"What was that all about?" Nathan wanted to know as we trudged back to his car. "Why all the fuss over some stupid cowboy hat? At least it's a lead."

"Maybe it's more *mis*leading than you think." Thank God I hadn't mentioned Burton's hat to Nathan. All I'd told him was that some goon took a shot at him without going into detail.

"Leave the murder investigations to the police." He gave me a stern look, as if I were an unruly child. "Jazz, you know better than to tangle with a sheriff. What were you thinking?"

"OK, so I wasn't thinking. But that cowboy hat has nothing to do with the murder."

"How can you be sure?" Nathan eyed me.

"Think about it. If the victim tried to shoot the robbers at close range, why did he miss?"

"Good point. Unless they attacked him from behind and a gunshot hit the hat by mistake?" Nathan mulled it over. "Maybe Mack can figure it out."

Always Mack to the rescue. Wouldn't it be nice if *I* found some clues for a change? "Say, didn't you think it was convenient that the killers left the bat by the body?"

"I heard the cops found it out in the alley, behind the bar. Seems those guys left in a big hurry." He stopped to let a horse and buggy pass, waving at the driver who wore a top hat and dress suit—a less common sight these days. "So where to? Home or the daily grind?"

"Let's get back to the paper" I told him. "I want to see what the newsboys dug up."

While we drove down Market Street, I stared out the window at the now-quiet speakeasies, wondering: How in the world did Burton's hat appear at a murder scene? Were the killers after him too? That might explain why he was lying low, keeping out of sight.

Back at the *Gazette*, I nodded at Finn, glad to see his newspaper stack had dwindled to only a few left. "How's biz?"

"Could be better," he grumbled. "Hey, Jazz. Some guy came by looking for you this morning. Asked me all kinds of questions. What time you worked, what you did, stuff like that."

My heart skipped a beat. Was it one of the goons who attacked Burton last night? "Who was he? Did you get his name?"

"Naw, I figured you wouldn't wanna know a fella of his sort, so I played dumb. Told him I didn't know who you were." He grinned. "How'd I do?"

"You were swell." I smiled at my pint-sized protector. "What did he look like?"

"Average Joe, a lot older than you. Kinda had an Irish accent."

Irish accent? Who in the world would be looking for me fitting that description? A Beach Gang goon? Could it be Colin Ferris, that handsome devil?

"Thanks, Finn. How'd you know he was Irish?"

"He sounded like my dad." His face fell. "Before he left my Mom and me."

"Sorry to hear it, Finn." I patted his scrawny back. "Do you ever see him?"

"Naw. I'm the man of the family. That's why I gotta sell papers. So we can eat."

My heart went out to the little breadwinner, the weight of the world on his tiny shoulders. Glad to hear he wasn't an orphan, after all. I made a mental note to ask Mr. Thomas if we had any extra work for Finn. Surely we could find something for this bright boy to do, even if only to sweep around our dusty offices.

Instead of working, I watched the clock, shuffling papers, waiting for Mack to arrive and give us an update. Finally he showed up and made a beeline for my desk, closely followed by Nathan. "Your little outburst made quite an impression on the cops back at the Rusty Bucket," he said, blowing cigar smoke in my face.

"Just trying to be helpful." I shrugged, waving away the fumes. "So what did you discover? Any other clues besides a random cowboy hat?"

"Random? I think you know more about this Stetson than you're letting on." Mack studied me, eyes narrowed. "Any idea where your boyfriend was last night?"

"Agent Burton?" I frowned, acting puzzled. "In fact, he was with me. Why is it any of your business?"

"All night?" He gave me a sly smile, exchanging curious looks with Nathan.

"Of course not. I'm no vamp!" I huffed, my face flushed. "We ate at the Hollywood, then he took me home."

"Straight home? Well, then, how do you explain his hat being at the crime scene, only a few feet from the victim?"

"Good question." I squirmed in my seat, which suddenly felt hot as hell. "How do you know it belongs to Agent Burton?"

"Word gets around. Heard the bullet knocked his hat right off his head, but he walked away without a scratch." Mack stroked his stubble. "Besides, the cops recognized it, band and all. It's a small police station."

I tried to reason with him. "Mack, we all know Burton wouldn't go around bashing a bar owner, or anyone, in the head with a baseball bat. There's got to be a logical explanation. Obviously the gangs are behind the murder. Johnny Jack set him up."

"Oh yeah? Got any proof?" Mack raised his brows. "Say, if you can get me an interview, I'd like to hear Burton's side of the story."

So would I. "Sorry, Mack, he's on his own. I have no idea where he is. I'm sure he'll be back at work tomorrow."

"I doubt he'll show his face at the station. Last I heard, Sheriff Sanders wants to take him in for questioning. They're looking for him now."

"You don't say." My body tensed up, and I glanced away, avoiding his accusatory expression. "Keep me posted."

I was in no mood for Mack's insinuations. Flustered, I gathered my things and hurried toward the door. Nathan followed me outside, stopping me on the steps. "Sorry, Jazz. Why didn't you tell me Burton was involved? Anything I can do to help?"

"Thanks, Nate. He's being set up, I'm positive. But we can't do anything until we find him."

I stood on the sidewalk, looking for Finn, but he and his newspapers had gone. Even Golliwog, my dark shadow, had disappeared.

Dragging my feet, I headed to the trolley stop and boarded just in time. All the seats were taken, unusual on a Sunday. I wrapped my arm around a post and held onto my floppy hat, looking as droopy as I felt, and stared back at the nosy passengers.

At the boarding house, I trudged up the walk, feeling like a limp rag doll. Eva was cooking up a storm in the kitchen but I'd lost my appetite and my energy. I wanted to go to my room to take a nap, no longer willing to face the day. As I turned to go upstairs, I heard a slight tapping on the window, almost a clawing noise.

Nervously, I peered through curtains, and sucked in my breath: On the front porch stood Agent Burton, bruised and battered, a black eye starting to darken, his suit disheveled and torn.

CHAPTER NINE

My spirits lifted and sank at once. "What happened to you? I've been worried sick." Forcing a smile, I opened the door, and gave Agent Burton a quick hug. "Come in, come in."

He seemed surprised but pleased by my reaction. "Sure? I don't want anyone to see me," he said, glancing over both shoulders.

"Better than standing out here on the front porch." I took his arm and led him into the hallway, trying not to stare at the cuts and bruises marring his handsome features. "Let's go inside where we can talk." Sheepishly, Burton followed me into the parlor, head down, his ego clearly shattered.

My heart went out to him. I peeked out the door before shutting it tight. "Is anyone following you? How can I help?" I motioned for him to sit on the sofa, its horsehair cushions lumpy with age. Quickly I closed the curtains, a sliver of light illuminating the faded Persian rug and worn hardwood floor.

"I don't think so." Burton sat on the edge of the sofa, fidgety, as if ready to escape at any moment. "Jazz, I can't stay long. I just want you to know I'm OK."

I'd never seen him so shaken up. Burton usually epitomized the confident, cool, calm Prohibition agent glorified in news reels. "You don't look OK to me. Tell me what happened."

Frankly, I was dying to ask him a million questions, especially about the Rusty Bucket murder, but I held my tongue, hoping to hear his version of the events—if he was even there.

Luckily Eva seemed to be too busy in the kitchen to realize Burton was in the parlor. I could hear her banging pots and pans, water running in the background.

"After I dropped you off last night, I drove around the Downtown Gang's area, down Market Street, hoping to spot the shooter's car. I thought I was being followed, so I tried to lose them." Burton was breathing hard, looking down at the floor, then up at me. "Just when I thought it was safe, two hoods blocked my car, and tried to force my door. When I refused to get out, they knocked out one of my headlights with a baseball bat."

"A baseball bat?" My heart turned over. "Are you badly hurt?"

"They got in a few punches to the face and tried to rough me up, but I stayed in the car and managed to fend them off." He paused to catch his breath, and I noticed his bruised hands.

"What did you do?"

"They didn't want to kill me, just scare me a little. Still, they were able to reach in and snatch my hat. It was deliberate. What in hell do they want with my hat?"

"Your hat?" I held my breath. "Did you see their faces? Any idea who they were?"

He shook his head. "Their faces were hidden by handkerchiefs, like bank robbers. Who knows? Maybe they thought I saw some crime. They could be rival gang members or from out of town."

I couldn't believe the audacity of these thugs, attacking a Federal agent in public. While he was talking, I tried to imagine the scene, wondering how to warn him about the potential set-up. "No one offered to help?"

"I didn't see any witnesses." He shrugged. "If there were, they didn't want to get involved."

"I'm not surprised." When gangsters were on the attack, folks tended to look the other way, especially on Market Street after dark. "What happened next? Where'd you go afterwards?"

"A car came down the street so they ran off to the alley. I didn't want to go home so I drove around, finally fell asleep in my car, by the beach."

I pictured Burton sleeping under the moonlight, with the waves lulling him to sleep. A romantic image, except for the fact he probably used his gun for a pillow.

"Why didn't you come by last night? We have plenty of room."

"Jazz, I can handle myself. This goes with the job." He forced a weak smile. "Besides, I don't want to put you or Eva in any danger."

"You're the one risking your neck every day." I took his hand, noticing his bloody knuckles. "You can stay here for a while, until you feel better."

"I'd better not. I've already said too much. I don't want to get you involved."

"Bunk. I'm already involved." I touched his arm, recalling what Sammy had said, about being squired around town by the local Prohibition agent. Was he right—could I also be a target? "Want me to contact the police? What can I do to help?"

He shifted on the cushions, avoiding my eyes. "I hate to ask you, but I do need a favor. Between your pal Sammy and the newshounds, I hope you can locate my Stetson. I'm afraid the goons have something up their sleeve."

And how. Was that the real reason he showed up on my doorstep? Should I mention the murder now, or wait until I was sure he was safe?

"I'll be glad to help." Stalling, I told him, "Let me at least get you bandaged up first."

As I walked into the hall, Eva poked her head out the kitchen door. "Do you have a visitor or are you playing records? I thought I heard voices."

If anyone could help Burton, it was my aunt Eva who'd volunteered at John Sealy Hospital for years, and gotten used to seeing war veterans and victims of domestic abuse. As for me, I'm on the squeamish side, blanching at the sight of blood. When it comes to medical emergencies, I'm totally useless, preferring to act as helper, not a nurse.

"Agent Burton is here, and he's in bad shape," I told Eva. "He needs medical attention, at least a first-aid kit. Please don't ask him any questions. Not yet. He's in some kind of trouble and we don't want to scare him off."

Her almond eyes widened and she nodded in understanding. "I'll see what I can do."

I settled on the sofa next to Burton, cringing at the sight of his scrapes and bruises, scarring his once-flawless golden skin. "Aunt Eva is going to dress your cuts. She's practically a trained nurse so you're in good hands."

"Eva knows I'm here? I assumed she was still in church." A mild panic flickered in his blue eyes.

As if on cue, Eva appeared holding a bottle of alcohol, some gauze and clean cloths. She took one look at Burton, and sat down by him, dabbing at his features while he winced. "I know this may hurt, but it's nothing compared to that beating you took." Eva said it in a scolding manner, as if Burton had a choice.

"It could have been worse," Burton said, tight-lipped. "I was outnumbered two to one."

"Not to mention the baseball bat. Those goons don't play fair." I didn't want to think about what could have happened earlier that night, how close he came to being killed.

"A baseball bat? I'm surprised you don't have any broken bones." Eva examined his neck and patted his torso. When he flinched under her touch, she told him, "Take off your shirt."

He hesitated for a moment, then slowly unbuttoned his shirt, dutiful as a child. I couldn't help but admire his sun-tanned muscular frame, averting my eyes so he wouldn't catch me ogling his hairy chest like a peeping tomato. I cringed when I saw the cuts and bruises on his upper body, arms and shoulders, hidden by his shirt.

"Just as I thought," Eva said.

With the efficiency of a war-time nurse, she tended to his wounds, applying ointment and wrapping his arms with gauze. At first tense and upright, Burton seemed to relax under her care, remaining silent, but I could tell he was grateful for her attention.

"Jazz, please bring me the aspirin bottle. James, would you like some lemonade?"

His face brightened. "Lemonade would be a treat."

As I turned to go, I heard a knock at the door, and put my finger to my lips. Burton and Eva sat motionless, eyes wide.

Then I crept across the room and pushed aside the curtains:

Sheriff Sanders stood on the front porch, hat in hand, peering through the stained glass door.

CHAPTER TEN

I froze, still as a statue, signaling Eva to answer the front door. Puzzled, she jumped up, smoothed out her cotton frock, shutting the parlor door behind her. "Why, hello officer!" I heard her say. "Is something wrong? Has there been any trouble in our neighborhood?"

I tiptoed to the door, opening it a crack, straining to listen. Burton quickly buttoned up his shirt and put on his jacket. He frowned at me, hands upturned, shaking his head, mouthing, "What's going on?"

"Wait." I held up my hand like a stop sign. Why hadn't I warned him first?

"No trouble here, nothing like that, ma'am. I'm Sheriff Sanders," he bellowed. "Just looking for your sister. Jasmine Cross, right? I'd like to ask her a few questions."

I knew Eva was delighted with that slip. Still, I could only imagine what the neighbors thought with a sheriff's car parked in front, and his deep voice blaring, louder than a foghorn.

"My sister? No, Jasmine isn't here. Is she OK?" Through the door crack, I could see Eva touching her throat, not bothering to correct him. I had to hand it to my aunt, she was on the trolley, covering for us, lying as if it was a regular habit, not a sin.

"She's not directly involved, ma'am." His voice softened. "We just want to ask her a few questions about Treasury Agent James Burton. Do you know him? Is he her fella?"

Fella? I sure hoped Burton couldn't see my face turn beet-red.

"They're good friends. Why? What's the matter?" She paused. "Such a nice, brave young man. I hope nothing's happened to him."

You'd think Eva was Burton's sweetheart, the way she gushed on about his attributes.

"We found his hat and wanted to return it to him. I hoped your sister could help locate him, that's all. Please give her my message." The sheriff tipped his hat, similar to Burton's Stetson.

"I'll be glad to, Sheriff," Eva agreed.

"Well, ma'am, I'd best be on my way. If you hear anything, let me know." He shuffled his feet, then looked up at Eva from under his hat brim, almost shyly. "I may come back tomorrow, if your husband doesn't mind me talking to his wife?"

I shook my head in disbelief. Was he flirting with my aunt or buttering her up? Guess he didn't want to alarm her by mentioning the murder investigation.

"I'm not married, Sheriff, and even if I was, I wouldn't let my husband make those kinds of decisions for me. I speak to whomever I want, whenever I want." Aunt Eva squared her shoulders, holding her head high. I had new respect for Eva, standing up to authority, when she was such a by-the-good-book, law-abiding citizen. "Now if you'll excuse me..." She attempted to shut the door, but the sheriff stuck out his beefy paw.

"I'm sorry, ma'am. Such a pretty little lady like you, I just assumed...I'm sorry, I didn't want to make you mad...I mean, I was just being polite." Sanders turned red, tongue-tied, clearly awed by my aunt's radiant beauty.

I exchanged confused glances with Burton, who'd edged closer, listening to every word. Was Sheriff Sanders badgering my aunt for information or asking if she was available?

"Not at all, Sheriff. Actually I'm quite flattered. Please feel free to come by again."

Sanders perked up. "Thanks, ma'am. May I ask your name?"

"I'm Miss Broussard, but my friends call me Eva." She held out a dainty hand and I noticed Sanders studying her ring-less ring finger.

"Such a pretty name, to go with a pretty face." Sheriff Sanders stood on the porch for a minute, fingering the brim of his hat. "Good day, ma'am. Can I call you Eva?"

"Of course." Slowly Eva shut the door, lingering a while, watching the sheriff walk down the brick path. I rushed back to sit by Burton, both of us grinning like mischievous children.

Clearly, Eva had turned Sanders' head without even trying. She was all smiles when she returned, blushing like a schoolgirl.

"Who was that?" I teased. "Sounds like someone has a crush."

"I doubt it." She frowned, trying to regain her composure. "The sheriff was buttering me up just to get information."

"Baloney!" My spinster aunt was more cynical than I thought. "I saw the way he looked at you. He was being sincere."

"Were you spying on us? In any case, I'm not interested," she huffed, hands on her hips. "Tell me, Jazz. Why does the sheriff want to talk to you about Agent Burton?" Her blue-green eyes darted back and forth. "What is it you two aren't telling me?"

"Honest, I'm in the dark, too." Burton eyed me with suspicion. "Jazz, why was the sheriff here, looking for me? I don't believe that bull about returning my hat. What's the rumpus?"

"He's telling the truth about your hat." I sighed. "It's a long story, but I'll make it short."

Burton and Eva exchanged curious glances. "Take your time," Burton told me, crossing his arms.

"Mack got a call today about a murder on Market Street."

"Who? Where exactly?" Burton looked alarmed. "I was on Market Street last night."

I shot him a look, warning him not to blab in front of Eva.

"It didn't involve Sammy, did it?" Eva sounded worried.

"Thank goodness, no." There was no nice way to say it: "Turns out the owner of the Rusty Bucket was beaten to death last night with a baseball bat."

"Charlie Parker?" Burton leapt off the sofa, then sat back down, grimacing in pain. "He was a real nice guy. What a shame."

"How well did you know him?" I asked, watching his reaction.

"I raided his bar once, but all he had was near-beer. He couldn't afford the good stuff—too many mouths to feed at home."

Burton shook his head. "After he told me his sob story, I gave him a slap on the wrist, nothing else. Sad sack. He wanted to go to college, become an engineer or chemist, but he kept having kids. Eight at last count." He sighed. "Who in the world would kill a good egg like Charlie? And what in hell does this have to do with me?"

Aunt Eva tilted her head, puzzled. "Is that why the sheriff stopped by? Did he assume Agent Burton was hiding *here*?"

"He thinks I know something about the murder," I admitted.

"Why would he think that?" Burton watched me, rubbing his two-day-old stubble.

"Who knows?" I tried to stall, but they both gave me the evil eye. Finally, I had to blurt it out: "They found your cowboy hat at the crime scene, so they assume you're involved."

Burton jerked up off the couch, blue eyes blazing. "I knew it! Those goddamn gangsters are trying to frame me for murder!" Sheepishly, he lowered his gaze, bowing his head to Eva. "Sorry, ma'am. Excuse my language."

"Perfectly understandable, considering the situation," Eva told him. "So what will you do next?"

Burton shoved his hands in his pockets, pacing the parlor. "The only way I can prove my innocence is to find the real killer, or as the case may be, killers."

"You can't leave now. The sheriff and probably half the police force are looking for you," I pointed out. "Not to mention Johnny Jack and the Downtown Gang." I locked eyes with Eva and she nodded her approval, reading my mind. "Why don't you stay here for a few days? Maybe we can help you solve this murder?"

Good idea, Jazz. Invite the number-one murder suspect to spend the night, with the county sheriff hot on his trail.

"I take it you were at the murder scene? Figures." Burton stopped pacing, his eyes shifting back and forth, no doubt considering his options. "Sure it's safe? I hate to intrude."

"Of course it's OK," Eva nodded. "You're in no shape to leave now. It's too risky. Who knows what that sheriff really wanted?"

"I'll stay on one condition." Burton took a deep breath and turned toward me. "Jazz, you've got contacts at the paper, and your pal Sammy is chummy with Johnny Jack and the Downtown Gang."

"Chummy?" I frowned. "I wouldn't exactly call them friends."

"Fact is, Sammy has access to Johnny Jack and his men. And you can get into places I can't right now. If we work together, we can prove that I'm not guilty."

How could I refuse? "Absolutely. Ready to get started?"

CHAPTER ELEVEN

Aunt Eva's expression darkened and she shook a finger in Burton's face. "If anything happens to Jasmine, I'm holding you personally responsible, Agent Burton," she admonished him. "She's like a daughter to me. Don't you dare do anything rash or reckless!"

"Yes, ma'am." Burton half-bowed. "I promise not to put her in any danger."

She gave him a polite smile. "In that case, you're welcome to stay here for as long as you want. We've got an empty bedroom on the first floor." She acted as if he were going to be a permanent resident, not a temporary guest.

"I don't mind sleeping in the parlor," he offered. "Then I can leave early, without disturbing you or your guests."

"Fine, whatever makes you most comfortable." She nodded. "I'll bring you a pillow and sheets later. The bath is on the second floor."

"I'll be glad to show him around," I said, blushing. Seemed we'd be sharing a bathroom, among other things.

"Don't forget to turn out the lights tonight." She turned to go, her slender hands resting on the door frame. "Please be careful, both of you."

After she left, I racked my brain for ideas, thinking aloud. "Maybe you should go to the police station and explain what happened. Your bruises prove you were attacked with a baseball bat, same as the victim. Sure you don't want to go to the hospital? At least you can get checked out and they'll record your injuries."

"I'll live, thanks. Besides, the goons may be waiting there." He looked away. "I hate to let anyone know those gangsters got to me, and tried to beat me silly."

"Isn't there anyone you trust on the police force?" I wondered. "There's got to be some honest cops in Galveston."

"Look for the ones in the shabbiest shoes and clothes," Burton said, half-joking. "The cops on the gang's payroll dress just like them, like big shots."

His remark made me wonder about the crowd at the Hollywood Dinner Club Saturday night. Were any of the high-rollers actually cops in fancy suits and hats? If so, why hadn't they come to Burton's aid? "What about your car? Where is it parked?"

"It's in the alley behind the Camel Stop on Merchant Street, minus one headlight." He rubbed his arm and winced, clearly still sore from the attack. "I wonder if they used the same baseball bat? The car may still have traces of the victim's blood and hair."

A gruesome thought. "Couldn't that be used as evidence? The bat was pretty bloody so it probably left some marks."

"You saw the victim *and* the murder weapon?" Burton studied me. "I'll bet that turned your stomach."

"You said it." I made a face. "I felt like upchucking all over the sheriff's shoes."

"I'd pay good money to see that." He grinned, his first smile I'd seen today.

"Say, why don't I run over to the grocery store and make sure your car is still there? I can check for..uh...samples while you stay here." I thought of Nathan, who usually took crime scene photos, but what would a black-and-white picture of a dirty headlight prove?

"I hate to put you in this position." Burton worked his jaw, staring out the window. "I'd better go with you. The goons may be tailing me, looking for my car. They might have the same thought—that it contains evidence. For all I know, they smeared my hat with Charlie's blood."

"No, it was surprisingly clean." I gave him a reassuring smile. "Don't worry, I'll watch my step. I can pop in and buy some groceries for Eva as a cover. I'm sure she'll be pleased."

"I'll follow a few paces behind, just in case. To make sure nothing is out of order."

"Don't you think we'll be a bit conspicuous? After all, they may have seen us at the Hollywood last night. The sheriff already suspects we're a couple."

"You must admit, we do make a striking pair." Burton winked at me. "Not to worry, I'll keep out of sight. I'll take the alleys while you'd better stay on the sidewalk."

"Sounds good," I agreed, relieved. What if one of the killers was waiting by the car with a baseball bat? Burton was right: We stood a better chance united, rather than separate.

After I got a grocery list from Eva, who seemed surprised but pleased, Burton and I headed toward the Camel Stop grocers. "Just pretend I'm not there, that you're running an errand for Eva like a normal Sunday," he said. "I'll meet you behind the store in half an hour or so."

He'd put on a brown cap, similar to Finn's newsboy cap, completely altering his looks. With his torn shirt and scuffed-up shoes, he looked like an average working stiff instead of the nattily-dressed Treasury agent I knew.

As I made my way down the street, I admired the Victorian houses and churches which withstood the hurricanes and storms that had ravaged Galveston. Most buildings by the beach weren't so lucky. The infamous 1900 Storm struck everything in its path without any warning , destroying thousands of homes and buildings, killing more than 6000 people—including countless children.

Only three boys survived from St. Mary's Orphanage, while the nuns perished trying to protect the orphans. The hurricane hit with such force that 150-mile-an-hour gale winds uprooted huge palm trees, flying across the Island like deadly torpedoes.

Turning onto Merchant Street, I stole a glance down the alleys, hoping for a glimpse of Burton in his pseudo-disguise. I pretended to window-shop along the way, to give him time to catch up, drooling in front of the new bakery filled with sweet treats: German chocolate cake, apple pies, tarts and kolaches, a variety of cookies and cupcakes. Tempting! I waved to the plump, rosy-cheeked baker who wore a stained apron covered in flour and chocolate, but rushed past, afraid I'd come home laden with desserts if I lingered too long. Still no sign of Burton.

Walking across the street to the Camel Stop, I heard a loud honk and jumped back to the curb. Jeepers! Irritated, I turned to look for the impatient driver, when I heard my name called: "Jasmine Cross!"

My stomach knotted as I spied Sheriff Sanders easing his car to a stop in the middle of the street.

CHAPTER TWELVE

I guess the county sheriff could park his car wherever he liked.

"Just the person I wanted to see." Sheriff Sanders motioned me over. Great, I groaned. If the neighbors hadn't already seen the sheriff's car parked in front of our boarding house, all of Merchant Street would see us talking out here in broad daylight. Now tongues would wag all day and night. "Did your sister tell you I came by?"

Was he following me? Had he seen Burton in the alleys?

"You mean my aunt?" I hated to reveal Eva's secret—she was only 15 years older than me—but I wanted to douse his flames *and* his enthusiasm. "How can I help you?"

"Your aunt? How old is....?" He tipped his cowboy hat back, squinting up at me. "I was just wondering about your friend, Agent Burton. Any idea where I might find him?"

Up close, he seemed harmless and I suppose he could be considered handsome in a beefy, burly, ate-too-much-fried-chicken kind of way. I doubted he was Eva's type, though she did go for men in uniform.

"No, sir, I haven't seen him since last night." I gave him a sweet smile, trying not to act like an accomplice to murder. "He's not my steady. I don't keep tabs on his whereabouts. Why?"

"I just had a few questions about the Rusty Bucket murder," he drawled. "Won't take long."

"You don't think he's involved, do you? Agent Burton is such a gentleman. He wouldn't hurt a fly!" OK, so maybe I was overdoing the Southern Belle act, but I hoped if I could keep the sheriff talking, maybe Burton would see us and run the other way.

"Well, we'll see about that," he scowled. "Looks mighty suspicious when a Prohibition agent's hat is found next to a murder victim in a bar."

I couldn't bite my tongue any longer. "While you're at it, why don't you investigate the shooting outside of the Hollywood Dinner Club last night? Agent Burton could've been killed!"

"Yes, ma'am, I heard about that unfortunate incident. Did either of you see the gunman?"

"No, it was too dark." I hesitated, wondering how much he really knew. "Do you think it's somehow connected to the murder?"

The sheriff's eyes widened. "I plan to find out."

I leaned against the car, acting all neighborly. "Sheriff, do you really think a respectable Treasury agent like Burton would go after a small-time bar owner with a baseball bat? Doesn't that sound more like a gang killing?"

"We have to investigate all possibilities," he bristled, adjusting his hat. "If you see him, please convey my message."

"Yes, sir," I said, almost saluting him.

"Before you go, can you please give Eva my regards?" His broad face reddened and he cleared his throat. "Do you think she'd mind if I called on her again? If she doesn't have a fella, I mean."

Swell. Did we really want the nosy sheriff hanging around our boarding house, especially with Agent Burton staying there, even temporarily? But wouldn't it seem suspicious if I suddenly said she was taken?

"Give her time," I said, hoping to discourage him. "She still hasn't gotten over her fiancé, who was killed in the war."

"That was almost ten years ago! Maybe I have a chance?" Beaming, he looked in the rearview mirror, straightening his collar and patting his thinning hair. Then he carefully put on his hat and started his engine, no doubt noticing all the cars piled up behind him, their horns silent. "I'd best be on my way. Good day. Please tell Eva it was nice meeting her today."

I stifled a smile, wondering how she'd react if she knew the sheriff had a crush on her?

Glancing both ways, I entered the Camel Stop, my grocery list in hand. So far, no sign of Burton.

Had he seen me talking to the sheriff? I hoped Sanders had left the area. Was it safe to even approach Burton's car?

I glanced out the back window while I scrutinized the fresh produce along the last aisle, hoping for a glimpse of Burton. Sure enough, his car appeared to be parked behind the store, a wire dangling from the busted headlamp. From a distance, I couldn't tell if the car still had remnants of the victim's blood, but I intended to inspect it myself, with or without Burton.

"May I help you, miss?" The grocer asked me, his bushy eyebrows raised in suspicion. I was dawdling so long, he must have mistaken me for a shoplifter.

Startled, I replied, "No, thank you. There are so many choices!" I beamed at him as if I were shopping at an enormous Sears and Roebuck department store, not a small mom-and-pop shop.

Finally when I couldn't stall any longer, I paid for my groceries and started down Merchant Street. I turned on 24th Street, then ducked behind the alley, praying the sheriff wasn't around.

Gingerly I approached Burton's car, setting down my bag of groceries against the wood-spoked tire. Holding my breath, I leaned closer for a better look, noting the smeared blood, now dried, and remnants of hair.

Burton was right: The headlight was smashed with the same baseball bat used in the murder. I could only imagine the violence of last night. What kind of barbarian would kill with such brutality, then attack a Federal agent in public?

Shuddering, I turned away when I heard a voice say: "Fancy meeting you here."

Burton sat up in the back seat of the car, a devilish grin spread across his battered face.

I almost jumped out of my skin. "James! You scared me half to death!"

"How could I resist?" He grew solemn. "When I saw you gabbing with the sheriff, I had to find a place to lie low, literally."

"What was I supposed to do?" I put my hands on my hips. "I couldn't exactly ignore him after he called out my name, loud enough for everyone to hear."

He eyed me. "What were you two talking about, anyway? Me?"

"You and Aunt Eva. Seems he has a little crush on her." I took a quick look down the alley, but only spotted a scrawny orange tabby cat. "I hope he wasn't following us."

Burton got out of the roadster, and walked around to the front. "What do you think? Should I take the car in, and show it to the cops before all the evidence disappears?"

"Think you can trust them?"

"I know a few good old boys who have my back." He frowned. "At least I hope so."

"What are you going to do? Walk into the police station with your hands up, like a wanted criminal?" I stared at him, having second thoughts after my conversation with the sheriff. "They might arrest you on the spot."

"Why don't you leave that decision to me?" Sheriff Sanders appeared, his bulky shadow darkening the alley. "Thanks for your help, Miss Cross."

He said it so politely, with a straight face, that I couldn't tell if he was being sarcastic or sincere. "Agent Burton, you'll need to come downtown with me for questioning in the murder of Charles Parker. He was bludgeoned to death at the Rusty Bucket."

Burton worked his jaw. "Damn!" he muttered, glancing back and forth at me and the sheriff, eyes narrow as keyholes. "You mean as a suspect or as a witness?"

"Both." Sanders frowned, hooking his thumbs into his belt loops. "I'll follow in my car."

When Burton hesitated, the sheriff pulled out his gun and motioned down the alley toward the street. "Let's get going, Agent Burton. Now."

CHAPTER THIRTEEN

Was Sheriff Sanders bluffing or actually threatening Agent Burton? To distract them, I picked up my bag of groceries, and stood between Burton and the sheriff. "But Agent Burton promised me a ride home," I whined, going into damsel-in-distress mode. "This bag sure is heavy."

"I'd hate for him to break his promise to a lady." Sheriff Sanders tipped his hat. "We'll be glad to stop by the boarding house. It's on the way to the police station."

"I know where it is," Burton bristled. "No need to follow me."

"Best if I escort you in, son. If what you say is true, your car can be used as evidence in a crime. We can analyze the blood to see if it's the same type as on the murder weapon." He gave Burton the once-over, taking in his scuffed clothing and battered face. "Even if the blood type is a match, we can't prove it's the victim's blood or that you didn't commit the murder."

Burton looked incredulous, moving toward the sheriff. "Why in hell would I kill Charlie, then bash in my own headlight with the same baseball bat? You really think I'm that stupid?"

"To cover your tracks, boy." Sanders adjusted his pie-sized belt buckle, embossed with a longhorn, and took a step toward Burton, his face inches away. "I'm sure you know all the tricks by now."

"Tricks? What tricks? I'm telling the truth!" Burton's face flushed and I could see a vein throbbing in his neck.

I sucked in my breath, hoping both men could rein in their tempers. The last thing I wanted was to watch a showdown in the alley, like the gun battle at the OK Corral.

Whenever fights broke out at school, I tried to stop the unruly boys by saying, "Watch out! Principal's coming!" But that gag wouldn't work on two armed law officers.

"These groceries are wilting in the sun," I wailed, squeezing Burton's arm. "I'd like to get home before they go bad." Not very imaginative, but it was the truth.

Burton blinked at me, as if coming out of a trance. "Can't keep the lady waiting. Ready to go, Sheriff?"

"I'll be right behind you. You two wait here while I get my car."

Did we have a choice? Burton seemed embarrassed as he placed the groceries in the back seat and held open the passenger door. "He's treating me more like a suspect than a victim. I just wish I had a witness, someone who can back up my story."

"I'm sure someone saw the killers. How could they miss an attack like that?" I racked my brain, wishing Sammy could help. "Maybe you can ask around Market Street?"

"Obviously no one's claiming they saw or knew anything about the murder." Burton sounded frustrated. "Why else would Sanders be grilling me if he had another suspect?"

On cue, Sheriff Sanders pulled up behind us, honking his horn, as if we could ignore his squad car. When Burton pulled out onto the street, I asked, "I wonder why a county sheriff is investigating a local murder? Isn't that usually handled by the Galveston police force?"

Burton nodded. "Murders are generally under the jurisdiction of the local Homicide division. Frankly, I *am* surprised to see a county sheriff on this case."

"Maybe he's trying to help you. Why not give him the benefit of the doubt?"

"That's the least he can do for me," Burton scowled. "Hasn't he heard of 'innocent till proven guilty?'"

"Good question. Why would the sheriff suspect you when it was an obvious gang killing?" Was he as dirty as the local cops, or a neutral outsider?

Burton took his time driving, carefully turning corners, stopping to allow pedestrians to cross. Did he purposely wanted to irritate Sanders or prove he wasn't a flight risk? We turned onto our street and he slowed to a stop in front of the boarding house.

"Please call me and let me know what happens." I squeezed his arm. "We'll have the parlor ready for you tonight. See you later."

"Will do, if he lets me out of his sight." Burton picked up my bag of groceries just as Sanders pulled up behind us, and ambled over to his car.

"Here, let me help you with that," Sanders said, taking the bag from Burton. "It'll give me a chance to see your pretty aunt again. Can't believe she's not your sister."

I exchanged surprised looks with Burton. Though his job—not to mention his life —was in danger, all the sheriff wanted to do was to flirt with my aunt. Perhaps it was a tactic, an attempt to appear trustworthy and get us on his side.

I waved good-bye to Burton as I trudged up the walk. Eva flung open the door, staring at us, puzzled. "Why, Sheriff, what a nice surprise. Thanks for helping Jasmine with the groceries."

"My pleasure, ma'am." He shuffled his feet, handing her the bag. "This is for you."

She glanced at me, then outside at the parked cars. "I see you found Agent Burton. Is everything all right?"

"I hope so, ma'am," he said, tipping his hat. "Maybe I'll see you again soon."

Oh, brother! I couldn't decide if the sheriff was a lothario in disguise or looking for a sweetheart on the side. Didn't he have a wife? What if his schoolboy crush was just a ruse?

Blushing, Eva replied, "I'd like that."

What was she thinking? I crossed my arms and leaned against the door, glaring at Sanders until he got the hint and left. Finally!

Taking the bag from Eva, I huffed, "Why are you encouraging that sheriff?"

"I'm just being polite." She blushed. "How do you know he's not trying to help?"

"Now you're defending him? He practically accused Burton of murder!" I shook my head in disbelief. "Are you seriously interested in seeing him again?"

"If it helps Agent Burton, why not have a little fun?" She gave me a coy smile. "After all, you're not the only one who knows how to flirt to get her way."

Was that an insult or a compliment?

While Eva and I washed dishes that night, I waited for the phone to ring, waited for news of Burton's interview with the sheriff, waited for his explanation, waited for him to show up.

But the call, and Burton, never came.

Monday

The next morning, I arrived to work, late as usual, bleary-eyed and exhausted. I'd tossed and turned all night, worrying about Agent Burton, trying not to think the worst. Why hadn't he returned to the boarding house, after we offered to put him up for the night? What went wrong?

I picked up the morning paper, cringing at the headline: BARKEEP BASHED TO DEATH BY BRUTAL BASEBALL BAT ATTACK. Worse, a graphic photo showed the battered body next to the baseball bat. Thank goodness, the photo was taken from the back, without showing Parker's face.

I folded the paper and put it away. To be honest, I couldn't bear to read about murder and violence so early in the morning. What an unpleasant way to start the day.

"Morning, Jazz. Say, I heard your fella got pinched by the police." Mack greeted me as I settled in at my desk, loud enough for the whole staff to hear.

Boy, Mack had some big-mouthed snitch down at the police station. My boss snapped her head to attention, her spectacles dangling off her nose, hand cupped to her ear. Nathan hesitated by the darkroom, waiting for my response.

"So what?" I crossed my arms, facing him down. "For your information, the sheriff only wanted to ask him a few questions, as a possible *witness*."

"The sheriff?" Mack raised his brows, glancing around the newsroom. "Sounds serious."

"So the only one *pinching* Agent Burton is you," Hank, the cranky sportswriter, cracked. He snickered at his own joke, while the cub reporters laughed, eager to flatter their mentors.

"Is he ticklish too?" Pete added.

"You're a barrel of monkeys." I rolled my eyes at the newsboys. "Or should I say baboons?"

"Can't take a joke, Jazz?" Hank called out.

"Sure, if it's funny." I rolled my eyes at him. "Sorry, Hank, but you're no Buster Keaton."

"I'll say. You fellas sound more like Amos and Andy," Nathan cracked. Glad he finally shut them up.

After they quieted down, I made my way over to Mack's desk and plopped down in a nearby banker's chair. "Seriously, Mack. I'm worried about Agent Burton. What have you heard?"

He studied me over his Remington typewriter, brown eyes bright despite his thick glasses. "When was the last time you saw Burton?"

"Yesterday afternoon. I was there when the sheriff...uh...offered to escort him to the police station. Why?" Was Mack fishing for information or was he afraid to tell me something?

"Guess you haven't heard the latest. Keep this between us, OK?" Mack leaned over on his desk, elbows resting on his stacks of notes and papers. "I like the kid, too. I consider Burton a stand-up fella, a smart guy, but I swear he doesn't stand a chance against the Downtown Gang."

I jumped up, my back stiffening, almost afraid to ask: "What happened? Is he OK?"

Mack sucked on his pipe and blew out a plume of cherry smoke. "Apparently Johnny Jack and his thugs showed up at the police station last night, accusing Burton of killing Charlie Parker. From what I heard, you'd think they'd released the Ten Plagues of Egypt."

CHAPTER FOURTEEN

"Johnny Jack showed up at the police station with his goons?"

I leaned against Mack's desk, gripping the edge to steady myself. "What do you mean by the Ten Plagues of Egypt?"

"All hell broke loose." Mack glanced around the newsroom, then motioned for me to sit down close to his desk. "Look, this is third-hand information at best. All I know is Johnny Jack and his gang barged into the police station, hooting and hollering, swearing up and down that Agent Burton killed Parker in cold blood."

"What happened?" I held my breath.

"The cops may not like Burton, but they love a good fight. Any excuse to start throwing punches. And chairs. I hear the whole thing turned into a nasty saloon brawl. Gotta admit, wish I'd been there."

I could only imagine the chaotic scene, two groups of armed men facing off, like a Wild West gun battle. I swallowed, trying not to show my panic. "Did anyone get hurt? Is he OK?"

Mack shrugged and puffed on his smelly cigar, the sweet scent of cherry tobacco tickling my nose. "For all I know, he's still at the station. I heard the sheriff ordered Burton to spend the night there, for his own protection. It wasn't safe to leave after that ruckus."

"In a jail cell?" No wonder I hadn't heard a word since Sunday afternoon. "Think I can go see him?"

His eyes gleamed under his bushy brows. "Sure, why not? It's a public place. I'll drive you over if you want."

I knew Mack wasn't trying to be nice: What he really wanted was an exclusive scoop, and figured I'd help him get Burton to talk. He paused to suck on his cigar, blowing smoke until I started to cough.

I glared at him. "Thanks, but I think I'll go alone. I doubt he's in the mood to be sociable."

Nathan walked by, clearly trying to eavesdrop, wriggling his eyebrows up and down like Groucho Marx. Funny, since he was the polar opposite of the Marx brothers, with his fair sandy hair and pale skin. I wanted to ask if he'd take me to the station, since I didn't want to face the cops alone. Sure, he and Burton had their differences, but now Burton's life was on the line.

Before I could talk to him, Mrs. Harper called me over, removing her spectacles.

"Is it true, Jasmine? Is Agent Burton in jail—accused of *murder*?" She blinked at me, giving me a sympathetic smile. So that's how rumors got started—via nosy gossip columnists.

"Hogwash! He's at the station for his own safety. The gangs are trying to set him up." My face flamed. "I know he's innocent."

"Of course he is." She nodded, reaching out with a gloved hand to pat my arm. "Hard to stay on the straight and narrow with so much temptation around. Such a fine young man, too."

Temptation? Apparently she'd decided Burton was guilty, just like the sheriff and Mack had already made up their minds.

"Two goons came at him with a baseball bat, probably the same one used in the murder. They bashed out his car headlight," I told her in a low voice, breathing hard. "So he went down to the police station to show them the evidence."

"You don't say," she replied, looking skeptical. "That's not what I heard. My sources say the sheriff picked him up on Merchant Street, and insisted he turn himself in."

"What sources?" My throat felt dry as I scrambled for words. All of my explanations seemed to make things worse. "I'm going down to the station right now to find out what really happened. I'll do whatever it takes to help prove he's innocent."

"Hold your horses." She tapped her long nails. "Have you finished checking my columns? We can discuss your plans to get your fella out of jail later. I just pray he's not guilty."

There she goes again, I fumed, making up stories, spreading lies. My boss loved to knock people off their pedestals, especially the bold-faced types she envied.

"He's not in jail," I fumed. "He's working."

"Is that so?" She swiveled around in her squeaky banker's chair, and resumed pounding her typewriter, cutting me off. How she typed so fast in those bulky gloves, I had no idea.

No use arguing with her. I decided to skip lunch so I could type up a week's worth of columns, working until my fingers ached. Then I had to call various sources to verify a few facts, to make sure the newest debutantes were still engaged to the same future financiers, doctors, engineers and lawyers, preferably sons of Galveston's old money families.

Fortunately, columns could be cut or revised with enough notice, especially after the betrothed had a dreadful argument or a change of heart—or a long-lost love suddenly appeared.

A few hours later, I handed my stack of stories to my boss, watching her cluck over the copy and mark them up with bloody red ink. "That'll do for now. I know you're anxious to visit your beau."

She acted like he was serving time in prison, not at work where he belonged. Finally I could call it a day, and check on Agent Burton, *if* I could convince Nathan to give me a ride.

Half an hour later, Nathan and I were on the way to the police station in his old jalopy. "They don't really think Burton killed that barkeep, do they?" He paused to let a few schoolchildren cross the street, neat and tidy in their Catholic school uniforms. "I mean, I can understand if a raid got out of hand, and he had to defend himself…"

"He didn't do it!" I frowned at Nathan. "Why can't anyone believe he was set up?"

When we arrived at the station, a bare-bones red brick building with a few desks and jail cells, it was mostly empty. A few cops wolf-whistled as we walked in, and a young guy with wavy chestnut hair looked me up and down, flashing his best matinee-idol smile.

"I'm at your service, ma'am. Whatever you want, I've got it," the cop razzed me. Same cheeky group of jokers as the newsboys, but these smart-alecks carried guns.

"Buzz off, buster." Nathan glared at him, stepping forward. Despite his small stature, he never backed down from a fight.

Out of the corner of my eye, I saw Agent Burton charging toward us from a back office, wearing the same clothes he had on the day before, minus a hat.

"I'll take it from here." Burton elbowed the rookie aside.

I cringed at his fresh cuts and bruises, his swollen eye a deep black and purple.

"You look terrible," I blurted out. "Are you hurt?"

"Let's just say I had a rough night." Burton looked apologetic. "Now you know why I didn't call."

CHAPTER FIFTEEN

"Can we go somewhere and talk?" I glanced at Nathan, who got the hint and left to explore the police station.

Agent Burton led me to a small, simple office in back overlooking the Strand. "Have a seat. It's not the Hollywood, but it works." I noticed its sparse, worn furnishings: an old typewriter and gooseneck lamp sat atop an old roll-top desk, a few papers and books stacked neatly to the side.

Unlike Mack and Mr. Thomas, my editor, Burton didn't even have his own hat rack. No personal photos or mementos or pictures of any kind, as if he were a temporary visitor. Was it an oversight or was the job so dangerous, the police chief didn't expect him to stay very long? I didn't want to speculate on the obvious.

"Sorry I couldn't stop by last night, but some uninvited guests showed up here and I got delayed." He stretched out his long legs and attempted a smile.

"What happened? I heard there was a big brawl." I settled in his oak banker's chair, moving as close as possible to him, ignoring the cops' stares as they passed.

Burton's blue eyes glinted. "I'd call it a knock-down, drag-out fight. Seems Johnny Jack likes to make a scene."

"Glad you're OK." I touched his hand, mulling it over. "Was anyone else hurt?"

"You can say that." Burton winced when he tried to smile. "This station became our own personal fortress, like the Alamo, but with better results. A few goons got so worked up, they were throwing chairs across the room."

"Chairs?" I gasped. "What did y'all do?"

"We fought back, what else? Finally Sheriff Sanders fired off a few rounds to get their attention, and the thugs ran away like scared mongrels. Luckily he was shooting blanks." He motioned to the young cops with gratitude. "Thanks to these fellas, I'm still here."

"Hard to imagine Johnny Jack is scared of anything. Maybe it was just a warning to stay away from his turf?"

"Well, it worked. The guys here are plenty spooked."

"So what happened with Sanders? Did he interrogate you about the murder? Does he believe you, that you're innocent?"

"I think so, but he's not letting on to Johnny Jack. Officially the case is still under investigation." He grinned. "Turns out the sheriff is full of hot air, just like his gun."

I began to breathe easy. Still, I wondered about Sanders' good-old-boy image: Was it all an act to catch folks off-guard?

"What about your car? Did they test the blood and hair samples on your headlamp?"

"They're still in the process of evaluating the residue, so I'm stuck without transportation or a place to live for a while." Burton rubbed his day-old stubble, and I noticed the cuts and welts on his hands and knuckles. "What I really need now is a shower and a shave, but I'd rather not go home. Johnny Jack's goons may be waiting for me."

"You can't stay here forever. It's not livable. Where did you sleep—in a jail cell?"

Burton nodded. "We had no other choice. Johnny Jack's men surrounded the station."

"You don't say!" I leaned forward, touching his hand. "Say, why not stay at the boarding house tonight? Our offer still stands."

"It's too risky. I'd rather not put you or Eva in any more danger."

He had a point. "What about staying at the Hotel Galvez? The least they can do is let you spend the night after you helped with the bathing beauty pageant."

"I'd like a nice soft bed after that rock-hard cot. But I think the Galvez is too public, not to mention too pricey for a police budget. I'd be better off in an out-of-the-way place without so many tourists." Burton gave me a sly smile. "Maybe you'll come visit me?"

"It won't be the first time we've been in a hotel room together," I teased him. "Why don't you suggest the idea to your boss?"

"What boss? I'm my own boss. But I may need to square it away with Chief Johnson."

"I'll ask Nathan to give you a ride there—less obvious than a police car."

"You're just full of ideas today, aren't you?" He winked. "Glad I've got you on my side."

While he talked to the police chief, I noticed a gold cuff link on his desk, engraved with some type of family crest and scrolled letter. Seemed a bit fancy for a flatfoot. Maybe one of the gangsters lost it during the fight? I made a mental note to ask Burton about it later.

Getting restless, I decided to wander around the station, taking note of the messy desks and cluttered offices. Except for the cowboy hats and holsters and lack of newspapers, their work space didn't look that different from the *Gazette* newsroom.

"What'cha doing, girlie?" a ruddy-faced cop sidled up to me. "Poking your nose where it don't belong?"

"Just looking for my friend, Nathan," I stammered, motioning for him across the room.

"Say, aren't you Burton's gal? Jasmine, is it?"

How did he know my name? "We're just friends." I tried to brush him off, my face flushed.

"If you say so." He shrugged, looking skeptical, and walked off.

Swell. These coppers were as gossipy as my boss.

Nathan seemed to be in a serious discussion with a silver-haired cop who I recognized from the crime scene on Sunday. I presumed Nathan was questioning him for Mack's sake.

When I approached them, the cop tipped his hat politely. "I'm Deputy Chief Doug Connors. And who's this pretty little lady?"

"Jasmine Cross." I stuck out my hand. "I work at the *Gazette*."

"Secretary?" he asked. "Gossip columnist?"

I admit, his assumption stung, but I stood tall. "I hope to be a news reporter."

"My, my." Connors gave me the once-over. "A girl reporter. I'll bet you distract all the fellas at work."

"She sure does," Nathan said. "In a good way."

I shot him a go-to-hell look and they both got the telegram. After Connors left, I smiled brightly at Nathan. "Say, will you do me a big favor? If Burton gets the OK, can you give him a ride to a hotel? Where, I don't know."

"This place is loaded with squad cars. Why me?" Nathan frowned. "I don't want to be Johnny Jack's next target."

"Keep it down!" I hushed him. "No one will notice him in your old Ford. If a cop car pulls up with Agent Burton inside, he may as well be in a parade."

Burton appeared then, patting my back like I was his kid sister, no doubt to keep the cops from razzing us. "Good news. The captain approved your idea, saying it's probably safe for me to stay in hiding a while. He suggested a small motel by the old Tremont Hotel. No need to stop by my place. It's not safe to go home."

I elbowed Nathan a few times until he finally piped up: "Come on, I'll give you a lift."

Burton beamed. "I knew you were a good egg. I'll go get my gear and meet you outside."

Gear? Did the sheriff allow him to keep his gun? I didn't want to ask for fear of embarrassing him, but I suspected the sheriff confiscated any weapons. Still, baseball bats were in ample supply at any dry goods store.

"So where to?" Nathan asked as we climbed into his Model T.

"A hole-in-the-wall called Lafitte's Lair," Burton told us. "Supposed to be named after some famous local pirate."

"You mean Jean Lafitte," I said. "Wouldn't it be nice if we found buried treasure there?"

"Count me in," said Nathan. "We can all share the bounty and run away to Greece."

Burton remained silent, staring out the window, no doubt pondering his fate as we drove.

Indeed, the hotel had the weather-beaten, windswept look of an old pirate ship, but at least it seemed neat and clean. "Well, it's not the Hotel Galvez, but it'll do." Burton sounded disappointed.

After Nathan parked in front, a young bellman came to open my door, but Burton jumped out. "Only me checking in."

"Your valise, sir?" Puzzled, the valet began to open the trunk.

"No luggage." Burton flashed his badge. "This is all I brought."

Startled, the valet backed away, and rushed to open the entrance. "Yes, sir."

Burton lingered by my car door, squeezing my hand. "Thanks for everything, you two."

"Call if you need anything. You know where to find me," I said, trying to act cheerful, trying to ignore the fear, the dread, in the pit of my stomach. What if Johnny Jack and his gang found out where he was staying? Would I ever see him again?

"Same goes for you." He grinned as walked inside, giving us a quick wave. I waved back, forcing a sunny smile, hoping he'd be safe for at least a few more days.

"Gotta admit, I wouldn't want to trade places with Burton," Nathan said, driving off. "I couldn't live that way, looking over my shoulder every minute."

"You said it. He's just trying to do his job and the gangs want to kill him for it."

"Tough break." Nathan turned on Seawall Boulevard, slowly driving by the beach, the sky a dusky blue shade. I watched families playing with big colorful beach balls, young couples lounging on the pale sand under pastel parasols, wishing I could join in the fun.

"Say, are you ready to head home or do you want to grab a bite to eat? I wouldn't mind some fresh fish from Gaido's."

Nathan couldn't last half an hour without thinking about food.

"I've got a better idea. How about going to the Oasis to see Sammy? Bernie's a great cook—and besides, the food is free."

"Can't beat free." He grinned, and turned right on 23rd Street. "Now? Wouldn't you rather go later, when the joint is jumping?"

"I want to ask him about the murder, see what's new."

"Isn't he on the outs with Johnny Jack? If he did know anything, I doubt he'd blab to a society reporter, even if you're friends." I'd never told Nathan, or really anyone besides Amanda, that Sammy was my half-brother—and I wanted to keep it a secret, to be safe.

"Don't worry, he trusts me. We won't stay long."

Nathan parked halfway between the Oasis and the now-closed Joe's Bar, and opened my car door. After I knocked a code on the heavy wooden door, Dino peered out the window slot. "What are you two doing here?" He acted surprised. "The sun hasn't even set."

"Hello to you, too. Where's Sammy?" I asked. "In his office?"

Dino shrugged and cracked open the door, avoiding my eyes. "He's downstairs."

"Is everything OK? Johnny Jack didn't show up again, did he?"

"See for yourself." Dino wasn't known for being chatty.

I exchanged worried looks with Nathan as we made our way down the stairs, adjusting my eyes to the darkened room Strange that no one was tending bar. Doria, our wooden mermaid mascot, held court over the walnut counter where a few sad sacks drowned their days and nights.

Something looked different. Then I realized that a bright new slot machine had been installed right by the bar, ready and waiting to collect coins or tokens. Worse, the grand piano had been moved from its prime spot and pushed into a corner.

In its place, a group of men sat with Sammy, playing poker around a huge table piled high with chips and cash, acting as if they were enjoying an innocuous game of Mah Jong or gin rummy. Were they customers or part of the Downtown Gang? Was this a friendly game of cards or were they settling a score or bet?

A couple of gold diggers sat at a nearby table, staring at their enameled compacts, fidgeting with their frocks and fussing with their bobbed hair. In their extravagant glad rags and headpieces, they seemed a tad overdressed and overeager for a simple speakeasy like the Oasis.

Standing by the bar, I watched the men play for a few minutes. From the looks of the poker players, they appeared to be serious card sharks, not your run-of-the-mill amateurs. Sammy had made it a policy to never to allow gambling in his bar. Since when did he start playing poker with hard-boiled thugs?

CHAPTER SIXTEEN

"I didn't know Sammy liked to gamble," Nathan whispered. "Those dames look expensive."

"I'll say." I fingered my bead necklace, trying to assess the situation. "No doubt this was Johnny Jack's idea. Maybe we should hit the road?"

"Let's stick around a while," Nathan said. "I'm starving!"

Naturally, Nathan's hunger pangs took precedence over everything. Sammy must have noticed us then, because he placed his cards face-down on the table. He mumbled a few words to the men, then rushed over to greet us, acting guilty as a hooligan caught with his hand in the till. Luckily the radio was cranked up loud enough to cover up our conversation.

"Sorry to interrupt your poker game." I glared at him. "What's going on? Who are your new buddies—swindlers and cheats?"

"Look, Jazz, I had no choice." Sammy wiped his forehead with his hand. "Since Charlie's out of commission, Nounes forced me to hold the Downtown Gang's card games here. You know I can't say no to Johnny Jack."

"Isn't it enough that you're his bag man? What else does he expect you to do?"

"Who knows? But I don't want to make any trouble. Hey, I'm getting to know the guys in the gang. It ain't all bad."

That gave me an idea. "While you're at it, can you ask about Charlie's murder? And maybe you can find out who took a shot at Agent Burton."

"Wish I could help." Sammy shrugged. "The gang may label me a snitch if I ask too many questions."

My face fell. "That's not what I meant. Just let me know if the subject comes up."

"Sorry, Jazz. I'm just jittery after...you know. If the guys think I'm acting too nosy, they'll get suspicious. But there's no law against a guy listening to a conversation."

"Say, can I join in?" Nathan asked. "I play a mean game of poker, if I say so myself."

"I don't think that's a smart idea. You might lose your shirt, plus a few body parts if you don't pay up." Sammy shook his head. "Look at Parker. Can't believe his funeral is tomorrow."

Nathan blanched. "Forget it. I value my body parts too much."

No wonder Sammy couldn't turn down Johnny Jack. I didn't want to think what Johnny Jack would do to Sammy, or to anyone in the Downtown Gang, if they disobeyed his orders.

"Can't we at least get a drink before we go?" Nathan asked.

Sammy grabbed two cold Coke bottles from the ice-box. "You kids better scram. It's not safe for you to be here now."

"Thanks, Sammy." We both smiled in gratitude, taking a sip.

I heard heels clicking on the hardwood floor and the floozies came into view, frowning, creasing their careful face paint. "Let's blow this joint," I heard the striking marcelled brunette say.

She perked up when she saw Sammy, purring, "Hey, tall, dark and handsome. I'll be glad to roll your dice anytime you want." She leaned over and her bee-stung lips brushed his stubbly cheek. "Just make sure my man ain't around. See you later, Sammy."

Sammy blushed to his temples, but I could tell he secretly loved the attention. "Behave yourself, Flo. Don't take any wooden nickels."

"That's no fun," she laughed, wiggling her long fingers as she left. "Toodles!"

Good thing Amanda wasn't here to watch Sammy flirting with Flo. She'd have stripped off Flo's glittery gown and headband faster than she could say "Toodles."

"Flo? Who's Flo?" I razzed him, wondering where I'd heard her name before. "Your new flame?"

"Hell, no. Flo's a busy gal—she's got a cop on one arm, a gangster on the other. I'd be a fool if I got tangled up with a dame like her."

"You know Amanda has a mean jealous streak."

Sammy looked worried. "You won't tell her, will you? Either way, I'd be a dead man."

"You said it." Before we left, I took one last glance, wondering: Were any of these jokers playing poker responsible for setting up Burton? What about whacking Charlie Parker?

Sammy blocked my view and firmly took us by the elbows, nudging us toward the exit.

"I get the telegram." I held up my hands, and motioned for him to follow us upstairs.

When we got to the door, Sammy nodded at Dino, motioning toward the entrance. Taking his cue, Dino bolted the door, then lumbered down the stairs, out of earshot.

"Got some news." I pulled Sammy aside. "Did you hear Johnny Jack and his henchmen stormed the police station last night? They accused Agent Burton of killing your pal Charlie. Know anything about that little incident?"

He nodded. "I heard some noise, but kept my nose out of it."

"Any idea what they're planning next? Don't forget, Burton helped you with Johnny Jack not too long ago."

"Helped? Your Agent Burton is the reason I'm in this jam." His jade eyes narrowed. "Sorry, hon, but I gotta run or they'll send a firing squad after me too."

I wished he was only joking.

Sammy unlocked the door and practically pushed me and Nathan outside. I hated seeing him like this, taking orders from a ruthless gang leader, kowtowing to Johnny Jack like a servant.

In the car, Nathan turned to me. "I've never seen Sammy act this way. Normally he's cocky, hard-boiled. I don't know the guy very well, but seems to me he's shaking in his boots."

"Can you blame him?" I sighed. "What if these hoods try to set him up, make him lose all his dough? Then they can keep him on a short leash, ordering him around until his debt is paid."

As we drove, my mind flip-flopped between Burton and Sammy, afraid for both men. While Burton appeared to be safe, temporarily at least, now I worried about Sammy holding off Johnny Jack and his goons. Sammy was getting drawn deeper into the Downtown Gang, trying to appease his mob boss, and not cause any new rifts. What would Johnny Jack expect Sammy to do next—serve as a hit man?

"Say, we still haven't eaten yet and it's time for supper. You promised me a meal." Typical Nathan. Never mind murder and mayhem—food was at the top of his list.

I certainly didn't feel like going home and facing Aunt Eva or her gossipy boarders. "How about Star Drugstore? I think Amanda is working the evening shift."

"Sounds good to me. Haven't seen her in a while," Nathan agreed, turning down 23rd Street, and parking down the block.

At the diner, Amanda beamed when we entered, ushering us to a quiet booth in the corner. "What's new?" she asked, sitting next to me. "Is everything jake?" When I didn't answer, she tapped my arm "Why the long face? Is it Sammy? Or Agent Burton?"

Nathan took off to flirt with a cute blonde waitress behind the soda fountain, and I heard him order a root beer float. I lowered my voice to a whisper. Briefly, I filled her in on the latest news: "Guess what happened last night? Johnny Jack and his men showed up at the police station, gunning for Burton, but the cops fought them off."

"Jeepers!" Amanda gasped and covered her mouth, eyes wide as saucers. "Was anyone hurt?"

"Burton got a little black and blue, but Eva took good care of him. Don't worry, he's safe now."

Amanda raised her brows. "At the boarding house?"

"At a hideaway." I shook my head, not mentioning the hotel in case anyone was eavesdropping.

"Glad he's OK. So how's Sammy? Don't tell me he hired a new floozy at the Oasis?" She wailed, twisting her long blonde locks.

"Of course not. He's just busy." I let out a deep breath, wanting to share my frustration. "Busy doing Johnny Jack's bidding."

"What?! I knew he was in trouble." Her blue eyes widened in alarm. "I'd better get back to work. The manager is giving me a dirty look." Then in a loud sing-song voice, she asked, "What would you like for supper? I recommend the chicken and dumplings."

"My favorite." I glanced over at Nathan, who joined me at the table. "Make that two."

The chicken and dumplings were hot and spicy, with big chunks of white meat. As we ate, I thought about our conversation with Sammy, mulling over an idea.

"Say, Nate, what are you doing tomorrow?" I grinned, trying to butter him up.

"Working as usual. Trying to get a date with that new waitress. Why?" He looked suspicious.

I leaned over and whispered: "You've heard that criminals always return to the scene of the crime, right?"

"Sure. So what's on your mind?"

"I bet they also show up at their victim's funerals. Feel like going to a burial service?"

"Not mine, I hope," he cracked.

"You're a riot." I gave him a tight smile. "Why don't we go pay our respects to the late Charlie Parker?"

CHAPTER SEVENTEEN

"A mob funeral? That sounds like a barrel of laughs." Nathan scowled. "Why waste our time with a bunch of gangsters? I've seen enough ugly mugs for one day."

"I predict the killer will show up there, and pretend to be in mourning." I tried to convince him. "It's our chance to look around for anyone suspicious."

"All gangsters look suspicious. They're not exactly true-blue Boy Scouts."

"I'll say. But Burton told me Charlie was a nice guy, a barkeep trying to support his family. All he did wrong was get behind in his rent." Even Colin Ferris, the good-looking Beach Gang thug, had turned out to be an A-OK fella after all, though his methods were questionable.

"Charlie's dead, isn't he? Nice guys don't usually get whacked with a baseball bat."

Nathan had a point. "We're not going to socialize. I just want to check out the crowd, to see who turns up at the funeral."

"You're trying to get Burton off the hook." Nathan gave me a sly grin. "Admit it, you're stuck on him. Are you going steady now?"

Flustered, I motioned for Amanda to bring our check, but she waved me off. "I'm just trying to help a friend. Agent Burton can't very well show up on his own since he's the prime suspect." Anxious to leave, I left a dollar on the table. "My treat. Let's get out of here before someone overhears us."

Outside, the sky had turned a coral pink. Nathan tried to change my mind while I walked ahead of him toward his car. "Two clean-cut newshounds will stick out like flashing neon signs at a mob funeral. What if people recognize you? They'll wonder why a society reporter is attending a gangster's burial."

"They'll probably presume I'm a serious journalist covering the crime beat."

"Right—you're so tough, you were ready to upchuck at the murder scene."

So he'd noticed my greenish hue. "Fine, I'll find my own way there. Maybe I'll catch a ride with Sammy since he and Charlie were friends." I knew Sammy would be furious if we made an appearance, but I didn't bother to tell Nathan.

"OK, if you insist, I'll tag along. First we need to find out exactly where and when." He frowned. "But I still think it's too dangerous."

To be honest, I'd already started having second thoughts the moment I suggested the idea, but I couldn't back out now, not after I'd convinced Nathan to go. "I can check the *Gazette*, but I doubt they advertise gangster's funerals in the obituary section."

"I bet Mack will know. He seems to keep up with the latest gangster happenings."

Who exactly were his sources, I wondered?

As we neared the boarding house, I spied a familiar dark car parked in front and my stomach lurched: What was Sheriff Sanders doing here? I rushed out of Nathan's Model T so fast, I forgot to shut the door. Nathan followed me inside the boarding house, taking off his hat.

I found Aunt Eva and the sheriff sitting in the parlor and, in my usual diplomatic way, blurted out: "What's wrong? Did something happen to Agent Burton?"

"Why would you think that?" The sheriff frowned. "He's holed up at a secret location."

"Just wondering what you were..." I began.

"Why don't you join us for some lemonade?" Eva interrupted, and headed to the kitchen before I could reply.

"Sure, thanks," Nathan called out, settling on the couch. "Don't mind if I do."

I leveled my gaze at the sheriff. "Did you get the results back from the blood tests?"

"Eva tells me you're a society reporter." Sheriff Sanders bristled. "Why are you so interested in a murder investigation?"

"Agent Burton is a good friend, as you know." I sat on the edge of the couch, facing him, ignoring Nathan's don't-you-dare-looks. "So you've determined that it *is* a murder, not manslaughter. You believe it was premeditated, not accidental?"

"Now, miss, I didn't say that." He looked down at the worn Persian carpet. "During the robbery, it seems the victim struggled with his killers since his fingerprints were on the baseball bat. Clearly he acted in self-defense and tried to strike back. We don't know all the facts yet."

Struck out was more like it. "Do you have any leads yet? Any suspects? I assume you've eliminated Agent Burton by now."

He stared at me, stone-faced, crossing his arms. Eva must have overheard us because she popped in the door that moment, holding out a glass of lemonade. "Jazz, can you please help me in the kitchen? I need to refill the sheriff's drink."

"No need, Eva. I'd best be going." Sanders stood up abruptly, hat in hand, and glared at me in warning. My eyes skimmed over his receding hairline, and he thrust his hat atop his head, his face florid. "Thanks for your hospitality."

"Glad you stopped by, Walter. Come again soon." Eva followed him out the door, still holding her glass.

Walter? Eva? Since when had these two become so friendly?

I rolled my eyes at Nathan who seemed just as mystified. Was my aunt falling for the sheriff or was she only being polite?

"What's going on between you and the sheriff?" I demanded when she returned.

"You mean Walter? Nothing. We had a nice chat, that's all." Her pale face flushed.

"He showed up here, out of the blue, just to *chat*?"

She turned crimson. "What's wrong with a nice widower paying a little attention to me? I'm not an old maid, you know!"

A widower—no doubt looking for a new wife? Aha!

Sad to say, by society's standards, an unmarried woman in her mid-thirties *was* considered a spinster. Perhaps she was more sensitive about her single status than I'd realized.

I softened my tone. "Sorry, Aunt Eva. I'm just worried about James, staying at a run-down hotel, not knowing if he's still considered guilty or innocent."

"Well, I doubt they would've released him if they thought he was a killer," she pointed out. "But the sheriff did admit they wanted to keep him in a safe place until Johnny Jack calmed down. They're hoping to appease him by..." Her voice trailed off.

"By what? By letting him get away with murder?" I flared up.

"Not at all." She cleared her throat. "Walter did let some information slip out concerning Agent Burton."

"He did? What did he say?" I perked up. "Did he admit Burton is innocent?"

"Not exactly." She paused. "Seems Johnny Jack is expecting a big shipment of rum during the next few days. I think from Cuba?"

"The sheriff told you that?" Nathan looked shocked, giving me a wary look.

Eva nodded, clearly pleased with herself. "So the police plan to look the other way and allow him to pick up his stash, just this once."

"What?" I was flabbergasted—not only by her statement, but by the fact she got the sheriff to talk to her at all. "Are you serious?"

"Walter swore it was true."

Frankly, I wondered how Burton would react, knowing Sanders was making deals with his nemesis behind his back.

"Thanks, Eva. I could learn a few tricks from you."

"Of course you could. You know the expression, 'Kill them with kindness?'" She wagged her finger like an overbearing nun. "I heard the way you were questioning Walter, drilling him, as if he was a suspect himself. Why don't you try a softer approach, treat your interviews as a conversation, the way your mother taught you?"

"You mean her other favorite saying: 'You can catch more bees with honey?'"

"Exactly." Eva nodded. "So you see, Walter isn't such a terrible man, after all. He's simply trying to help save your beau from Johnny Jack and his gang."

"I doubt Agent Burton will be too happy when he finds out the cops are giving in to Johnny Jack," I snapped. "If he stands by and does nothing, it'll undermine his authority—for good."

Frankly, I was getting suspicious. Why would the county sheriff confide private police business to my aunt? Did he assume that she'd tell me so that I'd try to reason with James, convince him to go along with their scheme?

"Jasmine, you know how I feel about Prohibition. I don't condone drinking that demon rum, or any of that rotgut." Eva placed a hand over her chest as if praying. "But if one more cargo of illegal liquor is allowed into Galveston, what difference does it make if it helps save Agent Burton's life?"

I couldn't disagree with her logic. Still, Burton may be spared for now, but giving Johnny Jack *permission* for a booze drop "just this once" wouldn't help Burton maintain any sense of control or power in the long run.

Tell the truth, I hated to think what Johnny Jack might do to Agent Burton the next time he tried to stop a rum-runner from coming into Galveston Bay.

CHAPTER EIGHTEEN

Tuesday

The next morning, I dressed in a navy linen frock with a sailor's collar and white piping and a wide-brimmed navy straw hat with a white band, tucking my white gloves into my leather clutch. I hoped I looked respectful enough for a funeral, since wearing all black at work seemed too conspicuous, especially for summer.

When I arrived, late as usual, Mack called me over to his desk, keeping his voice low. "Say, I heard your beau is staying at a swanky hotel for a while. Must be nice, living high on the hog on the taxpayer's dime."

Swanky—Lafitte's Lair? "Where'd you hear that?" Was he razzing me or fishing for information? "As you know, he's not a guest, he's in hiding."

Mack ignored my jab. "So have you heard from him?"

"Not lately. Why?"

"If you do, tell him to stay away from Charlie Parker's funeral today. It's not safe. I hear it'll be loaded with mobsters, all the way from Houston. Apparently Charlie was a popular fella."

"You don't say. Are you attending the service?" I asked innocently.

"Hell, yes. You know what they say about criminals returning to the scene...I'm banking they'll also be at the funeral. What a story." Funny, I'd just used that same line on Nathan.

"If it's so dangerous, why are you going?"

"Think about it. How often do you see so many wiseguys in one place? It's a crime reporter's dream."

Mack frowned, giving me the once-over. I must have looked nervous because he added, "You're not thinking of showing up, are you? I wouldn't recommend it, not for a dame like you. Since when do society reporters cover gangsters' graveyards?"

"Why not? Speaking of, where's it being held?"

"Look it up in the obits," he scowled.

"Maybe I'll see you there." I faked a smile, acting as if a mob funeral was the social event of the season. Mack was blowing so much smoke, puffing on his smelly cigar, I couldn't read his expression. I rushed off before Mrs. Harper noticed I wasn't at my desk. What excuse could I use to get off work early?

Frankly, I was surprised to see a two-line notice in the paper, next to a grainy photo of a young, good-looking Charlie Parker: The service was being held at 3:00 o'clock at the Wood Lawn Funeral Home, safely ensconced on the Downtown Gang's turf. His photo had to be at least ten years old, when he was still in his prime, roughly his late thirties.

You'd never know it was the same man I saw at the Rusty Bucket. His features were puffy and soft, no doubt from years of drinking away his profits—not to mention the fact that half his head was caved in. I shuddered at the memory, wondering if I *should* play it safe. If I had any sense, I'd take Mack's advice and stay away from the service.

Mrs. Harper placed a stack of stories on my desk that needed to be proofed and fact-checked. The thought of spending a nice sunny day grinding away, typing up tidbits about charity balls and tea dances and engagements, made me yawn: I had to break the monotony, even if it meant risking my neck *and* my job.

"By the way, Jasmine, how is Agent Burton?"

I noticed she didn't call him my "fella" anymore, since now she considered him a murder suspect.

"Wish I knew," I half-fibbed. "I haven't heard from him lately."

"Oh, my." She tsk-tsked. "I do hope he's all right."

At noon, Nathan stopped by, holding his straw boater. "Want to grab some lunch?"

"Maybe later. What about our plans?"

He glanced around the room and I followed his gaze to Mack's empty desk. No doubt he was taking his typical two-hour lunch. "By the way, Mack asked me to go with him to the, uh, event today to take photos. Discreetly of course. Sure you still want to go?"

"Nothing's changed. Besides, you promised," I said putting on my best pouty face.

"OK, you twisted my arm. I'll meet Mack there."

I worked through lunch without a bite, trying to crank out my boss's silly society stories. All afternoon, I'd racked my brain, trying to invent a plausible escape plan. Luckily, Nathan showed up at half past two, *sans* Mack. "Ready to go?"

"Come with me. I need to convince Mrs. Harper to let me out of my cage," I whispered. Typed pages in hand, I placed them gently on her desk. "Mrs. Harper, can I leave for the day since I finished my work early? We want to visit Agent Burton to make sure he's OK."

"Fine." She beamed her approval, then stared at Nathan, looking puzzled. "I didn't realize you and Agent Burton were friends?"

"Yes, ma'am. He's a swell fella. Just ask Jazz." He forced a smile.

Did he have to be so obvious?

In the car, I asked Nathan, "So what did you tell Mack?"

"I told him I was developing some photos and I'd see him at the funeral." He shrugged. "Mack's a big boy. He has his own car."

"Thanks, Nate." I smoothed out my navy frock and pulled on my gloves. "Say, why don't we stop by the Rusty Bucket on the way? Now may be a good time to search the bar."

"Sure that's wise? The cops won't like a dame snooping around a crime scene."

"Don't worry, we'll be careful." What did I expect to find—a calling card with the killer's name and address?

"We? Count me out. This is your hare-brained idea."

"Hare-brained?" I motioned toward Market Street. "Take a look. Obviously the cops had the same plan."

Police cars had blocked the area by the Rusty Bucket so we stopped in front of the Brown Pelican. What was going on? As we watched, a couple of cops struggled with a bulky one-armed bandit as they carried it to a squad car. Some held several boxes and files bulging with paper, and what appeared to be crates of liquor, followed by two cops juggling a big brass cash register.

"Must be a raid. Looks like they're clearing out the bar, slot machines, booze and all."

"The cops may be searching for evidence. A motive for murder." Nathan paused. "Or are they just helping themselves to the loot while no one's watching?"

"I'll bet. Wonder why they waited so long to empty it out?"

"I'm sure the Downtown Gang had eyes on the place. What better time to confiscate the contents than during a funeral?"

"Makes sense," I agreed. "While the gangsters are away, the police come out to play. I wonder what else poor Charlie Parker was up to besides hosting poker games?"

"Beats me. I don't buy the 'just a robbery' story. Too bloody. Seems like the killers had a score to settle."

"True. This seemed to be more about vengeance," I nodded, shading my eyes. "Say, let's skedaddle before the cops spot us."

Too late. A chestnut-haired cop with a ruddy complexion waved us away, then did a double-take and approached the car. "Well, if it isn't Nathan and Jasmine. Remember me from the station?"

Swell. How did he remember our names? I glanced at his badge, avoiding his gaze: Sergeant Something.

"Sure do." Nathan faked a smile. "Say, what's going on here?"

"Just routine police business. You kids better get out of the way and let the cops do their job." He paused, his expression wary. "Did you two know Charlie?"

"Not really." Nathan shook his head.

The cop thrust out his chest, threatening, like a rooster in a cockfight. "So why are you two hanging around here? Why'd you show up at the station house?"

"We're doing our jobs, same as you." Nathan saluted the policeman, taking his cue to leave. "Keep up the good work!" With that, he made a sharp U-turn and headed in the opposite direction. "Boy, did you see his face? He was ready to blow his stack!"

"I'll say. Whatever Charlie was involved in, the cops must be trying to cover it up."

Nathan snorted. "Yeah, covering up the fact they're stealing all his stash and cash!"

CHAPTER NINETEEN

As we neared the funeral home, I noticed the fancy new Studebakers and Bentleys and Cadillacs parked around the block. For a humble owner of a hole-in-the-wall, Charlie sure had some high-falutin' friends. We slipped inside the gilt-laden parlor, trying to blend into the sizable crowd, remaining on the outskirts of the service.

The family stood in front, and I counted at least half a dozen fair-haired children of varying ages and heights surrounding the simple casket, closed of course. Sadly, Parker's face was so bashed in, he looked like the monsters in *Frankenstein* or the *Phantom of the Opera*, two horror flicks I wished I'd never seen.

While the priest droned on, I had a chance to observe the crowd. I noticed quite a few floozies milling around, dressed a bit too bright to be in mourning, no doubt girlfriends or gold diggers hoping to land a sugar daddy. Some faces seemed familiar, but hard-boiled gangsters tended to look the same after a while, the way they held themselves, their defensive stance, ready to knock off an enemy without warning.

Strange that Mack hadn't shown up yet since he covered the crime beat. Gang activity provided fodder for most of his stories.

Scanning the crowd, I spied Sammy and Dino next to some goons across the room, and shifted out of their view. Were they the same wiseguys I saw playing poker at the Oasis?

Unfortunately, when the priest told the crowd to kneel, I was so lost in thought that I remained standing, so Sammy saw me clear as day. He frowned and looked heavenward, as if that could make me disappear. Nathan yanked at my dress, hissing, "Pay attention!"

That's one problem with Catholic churches and funeral homes: You had to continually stand and sit and kneel throughout the service, popping up and down like a jittery Jack-in-the box. Speaking of, I didn't notice Johnny Jack in the crowd. Of all people, shouldn't he be the first one to pay his respects? The least he could do was make an appearance for the family's sake.

A couple of hoods got up, saying Charlie was a swell guy, and a good friend. Near the end, a handsome young man stood by the casket, his eyes red-rimmed, and choked out a few words about his beloved father. I couldn't help but blink back a few tears after his short and heartfelt speech.

After the service, friends, family and hoods filed out of the funeral parlor, toward the burial grounds. Sammy made a beeline for me, disapproval written all over his chiseled features. He yanked my elbow, pulling me away from the group, out of earshot.

"What in hell are you two doing here?" he snapped. "Don't tell me you're on an *assignment* because I doubt your society editor would be interested in a *private* gang funeral."

Despite his threatening tone, I knew Sammy was more worried than angry. "We just wanted to pay our respects." I avoided his gaze but finally admitted, "OK, so I wanted to check out the crowd, see who turned up."

"Who were you expecting? Rudolph Valentino, rising from the grave?" His voice softened. "What were you thinking, turning up at a Downtown Gang's funeral?"

"I'm not here for fun," I whispered. "For Burton's sake."

"Don't you realize how dangerous it is?" He shook his hands. "If these wiseguys find out you're Burton's gal, who happens to be the prime suspect, they may try to take you out, too."

"Take me out? Why?" I blinked, never considering that possibility. "I was just curious."

"You know what they say—curiosity killed..."

"Lucky for me, I don't own a cat. Just a stray who follows me around." I tried to downplay his warning, thinking of Golliwog, my scrawny black stray, with a pang of guilt.

"I'm serious, Jazz." Sammy shook his head. "Now they've all gotten a good look at you. What if you're out with Agent Burton, and you run into one of these gangsters? Look what happened at the Hollywood. Could be your funeral instead of poor Charlie's."

What a pleasant thought. I had to change the subject—and fast.

"Burton is just a scapegoat. Maybe it *was* a random robbery or a Beach Gang hit. Who knows what your pal Charlie was really up to?"

I leaned forward. "In fact, the cops are raiding his place right now. We passed by the Rusty Bucket on our way over here and saw half a dozen cops loading up all sorts of stuff into their squad cars. Any idea why?"

Naturally, I didn't mention we took a deliberate detour to peruse the place.

"Now?" Sammy's hazel eyes flashed. "What were they taking?"

"Boxes, file cabinets—all his papers, too. Even the slot machine and cash register."

"Damn it!" Sammy slapped his forehead. "Everything?"

"Seems that way." I nodded. "Why does it matter?"

Sammy pulled out a Camel cigarette and lit it, shuffling his feet like he wanted to run away. "Last week, Charlie asked if he could borrow some money to pay off Johnny Jack. He's a nice guy so I thought, why not? So I let Charlie write me an IOU, told him to keep a copy in his cash register as a reminder. Now the cops are gonna find it and think I'm the real killer." He swallowed so hard his Adam's apple bobbed up and down.

"Don't worry, the gang still thinks that Burton's their number one suspect. Fortunately, he's holed up in a safe location."

I hated withholding information from my own brother, but he didn't need to know where Burton was staying. What if a gang member overheard the location?

"You don't say. Too bad for him, but lucky for me." Sammy paused to drag on his Camel. "Hey, did the cops see you two spying on them? Let's hope they think you just got lost."

My face flushed. "I think one cop recognized us from the police station yesterday."

"What? Who was it? Jazz, first you show up at the station house, then the next day you attend a Downtown Gang funeral?" He stared at me, incredulous. "Are you nuts?"

"I'm a reporter. They'll think I'm just doing my job." I began to mentally retrace our steps, wondering if my efforts to help Burton were all a big mistake.

"A *society* reporter. What if you're being watched? They may wonder if you're a snitch, trying to play both sides." He blew out a billowy puff of smoke. "Sure doesn't help any if you're seen here talking to me."

"A snitch? Me?" I had to savor the irony: Not long ago, Sammy had been suspected of that very thing.

Then Dino walked up and grunted, saying, "Make it quick. Burial will start soon."

"I'll be right there." Sammy glared at me. "You and Nathan better leave. Now."

"Fine with me. This isn't my kind of crowd anyway." I paused, noting his furrowed brows. "What's wrong, Sammy?"

Before he could reply, a nattily-dressed hood in a fez walked over, greeting Sammy with a hearty handshake, slapping his back. Who did he think he was—the Sheik of Araby?

Turning to me, the gangster said, "And who are you, little lady? You look familiar."

Sammy gave me a warning look behind his back, fingers to his lips, warning me to keep quiet. "A friend of the family." I pasted on a smile, wondering where I'd seen him before. Was he at the Oasis, or was it the Rusty Bucket?

Before I could pull away, the fez fella grabbed my hand and kissed it, his spiky moustache scratching my skin. He gave me the heebie-jeebies with his pseudo-sophisticated manner, his grubby hands rough as fish scales. How did he know Sammy?

"Nice meeting you." I yanked my hand back, wishing I could wash it immediately. Up close, I noticed a few bruises, red marks on his cheeks. Then it occurred to me: Was he the high-roller Maceo kicked out of the Hollywood Club last Saturday night?

To escape, I made my way over to the young widow, who stood in a sort of receiving line with her multitude of kids. She reminded me of a fresh-faced farmer's wife, with her simple black frock and thin straight blonde hair she'd put up in a loose bun, a few strands sticking out like loose straw.

I wanted to express my condolences, but when I saw her swollen face and red eyes, I immediately became tongue-tied. "I'm so sorry for your loss" was all I could muster.

Mrs. Parker squinted at me, as if trying to recall my name. "Were you a friend of Charlie's?"

"He and Sammy were friends. Feel free to call him if you need anything," I blurted out.

What was I saying? I doubted Sammy would appreciate the fact I'd volunteered his help, especially since babysitting a big brood of kids wasn't exactly his favorite hobby.

For a moment, she brightened. "Sammy Cook? How nice of him. Thank you, Miss...?"

"I'm Jazz Cross. Take care, Mrs. Parker." I squeezed her hand and turned away, feeling sad and foolish, but in a way I empathized with the poor widow. The same men who'd killed her husband probably attacked Burton later that night. And although our circumstances were entirely different, I could understand her sense of grief and loss.

I looked around the grounds for Nathan, who'd managed to blend in a bit too well. Scanning the area, I noticed a nondescript black Ford with dark windows cruise down the street as if in slow motion. Squinting, I did a double-take: Was that a Tommy gun sticking out the window? Instinctively I ducked, screaming my head off as loud shots blasted into the crowd.

CHAPTER TWENTY

I wasn't the only one ducking and screaming bloody murder. Dozens of people crouched down or dove to the ground, arms covering their heads. Some folks hid behind trees and bushes while a few mothers huddled over their children, who cried and wailed at the commotion.

Shaking, I kept my body still, lifting my head slightly to get a better view of the action. My first thought was of Sammy, Nathan and Dino: Were they OK?

A few men bolted on foot after the Ford, arms out, firing off shots, but the car sped up, its tires screeching as it turned the corner. Was that Sammy in the lead? Frankly, I couldn't tell all the dark-haired men apart: Were they mourners or mobsters or both?

After the shots and chaos subsided, I scrambled to my feet and smoothed out my frock. Frantic, I looked around the crowd as if staring through a blurred lens: Everyone seemed to walk around in a daze, mouths open in disbelief. Several people rushed to their cars, others returned to the funeral parlor, no doubt for sanctuary.

In an instant, the boundaries between us had dropped. Now we were a collective group of victims, bound together by tragedy.

I'd never seen or experienced a war zone but I imagined this scenario seemed similar. My legs felt wobbly and weak, yet I slowly managed to regain my senses. Loud shots still rang in my ears, and my whole body seemed shaky. Trying not to panic, I scoured the grounds, searching for familiar faces, afraid of what I might find.

So far I didn't see anyone hurt or wounded. Were they merely warning shots—a scare tactic to frighten the crowd? Or had the shooter missed his mark?

Across the grounds, I saw the widow sitting on a bench with her children, a few kids at her feet, clutching at her hands and clothes for safety. She appeared to be in semi-shock, eyes glazed, staring straight ahead, perhaps trying to comprehend what exactly had happened.

Who was the intended target? Was it the Beach Gang or an inside job? What kind of sick bastards try to gun down mourners at a funeral? My mind raced with questions that might never be answered, especially in Galveston, where most people and police minded their own business. But I wasn't most people.

Thank God I spied Sammy and Dino coming down the street toward me, chests heaving, still holding their guns. "Those goddamn assholes," Sammy snapped, breathing hard. "What in hell were they doing, trying to massacre the whole crowd?"

"Any idea who it was?" I asked. "Who'd want to target Parker's funeral—a rival gang?"

Sammy and Dino exchanged worried looks, and I knew they wouldn't say a word, as usual.

Still, I had more pressing matters on my mind now. "Have you seen Nathan? Help me look for him," I pleaded.

If anything happened to Nathan, I'd never forgive myself. Why had I insisted he tag along on my Quixotic quest to help Burton? What was Mack thinking, asking Nathan to take photos of a gang funeral—then never showing up himself? Strange. He'd tried to warn me to stay away, but I refused to listen.

"Glad to see you, kiddo!" I heard a familiar voice and turned around to see Nathan, a bit shaken up, but grinning from ear to ear.

"Nathan!" I gave him a big bear hug, relieved. "Where were you? I was worried sick."

"I got my camera so I could sneak in a few shots. I swear, this is the most exciting funeral I've been to in years." His face grew grim. "Unfortunately, not everyone fared so well."

Sammy moved toward him, alarmed. "Who got hit? Show me."

"You sure?" Nathan motioned for us to follow him. "At least the poor sap doesn't have to go very far. He can have his funeral right here."

"He's dead?" Sammy grimaced. "Anyone we know?"

Nathan shrugged and led us toward the funeral parlor's front entrance. By now, most of the crowd had dispersed, but we noticed half a dozen or so people staring down at a prone body on the ground. The priest knelt by the man, grasping his hand, talking softly.

As we edged closer, I heard him speaking in Latin, no doubt giving the victim his last rites. The group stood with heads bowed, while a few were praying and holding hands. Sadly, it was too late for prayers: A fez had fallen onto the ground, the man's dark, heavy-lidded eyes opened wide, a bloody bullet hole lodged in his forehead.

CHAPTER TWENTY-ONE

Who kills someone at a funeral? Gangsters, that's who.

Shuddering, I stared at the victim, blinking, as if seeing a mirage. And to think the guy had just kissed my hand moments ago.

The bullet hole was clean, without any messy residue or blood splatter—as neat as the bullet hole in Burton's Stetson. No doubt the work of a sharpshooter turned hit man. Very likely a war veteran. What was the connection?

Sammy threw his arms up in the air, leaning over the body. "What in hell? Not you too?"

"You knew him?" The priest asked Sammy.

"Not well." Sammy leaned over the man, examining his wound, shaking his head. "But he was a good guy. Tony Torino, a businessman from Houston."

"Let's all pray for Mr. Torino, may he rest in peace." The priest crossed his heart before bowing his head and chanting in Latin.

After we all pretended to pray, Sammy grabbed my arm and led me away while Dino and Nathan trailed behind.

"I can't believe they'd carry out a hit, at a funeral for God's sake, in broad daylight," he muttered.

"How'd you know the victim?" I asked when we were out of earshot, wondering who *they* were. "What was he doing here?"

"Tony was a bookie from Houston. Charlie served his Galveston clients." He scowled. "Then Tony became a goddamn loan shark on the side, one of the worst kind. The deeper in debt, the higher the interest rate."

"Really?" I stared at him in surprise. "But I heard you tell the priest he was a good guy."

"What else would I tell a priest over the sap's dead body?" Sammy gave me a tight smile. "It was the least I could do for the sorry bastard."

"You're such a diplomat." I shook my head, marveling at his white lies. "So how exactly was Parker involved?"

"Tony picked up his envelopes at the Rusty Bucket. Charlie was the go-between."

"Envelopes? You mean bets?"

Sammy nodded. "Tony tried to get me to take some of his Galveston action, but I told him to take a hike. I didn't want any part of his scam."

"Scam? Who were his clients?"

"You name it—gangsters, cops, politicians, fat cats." Sammy raised his brows. "Guess he got too greedy. They all do."

"You think your pal Tony was helping himself to the cash? Not paying off his bets?"

"I wouldn't be surprised. I hear both gangs were after him for fleecing their own."

"Figures." A thought hit me: What if Johnny Jack insisted Sammy take Parker's place, no doubt with a new crooked bookie? Would he become the go-between for under-the-table bets as well?

So how was Torino's hit related to Charlie Parker's savage beating? His murder had to be a warning to the gangsters and gamblers at the funeral. Since the MOs weren't the same, were the hits ordered by different gangs—or perhaps a Houston gang?

When Nathan and Dino walked up, Sammy stopped in his tracks. "Damn, that reminds me. I forgot to check Tony's pockets!"

"You're going to pat him down in front of a priest?" My mouth dropped open.

"Sure, why not? I'll pretend I'm helping the family, getting his personal effects."

"You think he'll buy it?" I hoped the priest would pray for Sammy as well. "Let me know what you find. Be careful."

"Same to you." He stuck out his thumb like a hitchhiker, pointing down the street. "For now, you kids better scram. Pronto."

I saw him walk with Dino over to Torino's body, hoping Sammy wasn't asking for trouble. Was he really going to dig into a dead man's pockets under the priest's nose, literally? What was he looking for—cash? Betting slips? IOUs? What did bookies carry in their pockets? A list of clients and their code names? A gun?

I stifled a smile, moving closer to the victim, trying to watch Sammy in action. If anyone could pull it off, it was my crafty brother.

"What's so funny?" Nathan asked me.

"Sammy. He's trying to search the body while the priest is praying for his soul."

He grinned. "He must be taking lessons from his buddy Maceo."

"No doubt. Sammy's gotten out of more scrapes than a tomcat."

I hoped his good luck would hold out. Like Golliwog, Sammy needed all nine lives if he wanted to survive under Johnny Jack's rule.

"Say, any idea why Mack never showed up today? He seemed so eager to attend."

"Probably chasing a hot lead." Nathan shrugged.

"What's hotter than a dead bookie, shot between the eyes?"

"You said it," Nathan grimaced. "Say, hanging around a funeral home with a couple of stiffs is giving me the creeps. Ready to go?"

"Sure, but let's stop by Burton's hotel first. I told Mrs. Harper we'd visit, and I hate to lie to her face." Truth was, I hadn't heard from Burton lately, and was getting concerned.

"It wouldn't be the first time you lied to your boss."

I felt my cheeks color. "Those were white lies. All in the name of journalism."

"Whatever you want to call it," he snorted. "Withholding information?"

"What's wrong with a little white lie now and then? Society news is full of falsehoods."

The upper classes were masters at concocting lies and keeping secrets—and how! Euphemisms and excuses were *de rigueur* in high society. A marital separation turned into a "vacation," a bigwig's mistress masqueraded as a "friend," and a bad investment became a "tax write-off."

As we made our way to Nathan's car, I heard police sirens and saw a few cop cars pull up and park in front of the funeral home. Two uniformed officers raced out of the first car, guns by their sides, while three plainclothes cops emerged from the second car.

I blinked in surprise as Agent Burton rushed toward me: Why had he come here, of all places? Didn't the gangs consider him the prime suspect in Parker's murder?

Burton stared at me, dumbfounded. "Jazz, what in hell are you doing here? Go home—it's too dangerous!"

"Same goes for you. Isn't it too risky for you to be here? We're surrounded by mobsters." I scanned the grounds and saw Nathan, following the cops with his camera as they questioned witnesses. "By the way, we were coming by to see you. Why aren't you at the hotel?"

"They let me out for good behavior." He looked worried. "Did you see who fired the shots? Any idea who was the target?"

"I saw a black Ford drive by, and they shot a bookie from Houston, named Tony Torino. Ask Sammy. He knew the guy."

"Figures Sammy would know the victim."

I ignored his jab. "Only as an acquaintance, not a friend." To change the subject, I asked, "Any word about your car yet?"

He nodded, his face relaxing. "The research lab determined that the stains on the bat and my headlight were the same blood type, so I'm no longer a suspect. They even gave me my badge and gun back today. Everything's copacetic."

"Good to hear." I breathed a sigh of relief.

"Speaking of, I'd better do my job or the cops will put me back on probation." He gave me a sly look. "Say, I missed you. I was getting bored at the hotel without any company."

My heart skipped a beat. "I promise, we were stopping by after the funeral."

"We? Why bring Nathan along?" He grinned. "You're the only one I invited."

"How would it look if I'd shown up at a low-rent hotel, alone, looking for you?" I felt my face flush. "Besides, I had to make up a story so Mrs. Harper would let me get off work."

"So I'm your alibi now?" His blue eyes danced, and I could tell he enjoyed teasing me—a bit too much. "Say, why don't we celebrate my good news? Maybe tonight?"

"Swell." I smiled, glad Burton seemed to be safe, back to his old self. "See you later."

As he turned to go, a bully in a pin-striped suit and red carnation ran up and shoved Burton with both hands, almost knocking him off his feet.

"What in hell are you doing here?" the well-dressed goon shouted in a distinct Irish accent. "Officers, arrest this Fed! He killed Charlie Parker!"

CHAPTER TWENTY-TWO

"Does anyone really believe this palooka?" Agent Burton scowled. I froze, wondering how the cops would react to these false accusations. Ironic that this goon was accusing a straight arrow like Burton of murder. All heads swiveled, staring as the cops circled both men, guns drawn.

"Says who? Got any proof?" An older cop with wire-rim specs addressed the goon.

What? Were they really taking this sap seriously?

"Sure do," the man boasted. "What about his cowboy hat? It was right there by Charlie."

No one said these two-bit hoods had any smarts. The gang leaders, maybe, but even that was questionable.

"And how would you know that?" The cop's eyes narrowed. "Were you there? I don't recall seeing you at the crime scene."

"Yeah. I mean, no," the wise guy stuttered. "I heard about it...on the street."

"Oh yeah? Well, we'd better question you downtown, to be sure." The plainclothes cop turned to a young officer in uniform. "Jack, handcuff this suspect and put him in the squad car."

"Suspect?" He spat out. "Not me, I'm a witness! I mean, I'm innocent! I don't need no bracelets."

I watched the young cop handcuff his wrists, noticing his fancy gold cuff links glittering in the sun. Where had I just seen similar cuff links? Did they match the one on Burton's desk?

The cop narrowed his eyes. "Tell us what you know and maybe we'll let you off easy."

"I don't know nothing!" The man squirmed under the young cop's grip. "Honest Injun!"

"We'll see about that," the officer said. "Jack, take him away."

I tried to get a closer look at the goon's shiny cuff links, but the young cop yanked on his arm, blocking my view. Wait, didn't Finn say a hood with an Irish accent was looking for me?

Trying to help, I pulled Burton away from the group. "Maybe it's a good idea if you left right away. You don't need another outburst right after you were cleared."

"I'm not afraid of these petty hoods." Burton bristled. "Besides, I still don't have my car. The cops had just arrived at the hotel when we got a call about the funeral hit."

"Sure you can trust them? Nathan and I saw your pals clearing out the Rusty Bucket today. When we drove by, they were carrying out loads of paper, equipment, files, even the cash register. Looked pretty fishy to me."

"You don't say. I'll have to figure out what they took. Later."

Nervously, I studied the officers, wondering if any of them helped clean out Parker's bar earlier. Perhaps that explained their late arrival to the crime scene.

Burton rubbed his chin and motioned to Sammy. "Say, I'd like to ask Sammy a few questions. Think he'll talk to me?"

"Not now. Not in public," I hissed. "You know how bad it looks if you're seen together. In case you didn't notice, we're surrounded by gangsters and cops."

"OK, you made your point. Guess I'll have to take him in for questioning, like the character in the car," he said dryly. "Maybe he'll confide in Sammy if he won't talk to us?"

"Don't you dare!" I shot daggers at Burton, hoping he was just pulling my leg. "Sammy's spent enough time in jail."

To distract him, I mentioned Sheriff Sanders and the fact he seemed sweet on Eva. Did Burton know about his bargain with Johnny Jack? Was Sanders even telling Eva the truth? Still, Burton had a right to know what was going on behind his back.

"By the way, have you heard about a booze drop from Cuba this week?" I asked, watching his reaction.

Burton's eyes flashed in surprise. "I plan on stopping the Cubans before the booze gets to shore. How'd you know?"

"Sheriff Sanders told Eva they had to work out a compromise with Johnny Jack to appease him." I paused. "To save your hide."

Burton blanched. "Is that so? What kind of compromise?"

"Why not ask Sanders yourself?"

"Tell me what he told Eva, and why."

Did I have to be the one to spill the beans? "He agreed to allow the Cubans to make their drop. Just this once."

"Oh yeah? Bullshit!" His eyes narrowed. "Why would Sanders tell your aunt such private police business?"

"Guess. He knew she'd tell me, and probably hoped I'd convince you to let it go."

Burton worked his jaw, averting my gaze, clearly getting steamed as the words sank in. "Why in hell would Sanders make that kind of promise to a gang leader? We can't let Johnny Jack get away with it, not even once. Prohibition is my department, not Sanders. He has no right to interfere with my business."

With that, he stomped away from me, toward the small group still gathered around the entrance. Thank goodness, they'd removed the body and taken it inside. Tell the truth, I was getting the heebie-jeebies just being near a funeral home, the graveyard only a few yards away. Was I standing on any old graves now?

Galveston was known for its beautiful cemeteries, but this wasn't one of them—it was more creepy than serene. I wasn't the superstitious sort, but you could never be too careful around graves: you didn't want to disturb any lingering ghosts with axes to grind.

Nervously, I looked around for Nathan and saw him talking to Sammy and Dino. Burton spoke to Sammy, and he drew back like he'd been struck, his hands balling into fists.

Moving closer, I heard Burton tell Sammy, "I'm not arresting you. I only want to take you downtown for questioning."

My heart sinking, I watched Sammy struggling with Burton, praying he wouldn't punch him—especially not in front of his fellow lawmen, dirty or not. The scene was all too familiar.

I started to speak, ready to defend Sammy, but he only scowled at me, as if I were to blame. "I'm sorry," I mouthed, mystified as Burton grabbed Sammy and led him away, his head down.

Damn it! Burton was treating Sammy more like a suspect than a witness. He shoved Sammy into the first squad car, crammed next to the goon in the striped suit. Sammy's olive eyes blazed, a look of resigned indignation on his face.

Worse, Nathan began snapping photos with his stupid camera, aiming at the men who sat side by side in the cop car, hiding their faces. He was so animated, you'd think he was taking pictures of more bathing beauties. Difference was, these guys weren't exactly smiling and mugging for the paper.

I admit, I felt like grabbing his precious camera and stomping it into the ground. Apparently I couldn't trust anyone now, least of all my so-called pals.

CHAPTER TWENTY-THREE

"What was that for?" I flared up, hands on my hips. "Did you have to humiliate Sammy in front of everyone?"

Burton frowned, clearly puzzled by my tone. "I had to make it look good, didn't I? You said we shouldn't be seen together. What should I do, ask Sammy to dance the tango?"

"You're a riot." I glared at him, not amused. "Don't you get it? You practically arrested Sammy in public, then shoved him in a cop car next to a gangster, so he seems just as guilty."

"Guilty of what? We didn't handcuff him. We only want to ask him a few questions."

"Well, you didn't have to turn it into a public spectacle. I told you about Torino in confidence."

His face fell. "You volunteered some information. What's wrong with trying to help?"

Burton seemed hurt by my reaction, but I was just as upset. If that's how he treated my friends, how would he react if he found out Sammy was my *brother*? Would he expect him to rat out his pals, act as his informant? He'd already tried that before, to no avail.

"Like I've said, I won't be your spy or your snitch, and neither will Sammy. Better to solve your problems by yourself, Agent Burton, and leave me alone."

"You've got it all wrong." His intense gaze bore through me, until I looked away.

"Oh yeah? You just got cleared and the first thing you do is accost Sammy? Take him downtown to the police station for *questioning*, like he's a murder suspect?" I knew I was being melodramatic, but I had to get it through his thick skull.

Frankly, I felt as if I'd let down both my father and Sammy. Upset, I turned on my heel and walked off, hoping he'd finally get the telegram. My first instincts regarding Burton were right: I had to keep my distance or someone could get hurt.

Nathan stood by his Model T, fiddling with his camera. Without a word, I got inside and slammed the door.

"What's wrong, Jazz? Did you and Burton have a falling out?"

"I'll say." I heaved a sigh. "You saw Burton drag Sammy off and shove him in a squad car like a murder suspect. Boy, I wanted to wring his neck. Why couldn't he act more civilized?"

"Hold your horses, Jazz. What did you expect him to do—send Sammy an engraved invitation?" Nathan snorted. "He was just trying to impress his cop pals. We both know Burton can act like a hard-boiled tough. Remember the raid at the Oasis?"

How could I forget Burton's face-off with Sammy? Not a great first impression.

"Maybe you're right. Guess I overreacted." I mulled it over. "Still, even if it *was* all for show, why did Burton have to make it look so damn convincing?"

"I wouldn't worry about Sammy or Burton," Nathan reassured me. "Those two fellas can hold their own."

"Well, your photos won't help. Thanks to you, Sammy's already been embarrassed enough to last a lifetime."

"I was taking shots of that goon, just in case. He looks familiar."

"Please try to crop Sammy out of the pictures," I pleaded. "He doesn't need to be linked to another jailbird. Say, did you notice the guy's cuff links? I saw one like it at the station, after the Downtown Gang showed up, guns blazing."

"I'll take a closer look at my photos. Why?"

"I'm just wondering how a two-bit gangster like him can afford such pricey gold cuff links?" I mused. "Who does he work for? Who lost the other missing cuff link? What's the connection?"

By the time we neared the boarding house, I'd simmered down a bit. I hoped Amanda was home so I could get a clear perspective. If anyone could cheer me up, it was my best friend and confidante—and Sammy's current squeeze.

Trouble was, first I had to contend with Sanders, whose squad car was parked prominently out front. His crush on Aunt Eva was grating on my nerves. What did those two have in common anyway?

Nathan rushed back to the *Gazette* to develop photos so I was left to fend for myself. I dreaded making small talk with Sanders. His idea of conversation was more like an interrogation.

I knocked on the front door, in case the sheriff was trying to get fresh with Aunt Eva. Heaven forbid I walk in on a sloppy smooch!

Eva blushed when she saw me, clearing her throat loudly. What was going on in there? "How are you, Jazz? As you can see, we have a visitor." The way she emphasized *visitor* made him sound like the ambassador to France, not some roly-poly local lawman.

Proudly she led me to the front room, where the sheriff tipped his hat. "Afternoon."

"Hello, Sheriff." I popped my head in and gave him a wave.

"Before you go, Miss Cross, I've got some good news." Sanders stood up, hooking his thumbs in his belt. "Your fella's been cleared of any suspicion in the Parker murder."

"My fella? You mean Agent Burton? Swell!" I acted surprised. "So what brings you here, Sheriff?" As if I didn't know.

"Well, since you brought it up..." Sheriff Sanders started fussing with his hat, tugging on his collar. "I wanted to ask Eva to be my date to the policemen's ball this Saturday."

"How nice!" I forced a smile, wondering why Burton hadn't mentioned the ball. Guess I didn't give him a chance. After my last tirade, I doubt he'd invite me to go anywhere as his date.

"Why, of course, I'd love to go, Walt." She blushed a soft pink and I wondered if Eva already expected his invitation. "I'll have to find a new frock just for the occasion."

"I'll be glad to go shopping with you. Sounds fun." Anything to take my mind off work and the aggravating Agent Burton.

As I turned to make my escape, I heard a loud knock on the door. Speak of the devil: Burton stood on the front porch, hat in hand, fidgeting like a nervous schoolboy. I tiptoed over to Aunt Eva, and whispered in her ear: "Please tell him I'm not here." She gave me a quizzical look before she got up to answer the door.

Frankly, the last person I wanted to see now was James Burton.

CHAPTER TWENTY-FOUR

Eva shot me a puzzled glance over her shoulder—meaning: Are you sure?—before she went into her gracious hostess mode.

"Hello, Agent Burton. I mean, James. Nice to see you again."

"Same to you, ma'am." He removed his hat. "Is Jasmine here? I'd like to see her."

She hesitated a moment and I wondered if she was going to blow my cover. Then in a shaky voice, she stammered, "I'm afraid she's not back from work yet."

"Work? But I just saw her at a f-f-f...function," he continued. Smooth move, I thought with gratitude. Imagine what Eva and the sheriff would think if they knew I'd attended a Downtown Gang funeral—with not one, but two corpses on the premises.

"Is that Agent Burton?" Sheriff Sanders shot up, flinging open the door and walking out on the front porch.

Oh no, now what? Would he squeal on me, tell him I was hiding inside like a coward? I peeked through the curtains, warily watching the scene unfold.

"Good to see you." Sanders pumped his hand like he was running for re-election.

Burton squared his shoulders. "Hello, Sheriff Sanders. What are you doing here?"

"Social call. Glad to have you back on the force. I knew you were innocent."

"I didn't realize I was guilty of anything," Burton said. "I was a victim, like Parker."

The sheriff's face colored. "Say, did you hear about the shooting at Parker's funeral today? Too bad I missed all the action."

Eva gasped and covered her mouth, but didn't say a word.

"I see you had better things to do." Burton's nod indicated Eva. "We've interviewed a few witnesses and gotten some leads. We have a couple of suspects, and a man in custody we're holding overnight."

Did that include Sammy, I wondered?

"Good work." Sanders patted Burton on the back. "I'll be there soon as I say my good-byes to the little lady here."

Little lady? I could imagine Eva cringing at his words.

"By the way, there's something I'd like to discuss," Burton told Sanders, blue eyes cold.

"What's that, son?" He crossed his arms, standing with his feet apart, like a linebacker.

"Not now, in private." Burton gave him an accusatory look. Did he want to confront the sheriff about the booze drop? Too bad I was hiding inside. What I'd give to eavesdrop!

Sanders turned to Eva, who'd come out on the porch. "I hate to leave, Eva, but duty calls." Then he reached over and kissed her on the cheek—right in front of Burton. Worse, she didn't even squirm or pull away.

I had to bite my lip to keep from shouting, 'What's the idea, you big lug? Take your grubby paws and mouth off my aunt!'

"See you soon, Walt. I'm looking forward to the policemen's ball this weekend." Then she smiled up at Burton, acting like a coquette. "Will you be attending the ball, Agent Burton?"

What a sly fox Eva was, fishing for information!

He shrugged. "No plans yet. Guess that depends on Jazz. Please tell her I came by."

Then he dashed down the walkway, the sheriff following close behind. They stood by their cars talking, Burton towering over the sausage of a sheriff, encased in his tight uniform.

As I watched out the window, the two lawmen appeared to be having words, or a "disagreement" as Eva would say. Wish I could be a fly, buzzing around their faces.

Sheriff Sanders seemed agitated, moving closer to Burton, beefy arms flailing about, while Burton kept his ground. Was I seeing things or did Sanders deliberately try to push him?

Luckily, Burton stepped aside and jumped into his car while the sheriff stood there, waving his hands in the air.

After they left, I asked Eva, "What was that fight all about?"

"I heard a few words here and there, mostly about Johnny Jack, that dreadful gangster. Honestly, I was ready to break it up if they had fisticuffs." Her face flushed. "Besides, you should be talking to Agent Burton in person, not spying on him from the parlor!"

She was right. Now I couldn't ask him about Sammy or potential witnesses or suspects—not even Tony Torino's gold cuff links.

"Burton thinks Sanders is sticking his nose in his business. He's federal, the sheriff is regional." I gave Eva a wary glance. "Guess you can almost call it a turf war."

"Agent Burton should be grateful Walt is trying to help," Eva told me. "One Prohibition agent is no match for these blood-thirsty bootleggers. They won't stop until everyone's blind drunk or dead from that demon rum!"

Now she sounded like a Women's Temperance supporter.

True, Burton seemed to be more of a figurehead, without much support from local police.

"Thanks for covering for me. I can't face James right now."

She settled on the porch swing and patted the seat next to her. "Jazz, you know I don't like to lie to anyone, particularly a lawman. What is going on with you two?"

I tried to sidestep the question. "I can ask the same thing about you and the sheriff. His visits are becoming a regular habit around here. What are his intentions?" I enjoyed teasing her, watching her get all flustered and tongue-tied. But not this time.

"I'm serious, Jazz. Why are you avoiding Burton? What's *really* the matter?"

I looked away from her intense gaze. "Let's just say he's in the doghouse right now."

"Why? Walt said he's cleared of any charges. Not that we suspected him for a moment."

"Wish he'd do the same for Sammy," I griped. "Give him the benefit of the doubt."

"Sammy? What about him? Did Burton raid the Oasis again?"

"No, nothing like that..." I hesitated, then saw Amanda rushing up the walkway. I could smell the greasy spoon from the front porch.

"Say, what's going on?" she called. "I swear I saw Agent Burton driving past with the sheriff on his bumper. Is he still in trouble?"

"Sheriff Sanders stopped by to ask me to the policemen's ball."
Eva beamed. "I assume it's the reason James stopped by, while
Jasmine hid in the parlor. Why are you angry at him?"

"You'd be mad, too, if you saw how he humiliated Sammy in
public today. Burton forced him to go downtown for
questioning...about some guy." I left out the *bullet between the eyes* bit.

"What?" Amanda started breathing, hard, her face twisted in
anger. "Of all the nerve!"

"What's wrong with asking a few questions?" Eva frowned.
"He's trying to do his job."

She was defending Burton again? "He treated Sammy like a
murder suspect—in front of everyone."

"A murder suspect?" Eva looked alarmed. "Who's everyone?
Where were you?"

How could I admit we'd attended a mob funeral full of gangsters
and gamblers?

Amanda headed upstairs. "Let's go to the Oasis and find out
what happened. Coming?"

"Sammy may not be there." I sighed. "For all I know, Burton
stuck him in jail overnight."

She gave me a smug smile. "If so, I doubt he'd have the nerve to
show his face here."

Good point. "OK, you talked me into it." I followed her
upstairs, ignoring Aunt Eva's disapproving look. "Let's shake a leg!"

CHAPTER TWENTY-FIVE

On the trolley, I gave Amanda a run-down of the day's events, including the fez-topped victim and Sammy being hauled downtown in a squad car. The car was practically vacant after the work rush, and we sat in the back, holding onto our hats as the trolley car squeaked and bounced along on its way to Market Street.

"You were there when that guy was shot down in cold blood?" Amanda shivered. "At a gang funeral? I've got the shakes just hearing about it. Any idea why he was murdered?"

"Sammy told me he was a bookie, so I doubt he had many friends," I said dryly.

"Only the kind who carry Tommy guns." Amanda tapped her head. "Say, what were you thinking, showing up at a mob funeral with Nathan? You're no dumb Dora."

"That's what Sammy told me. To be honest, I was looking for suspects in Parker's case. I didn't plan on a second murder." When the trolley made a sudden stop, I clutched my bag tight.

"What about Sheriff Sanders?" Amanda sounded exasperated. "Is he moving into the boarding house or what? Every time I turn around, there he is, making goo-goo eyes at Eva."

"You said it! I wish she'd show him the gate—and lock it when he leaves."

When we got to the Oasis, it was after seven o'clock, still bright outside. The nocturnal crowd didn't usually arrive until the bats did, closer to midnight. No waiting, no obnoxious drugstore cowboys feeding us stale pick-up lines.

After Dino opened the heavy door, I blurted out, "What happened with Sammy? Is he OK?"

Dino's face clouded over. "Everything's jake. Your Fed fella was showing off to his buddies. I picked Sammy up at the station thirty minutes later."

"What a relief," I sighed. "What else is new?"

"Not much," he muttered, looking down, which told me plenty.

Amanda elbowed me in the ribs. "Let's cut the chit-chat and go see Sammy."

We clattered downstairs, Amanda racing head-first, her cream floral print dress billowing out like a wedding dress train—not that I'd give her any ideas. Despite his appreciation of attractive women, my older brother seemed content to be a confirmed bachelor.

Heaven help the ladies who fell hard for his good looks, kind spirit and charm. Sure, I tried to warn Amanda, but she wouldn't listen, believing she was the one who'd tame him. Oh, brother!

Sammy stood at the bar, talking to Frank, and clammed up when we approached. Amanda rushed over and threw her arms around his neck, squealing, "I'm so glad you're OK!"

A few sad sacks turned around, leering at us, so sloshed they almost dropped their drinks.

Sammy removed himself from Amanda's grasp, tight as a bear trap. "Nice to see you ladies," he said in a wary tone. "Jazz, I thought you'd be at home, hiding under the covers."

"I admit, I almost lost my cookies. But how about you? He was *your* friend."

"Friend? That Houston hood? More like a vampire, wanting to suck his victims dry."

Nice image. "What happened with Burton?" I tapped my foot.

Sammy motioned for us to follow him to a back table. An old Negro man sat at the grand piano, playing a few rag-time tunes from memory, swaying in time. Half his teeth were missing but his bright smile was infectious. Even if he was zozzled, he sure knew how to hit those keys.

When we got settled, I asked Sammy again: "Did Burton or the cops interrogate you?"

"They tried." He shrugged. "They found out fast that I didn't know anything. I barely knew Torino. He found out I'm Johnny Jack's new collections man, and got real chummy, like we were lifelong friends. He was full of crap. And lead."

Amanda shuddered. "Glad I wasn't there today."

"Sure you want to hear all this baloney?" Sammy asked her.

She got the hint. "Guess it's time to powder my nose."

"What baloney?" I asked, sitting up.

"Keep this between us, OK?" Sammy leaned forward. "The cops can't figure out the connection between Parker and Torino. What got them whacked? Were they stealing the bets? Fudging the numbers? Cheating at cards?" He outlined some old scars and scratches on the table, studying the surface like it was a road map. "Let me know if you hear anything from your news pals."

"Are they sure their deaths are related? They were murdered in such different ways."

"The killers may want to throw off the police." He pulled out a Camel and lit it, blowing wavy circles of smoke to the sky. "I just want to know what they were up to so I can stay the hell away."

"Good idea. Say, what did you find in Torino's pockets? Anything interesting?"

"The usual, cash, calling cards, papers. Oh, and a few gaming tokens I didn't recognize."

"What kind? Can I see them?" I waited while Sammy dug in his pockets and pulled out a few assorted tokens. "Did the cops see you swipe these?"

He shook his head, taking a puff. "They were too busy watching that goon pick on your boyfriend. I left most of the stuff and just palmed these tokens."

"Can I show these to Mack? Turns out Parker had some tokens on him, too, but I didn't get a chance to see them." I fingered the cardboard discs, marked with initials. "Mack or his sources may know which casinos they're from, then we'll see if they're a match."

Sammy looked anxious. "Just don't mention my name. Say they fell out on the ground."

"Will do. Hey, did you get a chance to talk to the goon in the car? Some nerve, accusing Burton!"

"The creep? Sure, we shot the breeze a few minutes before the cops took us in. That bozo got the royal treatment, room and board, while I cooled my heels with Burton and some deputy. Lucky me."

"What did he say?" I perked up, straining to hear over the piano player who'd burst into a rousing number of *"When You're Smiling."*

"Keep it quiet, OK?" Sammy looked around the joint. "He admitted that he was paid to plant Burton's hat at The Rusty Bucket. Poor sap is too dumb to make it seem real. That hat looked brand-new, not a drop of blood in sight."

I sat up. "Did he tell you who hired him?"

"The cops came back before he could squeal. Too bad I couldn't bribe him to talk. Most small-time hoods can be bought for a few bucks and a pack of smokes."

"Framing a Fed agent isn't small time. Did you get a load of those gold cuff links he wore? They must've cost a mint."

"Sure, they were blinding. I figured he stole them off some big-shot, dead or not."

"Frankly, I'm surprised the gangs trusted a simpleton like him to set up a Fed."

"Who else would volunteer?" Sammy cracked.

"True." As long as Sammy was in the mood to talk, I was glad to pepper him with questions. "Say, how's the collections biz going?"

"No problems yet. The guys shell out the dough so fast, you'd think I was a stick-up man." He gave me a sad smile. "I guess in a way I am...But it helps that I bring Dino along. Everyone is scared of that baby grand. No one wants to end up like Charlie."

"They don't really think you or Dino killed him, do they?"

"I doubt it, but it seems to work in my favor." He grimaced. "A lot of barkeeps placed bets with Torino at Parker's bar and they got spooked by the murder. Both murders."

"Who can blame them?"

For once, I took pity not only on Sammy but also the rest of the bar owners in the Downtown Gang. Like Sammy, most were hard-working fellas just trying to pay the rent and feed their families. Sure, Sammy's "family" consisted mostly of lushes, floozies and gold diggers—so where did Amanda fit in? To his credit, he always looked out for me and Eva, helping us to make ends meet.

Buzz came over with two cold Coca-Colas and I handed him a quarter tip. Nice kid.

"How about some rum with my Coke?" Sammy held up his glass, while Buzz rushed off to comply.

Perfect way to bring up a taboo subject. "Speaking of rum, what do you know about a big booze drop this week? I hear Johnny Jack's supposed to get a huge shipment from Cuba, and the sheriff promised he'd look the other way. For Burton's sake."

"Oh yeah?" His eyes flickered, and I knew he was playing dumb. "Where'd you get your information—Burton or your pen pals?"

I shook my head. "Believe it or not, Sanders confided in Aunt Eva. Seems he's got a soft spot for her." He didn't need to know how soft and cozy that spot appeared to be.

"Why in hell would he tell Eva? Because of you and Agent Burton?" Sammy blinked, rapid-fire, shoving away from the table. "Well, I don't see Burton as a benchwarmer, sitting on the sidelines, waiting for permission to pounce."

"I'll say. If I know Burton, telling him *no* will only spur him on."

"Hey, I wonder what's keeping Amanda?" Sammy squirmed, looking around the bar.

Buzz reappeared with a bottle of rum, and I waited while he poured some into Sammy's drink. He tipped the bottle over my glass, but I held up my hand. Chocolate was my weakness, not alcohol.

After Buzz left, I said, "So tell me about this booze drop. Will it be dangerous?"

"Depends on whether or not Burton makes an appearance." Sammy exhaled, watching his cigarette smoke fade. "This doesn't leave the room. Swear?"

"Mum's the word." I nodded and crossed my heart.

His voice became a husky whisper. "Johnny Jack wants me to lead the whole operation. And it'll make my life a hell of a lot easier if the bulls never show."

CHAPTER TWENTY-SIX

"You?" My heart sank. I hated to imagine what might happen if Burton and Sammy faced off during a booze drop. Talk about the Ten Plagues of Galveston! "How'd you get roped into that job? Isn't being a bag man enough?"

Sammy scowled. "Johnny Jack gave me no choice. Claims he's training me for bigger and better things. I just hope to God he's not setting me up."

"You and me both." Sammy was getting in so deep, I was afraid he'd never get away from the Downtown Gang. Now I hoped Burton would take Sanders' advice and stay away. "So when is the drop taking place? This Saturday night?"

He stared at me, hard, hazel eyes narrowed. "You know a lot more than you pretend, don't you, Jazz? How'd you find out?"

It was more of a reprimand than a question.

"Take a wild guess. The policemen's ball is Saturday night. Johnny Jack knows the cops will be too busy kicking up their heels to bother with some Cuban rum-runners."

Sammy exhaled a plume of smoke. "So are you going to the ball with Burton?"

"No," I admitted, feeling like a wilted wallflower without a date to the prom. "He hasn't asked me, yet. Let's just say we're not on speaking terms." Why did I have to lose my stack with Burton? Even Eva's social life was going better than mine.

"I thought you two hit it off." Sammy sounded disappointed.

"Didn't you once tell me to steer clear of Burton?"

"This is business. I just hope he doesn't interfere with our plans." He raised his brows. "Bet you can find ways to distract him."

"You want me to act as bait? Gee, thanks."

"Jazz, you know what I meant." He reached out to pat my hand, reminding me of my dad. "Face it, Jazz, the Fed agent is sweet on you. I assumed he'd ask you to go."

"Sorry to let you down." I shifted in my seat. "Personally, I'd be more worried about the Beach Gang getting wind of the booze drop. Aren't they still sore at Johnny Jack for hijacking their Cuban rum?"

"Then we'll all have a big party, right on the beach." Sammy acted nonchalant, but I could tell he was worried, the way he sucked on his Camel like a lollipop.

I heaved a sigh. "I wish you'd change professions, Sammy. Open a regular restaurant."

A sore subject since I lectured Sammy at least once a month on the dangers of running a diner/bar and selling booze—even top-notch liquor—during Prohibition.

"You know I'm saving some dough for a showplace."

I didn't know which was worse, collecting commissions for a mob boss or leading a booze drop. Last time he dealt with a bootlegger directly, he almost got killed. Recalling that night on the docks, I winced at the memory of Sammy getting kicked around like a soccer ball.

"Say, what's keeping Amanda?" He repeated, clearly uncomfortable. We spotted Amanda sitting at the bar, talking to a nice-looking guy in a plaid shirt and suspenders, a real Joe College type. With their wholesome, all-American good looks, they both looked totally out of place in this dark, nautical-themed gin joint.

Sammy marched over and deliberately placed his hand on the back of Amanda's bar stool. Was he jealous or just marking his territory? "Are you kids enjoying yourselves?" he asked, eyes darting back and forth between the two. "Can I get you another drink?"

"I'm having a swell time," the youth told Sammy. "Amanda is very entertaining."

"I'll say!" Sammy said, smirking at his puzzled expression.

Amanda flashed her icy stare at Sammy. "Don't mind us, we're just getting to know each other, aren't we?"

The young man looked vaguely familiar. Where had I seen him before? With a start, I realized he was Charlie Parker's son, who gave that moving speech about his father at the funeral. All freshened up and in casual clothes, I hardly recognized the young man.

The two men eyed each other in the dark, and the young sheik gripped the counter as he tried to stand, picking up Sammy's cue. Tall, fair, young and handsome—not a bad combination.

"Guess I'd better head home. I've had one too many cocktails."

"Cocktails?" Sammy gave him the once-over, and I read his thoughts from his amused expression: What a lightweight. He patted him on the back. "You OK, pal? How about a strong cup of coffee before you go?"

"That'd be swell." He beamed at Amanda. "If Amanda here will keep me company."

"Sure I will." She cooed, touching his knee. "Don't you worry."

Finally I spoke up. "Aren't you Charlie Parker's son? I'm so sorry about your father. My condolences to your family."

He bowed his head a moment, then held out his hand politely. "You were there? Yes, I'm Chad Parker. Thanks for coming. Were you friends of my father's?"

Before I could reply, Sammy said, surprised, "Sorry, I didn't recognize you at first. Yes, your father and I were pals. He was a good egg. He didn't deserve to go that way."

Chad's face darkened. "No one does." He got to his feet, suddenly sober. "I hear you're the new collections man for the gang. Let me know if you hear anything, will ya?"

Sammy bristled. "Who told you that?"

"Word gets around." Chad shrugged, looking away.

Leave it to Amanda to break the tension as she touched Chad's arm, her dainty fingers stroking his sleeve. "Please let me know if there's anything I can do?"

"Maybe I'll see you later, toots. Hope we meet again soon." Chad tipped his hat, his gaze traveling from her long blonde hair, down to her cheerful floral frock and satin shoes.

I felt a pang of guilt for hogging Sammy all night, after Amanda took such great pains to get all dolled up for his sake. "I hope so," she smiled, making sure Sammy heard.

He'd heard every word, all right, evident by his scowl.

Both men had obviously forgotten about the coffee.

After Chad left, Sammy glared at Amanda, saying, "What are you trying to do, rob the cradle?"

Her face fell. "I had no idea he was Parker's son. Poor kid. Losing his father so young and in such a horrid way."

"You said it." I nodded. "He was all broken up at the funeral."

"Chad never mentioned his dad. He offered to buy me a drink and we had a nice chat. He's a sweet fella."

"Oh yeah? If he's so sweet, why isn't he at home mourning with his family? Instead he's trying to pick up dames like a damn lounge lizard," Sammy snapped. "What was he doing here in my bar?"

"Maybe he's trying to take his mind off things. Maybe he needs a break," Amanda bristled. "All that doom and gloom gets old fast."

Sammy had a point: Why did Chad show up *here* after the funeral? I couldn't resist asking, "What else did he say?"

"He just graduated from Ball High School and is saving up to go to college," she said, clearly impressed.

"He's only eighteen? Does he know how old you are?" Sammy razzed her.

"Twenty-two is not old," Amanda huffed. "Chad needed to talk and I was willing to listen. What else did I have to do? He told me he wants to be a doctor. I admire a guy with ambition."

I had to admit, I was surprised. The Oasis didn't attract a lot of doctors or medical types—and if they did make an appearance, they rarely returned for an encore. Guess they felt more comfortable in a sterile, stuffy environment.

"Oh yeah? And you believed him?" Sammy scoffed. "I bet it was just a line to impress the ladies." He knew all about lines and impressing ladies, not that he had to try very hard with his smooth Mediterranean features and confident swagger.

"Have a heart, Sammy," I told him. "We both know how painful it is to lose a father."

"Sure, I feel for the kid, but who knows if he's on the level? The way he glared at me...like he's spying on me, and my bar. How'd he find out I'm Johnny Jack's new bag man?" Sammy frowned, staring at Doria, our figurehead, as if she were a mystical seer with all the answers. "What if he thinks *I'm* the killer who whacked his dad?"

CHAPTER TWENTY-SEVEN

"Sammy, you're overreacting," Amanda insisted. "Chad was only making small talk. Don't be so suspicious."

"I'd better be if I want to stay alive." He headed up the stairs, motioning for us to follow. "Come on, ladies. I'll drive you home."

Amanda stood up reluctantly, sporting a huge pout, and trailed behind. Outside, we got into Sammy's roadster, and I sat in the back while they bickered in front, trying not to get involved in their lovers' spat. At the boarding house, he walked us to the door, refusing to even meet Amanda's gaze, then rushed to his car, stiff as a soldier.

"Thanks for the ride, Sammy," I called out. "Watch your back."

After we rushed upstairs, trying to avoid Eva, Amanda plopped on the edge of my bed and asked, "Say, what's eating Sammy? He sure seemed hot under the collar."

"With good reason. Sammy's got a lot on his mind."

"Obviously not me," she whined.

"He's worried after the hit today. Can you blame him?"

Amanda shivered dramatically. "If you ask me, that shooting was too close for comfort."

"I wonder who was behind the hit—Johnny Jack? Seems strange he didn't show his face today, out of respect." The dapper gangster was known as the life of any party, a showman who could turn even a funeral into a social function.

"You think he'd be so bold?" she asked.

"Johnny Jack is nothing if not bold. That's his style." I started removing my long beads and chandelier earrings. "Trouble is, all these wiseguys act suspicious. They start to look the same to me, like they all went to the same gangster school."

Amanda cracked a smile. "I'll say." She leaned forward, smelling the cockatoo perfume lamp on my nightstand.

After today, I definitely needed to relax, enjoying the subtle rose scent wafting from its ceramic feathers, lulling me into a stupor.

"So what were you and Sammy gabbing about today?"

Was it fair to burden Amanda with the truth? Still, I knew I'd blab eventually since I had a hard time keeping secrets from her, especially about Sammy.

"Don't let him know I told you. Swear?" I looked down at the quilted bedspread, fraying at the edges. "Johnny Jack asked Sammy to lead an important mission..."

She eyed me. "What kind of mission? Is it dangerous?"

I looked away, avoiding the question. "Lucky for him, it's taking place the night of the policemen's ball. He hopes I'll go with Burton, but we're not very friendly after our spat today."

"Is he meeting a bootlegger? Can't he send Dino in his place?"

"I think Johnny Jack wants Sammy to take on a..." I paused, trying to choose the right words. "A bigger challenge. To test him, give him more power."

"Oh no!" She covered her mouth. "You mean a booze drop? Is that why he needs you to keep Burton busy?"

I couldn't fool Amanda—she sure was on the trolley.

"Distract him is more like it. But I doubt he'll invite me now, not after I threw a temper tantrum."

"Jazz, you've got to make up with Burton—the sooner, the better! You have to help Sammy. The ball is only four days away!"

Maybe she was right. I admit, despite Sammy's dilemma, I really missed Burton and definitely wanted to go with him to the ball, booze drop or not. Why be a wallowing wallflower when you can pretend to be Cinderella for one night?

Wednesday

The next day at work, Mack called me over the minute I walked in. "Boy, am I glad to see you. Is Nathan around? I need to explain to you both about yesterday."

"You mean 'cause you didn't show up at the...thing?" I glanced around the newsroom and saw my boss giving me her "Get to work now" look. "Let's talk later, anywhere but here."

"Sure, kid." He lowered his voice, adding, "Afraid of the old battle ax?"

"And how!" I nodded.

When I told Nathan about Mack, he said. "Can't wait to hear his excuse. And it better be good."

Around noon, Mack slapped on his fisherman's hat and gathered us up like school kids going on a field trip.

Outside, a loud popping noise sounded down the street and immediately we all ducked for cover. Not again. Were the gangs having a shoot-out in the middle of the street?

Frankly, I was surprised to see Mack hiding behind the door, peeking out the window. Why was he so spooked?

"What the hell?" Nathan jumped up, shading his eyes, staring out at the street. "False alarm. Some old jalopy just backfired. You can see black soot all over the place."

Glancing both ways, Mack came outside, tugging on his wrinkled shirt, trying to act like he wasn't rattled by the noise. The big war hero, afraid of an old jalopy. Nathan and I exchanged grins as he walked ahead to a city park, with Golliwog tagging along, meowing for attention. We found a quiet bench away from the street, and faced Mack, who sat on our right.

"So where were you yesterday?" Nathan seemed suspicious. "You missed a great story."

"That kind of story, I can live without—literally." Mack shifted his bulk on the bench, staring out at the street. "OK, kids, I'll level with you. I got a tip about a possible drive-by shooting at Parker's funeral yesterday. Obviously, he was on the money."

"You knew all along?" Nathan jumped up from the bench and challenged Mack, while I sat there in stunned silence. "Who spilled the beans—the Beach Gang? Why didn't you warn us?"

"Sorry, it was last-minute." He blanched. "I was told to keep my distance. Those hoods know me by sight. They've seen my articles, know my name. I didn't want to take that risk."

"More material for your stories," I muttered. Honestly, I was disappointed in Mack. I didn't take the Great War veteran for a coward. "Who's your source? Which gang?"

Mack shrugged, avoiding my eyes and my questions. "Confidential. For now, I'd better lay off the gangster stories. I don't want to be next on their hit list."

"Too bad for Torino. The sniper aimed right between his eyes and didn't miss. One shot was all it took," Nathan said. "The work of a pro, a real marksman."

"Was Torino the intended target?" I asked Mack.

"Probably. I heard he had a thriving bookmaking business in Houston. Took over some Galveston action." Mack eyed me warily. "Why do you want to know?"

"Just curious. I'm not used to seeing people with bullet holes in their heads." I shuddered at the memory, recalling the victim's look of shock. "What provokes that kind of violence?"

"Bookies aren't exactly Boy Scouts." Mack took a deep breath and stood up, digging in his khakis for change. "Say, can I buy you kids a sandwich and soda?"

"Why not?" Nathan nodded. "Two hams and cheese on rye. OK with you, Jazz?"

"Sure." I was so stunned by Mack's admission, I didn't care what I ate for lunch.

After he left, I told Nathan, "What's eating Mack? It all sounds kinda shady to me."

"I'll say. It's not like Mack to back down from a threat. He usually thrives on dangerous conditions."

I sighed, thinking of Sammy and Burton, on opposite sides of the law, but similar in so many ways. "His story sounds fishy, like he's hiding something or covering for someone."

Nathan frowned. "Mack's always been straight with me, honest, above-board."

I knew Nathan admired Mack and his high standards, and clearly the feeling was mutual. Mack treated Nathan like the son he never had, asking him out on plum assignments, teaching him the rules and ethics of photojournalism, while I continued to sit on the sidelines.

"Good to know." I looked over Nathan's shoulder to make sure Mack wasn't listening. "But what if he got into some hot water, and his source bailed him out? Maybe Mack keeps his name out of the paper in exchange for leads, tips on gang activity."

"Sure, it's possible. How else would he get his scoops?"

Now I was improvising, thinking out loud. "Do you know if he's a gambler? Does he play poker or bet on sports?"

"Mack does like a good round of poker." Nathan nodded. "He often organizes games with the newshounds on weekends. In fact, he may host a game this Friday night."

"You don't say. Actual games with real cash?"

"We're not sissies. We don't play for fun. It's a battle. Winner takes all."

I leaned forward. "Does he ever play with his sources? His gangster pals?"

"What are you implying? That Mack owes money to the mob?"

I hated to think the worst of Mack, but being a top-notch reporter came with a lot of power and prestige—and possible corruption. "It's just a theory." I shifted my gaze to Mack as he walked up, holding our bags of sandwiches. "So far."

CHAPTER TWENTY-EIGHT

After Mack passed out our ham and cheese sandwiches, I pulled out the casino tokens from my purse. "By the way, do you recognize any of these tokens?"

Mack frowned, fingering the discs. "Where'd you get these?"

"I found them...on the ground. At the funeral home."

"Oh yeah? In plain sight?"

Nathan had a gleam in his eye. "I saw them on the grass, by Torino's body."

"That's right," I nodded. "Do you know if they match the tokens Parker was holding?"

"Where'd you hear that rumor?" Mack leveled his gaze at Nathan, who focused intently on his sandwich. Thank goodness he'd kept quiet about Sammy. If Mack showed up at the Oasis, asking his nosy questions, the Downtown Gang would really get riled up.

"I'll tell you if you fill me in." I stole a glance at Nathan. "Kinda like trading favors."

"Those aren't the kind of favors..." Mack began, then stopped himself, thank goodness. I wasn't in the mood to hear any lewd jokes or comments today, or any day. Gather a bunch of good-old-newsboys together and they soon become dirty old men.

"OK, yes, these match the ones found at Parker's place," Mack said. "The JP token is from the Jefferson Park Race Track, near New Orleans. Seems your *friend* likes playing the ponies. The others are from some craps tables at a remote casino in Louisiana. Obviously the victims were up to something since both places are conveniently located out of state."

I perked up. "Really? Like what?"

"Who knows? Maybe they were fudging numbers or fixing bets, and their clients found out. Lots of ways to cheat unsuspecting suckers from Texas."

"I'll *bet*." Nathan grinned.

I rolled my eyes at his pun. "So how do you fix horse races?"

"Keep this under your hat." Mack lowered his voice. "For starters, you can dope the horses or the jockeys, or both."

"Can't people tell if they're all doped up? Don't the officials get suspicious?"

"The race happens so fast, that it's hard to prove until it's over," Mack said, watching my reaction. "By then, it's too late. If that doesn't work, they can pay off the top jockeys to lose."

"They're willing to lose?" I blinked in surprise.

"Ever hear of the Chicago Black Sox?" Nathan piped up. "If folks are paid enough, they'll go along with most anything. It's a win-win situation: Guaranteed payment versus walking away empty-handed." He frowned. "Or is it more like lose-lose?"

"Depends on the jockey." Mack pulled out a fat cigar and lit it, puffing away. "Still, it doesn't always work. Racehorses are excitable, unpredictable. If a horse gets a burr under his saddle or is in a feisty mood and takes off, he can't always be controlled."

"Horses are smart, beautiful animals. They're not toys or playthings," I fumed. "They don't deserve to be treated like get-rich-quick schemes." Growing up in Texas, I'd always wanted a horse, but the upkeep and cost was too high and our property too small.

"You don't want to know what they can do to racehorses, especially if they're supposed to win. Shame." Mack shook his head.

He was right. I didn't want to know. How dare these jerks abuse horses for personal gain.

"I wonder if the tokens are related to Torino's death." I waved away the sweet smell of cherry tobacco, and blurted out: "Any idea why he was killed, and by whom?"

Mack frowned. "Why do you care? You're not an *investigative* reporter, are you? You don't cover the crime beat. Why don't you stick to society weddings and gossip?"

I bristled at his mocking tone, trying to control my temper. "You may recall my friend Sammy, who owns the Oasis? He said the barkeeps on Market Street are plenty worried."

"I forgot about your jailbird pal." He smirked. "Imagine that—a society reporter hanging around a Downtown gangster."

"What did you say?" I shot to my feet, trembling with anger. "You have no right to call Sammy names. That's slander. What about *your* sources? I doubt they're model citizens."

Nathan flashed me a "hold your tongue" warning so I stopped before I blew my top off completely. Mack's face turned stony and he glared at me, reminding me of a big, angry Buddha.

I spun around and walked off, my head high and my shoulders back, hoping my exit looked dramatic enough to shut him up. Just in time. A fresh-faced couple pushing a stroller sat down at a nearby bench, cooing over their baby. Newlyweds and new parents—what a contrast from Mack, a hardened, bitter journalist.

In any case, I had a few more answers to my questions—and Mack didn't even realize he'd been interrogated by none other than a sneaky society reporter. Or did he?

CHAPTER TWENTY-NINE

To calm down, I wanted to burn off some pent-up anger before I headed back to work. How dare Mack insult me and Sammy in one breath—no doubt showing off for his biggest fan, Nathan. He was as unpredictable as a racehorse. Why was he kind one minute, cruel the next? Typical arrogant male journalist.

I made a beeline for Post Office Street and Eiband's department store, hoping for some peace of mind. I needed time away from the office, a chance to think—as if I needed an excuse to shop. If I was lucky, maybe I'd find a bauble or bag I could actually afford.

As I entered the huge store, with its elegant décor, carved columns and tempting array of goodies, I immediately felt my shoulders relaxing, my breathing slowing down. After the past few days, I wanted to forget about gamblers, gangsters and guns, not necessarily in that order.

Eiband's maintained the hushed air of a library or a museum, its high ceilings and tapestries muffling any unpleasant noise. Occasionally you could hear a burst of excitement, ladies of leisure and means cooing with delight over the frothy frocks and gowns from Paris, the cut-crystal perfume bottles, the lacy undergarments, and the regal jewels from such houses as Cartier and Van Cleef & Arpels. With a sigh, I lingered over their vanity cases, made of real gold, pearls and gems, depicting Japanese or Egyptian scenes, each one a miniature work of art.

Not that I could afford any such extravagance on my measly salary, but as a society reporter, it was my job to know the names of the latest designers and fashion houses.

Sadly, most of the matrons wearing the chicest gowns in town looked frumpy, plump and over the hill. Of course I wouldn't mind a rich, handsome husband—though those two attributes rarely went together—if we were madly in love *and* I could still do as I pleased.

A gal has her standards!

Naturally, everything I coveted cost a pretty penny and more— far out of my reach. As I ran my fingers over the soft chiffon frocks and silk beaded gowns, a beautiful teal satin number caught my eye: sparkly beads adorned the neckline, the silhouette sleek and sultry, with a simple bow tie hugging a low-cut back, graceful as a lily.

Best of all, the gown came in the most attractive shade of peacock that I hoped might flatter my pale complexion, perfect for the policemen's ball! Yet my part-time Prohibition agent beau was nowhere in sight—all thanks to me and my big mouth.

Now I was more motivated than ever to charm Burton into asking me to the ball. One glance at the price tag and I returned to reality: $28. How on earth would I pay for such a stunning creation?

Then I had a brainstorm: Since Sammy had practically begged me to go to the ball with Burton, perhaps he'd pick up the tab. If not, I was worse off than Cinderella, with no escort and no gown.

A willowy blonde clerk came over and studied the frock with approval. "How lovely," she purred. "What a gorgeous shade of teal. This dress will look great on me! I mean, you..." She colored, grabbing it with her shell-pink talons. "Is it for a special occasion?"

"I'm going to a ball this weekend." I pasted on a smile, hoping it wasn't a total lie. No matter, I had to rescue my gown from her greedy clutches. Nothing wrong with being positive!

"The policemen's ball?" She looked me up and down. "Is your fella a copper?"

I tried biting my lip but it popped out: "He's a Federal agent."

Her face lit up. "You mean the new Prohibition agent in town? What's his name—Burton? He's a sheik. You're so lucky!"

Lucky if lightning didn't strike me for lying to her the moment that I stepped outside. How in blazes did she know about Burton? Was she cutting his photos out of the paper for her hope chest?

I tried to change the subject, my moxie fading fast. "Can I put this on lay-away?"

"The ball is this weekend! You only have a few days to pay." She sounded skeptical.

"I get paid on Fridays so I'll have the money by then." I figured I could always use it for a boring society soiree or event far in the future—since it would take at least a year to pay off.

I dug in my leather handbag and pulled out a five dollar bill, watching her eyes widen in surprise. Oh boy, I sincerely hoped my show of confidence wouldn't leave me in the poorhouse, with $23 left to pay. How would I make do till Friday, with only two quarters left to my name?

After filling out the paperwork, I raced down Post Office Street toward the *Gazette*, praying they hadn't noticed my absence.

As I barreled down the sidewalk, rushing past the throng of midday shoppers and housewives with baby strollers, I ran into the last person I expected to see: Agent James Burton. At six-foot-two, he was hard to miss, all decked out in a snazzy beige double-breasted suit and hat, looking like a tall, cool glass of lemonade.

"Fancy bumping into you." My heart pounded as I smiled up at his handsome face. "What are you doing here, stranger?"

"Looking for you. I wanted to ask you something."

He sounded serious. This was it—what perfect timing! If he only knew I'd just bought my beautiful ball gown!

"Anything." I held my breath, waiting for the magic words. While he hesitated, I tried to help him along, saying: "I'd love to!"

"I haven't even asked you yet." He frowned, puzzled. "I need you to do me a favor."

"What kind of favor?" Flustered, I watched the flower vendor bundle roses on the corner, unable to hide my disappointment. When was the last time I got a bouquet of roses?

"I wanted you to come down to the police station and give a statement regarding Charlie Parker's murder. It's just a formality." Finally a smile creased his face, just barely. "I need you to corroborate my story, explaining that we were together Saturday night at the Hollywood."

"Is that all?" I turned away, hoping he didn't notice my beet-red face. If only a sinkhole could suddenly appear and swallow me whole. The last thing I wanted to do was go down to the station, surrounded by cops who were all talking about the policemen's ball.

"What did you expect?" He fanned his face with his hat, the sun shining on his hair, like burnished gold.

"Nothing. I thought...you...we needed to talk," I stammered, feeling foolish. "Guess I wanted to make up."

"Make up your mind?" He raised his brows.

"You know what I mean." I looked away. "Can I give you a written statement instead?"

He nodded. "I'm sure that will be acceptable."

"When do you need it?"

"How about later today? I can stop by to pick it up."

"At the boarding house?" I suggested, hopeful. Should I finally admit that Sammy was my half-brother, to explain why I'd overreacted earlier?

"I'm thinking it's better if we meet at the *Gazette*." He stared at me without blinking. "Then I know you won't be hiding in the parlor, watching behind the curtains."

My face burned bright, again. How'd he find out I was there? Then I remembered that damn Sheriff Sanders—he probably spilled the beans. What a tattle-tale! What else had they discussed yesterday? Why did the sheriff push Burton? Now I'd never know.

"Fine." I straightened up, throwing back my shoulders, determined to save face and a tiny shred of dignity. I'd flung myself at him like an eager dime-a-dance dame and he turned me down. Honestly, could I blame him after the juvenile way I'd acted?

"How about six o'clock? I'll be finished by then." I tried to match his business-like tone.

"Swell." Burton gave me a grateful smile. "I knew I could count on you."

Count on me? He sounded just like a pal. Is that what we'd become, mere friends? Business acquaintances? How could I be so presumptuous, so stupid? Thank goodness I didn't have the dress with me, announcing my desperation for Burton and all the world to see. Then I'd really be left holding the bag—and a big fat bill to boot.

CHAPTER THIRTY

I trudged back to work, head down, feeling like a fool. Clearly I'd gotten so excited, assuming Burton was inviting me to the dance this weekend, that I'd misread all the signs.

Like a love-struck loon, I imagined I was Cleopatra to his Antony, acting out some silly romantic illusion. What a dumb bunny.

At the *Gazette*, Mrs. Harper called me to her desk before I had a chance to sit down.

"That handsome Agent Burton stopped by, looking for you." Her eyes twinkled. "Are you going with him to the policemen's ball? How ideal! You can provide an eye-witness account of all the festivities. The mayor and councilmen will be there so I know it'll be a first-class event. In fact, I wish I could go myself." She sighed and fluttered her lashes like Clara Bow. "I love to dance. Lucky you!"

She was the second person to tell me that. Unlucky in love was more accurate.

"Thanks!" I forced a smile, pretending to be pleased. I didn't want to burst her frothy bubble.

At my desk, I let out a sigh. How could I admit to Mrs. Harper, and the whole staff, that no, I wasn't invited to the ball. In fact, I no longer had a fella or any prospects at all. Yes, I felt sorry for myself—and how!

Truth be told, I seemed to scare off men on a regular basis. No wonder my last real beau took off for Los Angeles, seeking Hollywood stardom and gals pretty enough to be in the pictures. Meanwhile, I spent all day concocting stories about rich Galveston gals who didn't have to work and lived like movie stars. It wasn't fair, I pouted. Some girls got all the breaks.

That afternoon, I pounded out pages of Mrs. Harper's gossip column, taking out my rage on my poor innocent Remington Rand no-longer-noiseless typewriter. I shot Mack a couple of dirty looks, letting him know he was on shaky ground. If he ever wanted me to proof or edit his articles again, he could forget it.

Even Nathan noticed my foul mood, keeping a safe distance from my desk. So what? Since he worshiped Mack, he was no friend of mine. Finally after Mack left for the day, Nathan approached me. "Sorry about lunch. I don't know what was wrong with Mack today."

"He's a grouchy old man with no social skills," I grumbled. "He still lives in the Victorian era, his heyday. He thinks all women should get married and raise kids, cleaning and cooking round the clock, waiting on their husbands like maids."

Nathan grinned. "You may be right. And you may be asking too many questions." He bent over my desk, whispering, "Maybe you're onto something about his gangster pals."

"You mean his so-called sources?"

He nodded. "Your theory may be spot-on. Hate to say it, but Mack is no card shark. He owes us newsboys a pile of cash. What if he *does* owe money to the mob?"

"So he pays them back by keeping quiet." I nodded. "Can you find out for sure?"

Nathan shifted his feet. "Jazz, I don't feel right about spying on my pals..."

"It's not spying, it's gathering information," I pointed out.

"Can't promise anything." Nathan shuffled off, then turned around. "Need a ride home?"

"Thanks, but I promised Burton I'd write a statement, verifying we were together Saturday night." I forced a smile. "Can I take a rain check?" That reminded me: I hadn't even started writing my statement. I slid a clean sheet of paper in my typewriter, hands shaking. Damn, is that all I meant to him now—an alibi?

Just as I'd finished typing, a long shadow crossed my desk.

"Evening, Jazz. Got your statement ready?" I had to admit, the sight of Burton still made me swoon, but I had to be careful not to show it, not to him or the newsmen. Especially not now.

"Sure, here it is." I handed him the paper, hoping he didn't notice my trembling hands.

"Thanks for your help. Well, I'd better be on my way."

As he turned to leave, I said, "Wait. Aren't you forgetting something?"

"What?" His face looked blank.

"Me." I gathered my things in a hurry. "Can't we take a walk?"

"I'm parked in front," he said flatly, not bothering to offer me a ride home.

I felt like such a bug-eyed Betty and dumb Dora combined. When Burton wouldn't meet my gaze, I followed him out the door, fumbling to make conversation. "By the way, did you know Sheriff Sanders is taking Eva to the policemen's ball?"

Open big mouth, cram in big foot.

"That's nice. I hope they have a good time." His voice was monotone.

"Aren't you planning to go?" Oh no, that's not what I meant at all! I can't believe it slipped out. I was about as subtle as a bulldozer.

This time he stared right into my eyes, his face a mask.

"Sorry, but I've already got plans that night."

My heart dropped clear down to my feet. Did he have a date? A new gal? Or was he planning to show up at Sammy's booze drop?

Shaken by his cold reply, I stood there, staring at the worn floor, trying not to cry or show any emotion. Did he mean to upset me or was he still hurt? How would I know if he refused to talk to me?

Still, I knew it was my fault—losing my temper at the funeral and hiding when he came by to make amends. Not only was I acting childish, I was rude and thoughtless.

Finally I turned around, blinking back tears, chastising myself for acting so vulnerable in front of Burton. I stumbled down the sidewalk, bumping into Finn who took one look and said, "Hey, what's wrong, Jazz? You don't look so good."

"I'm OK," I muttered, not wanting to worry the young newsie.

"If you say so." He crossed his arms and blocked Agent Burton, twice the size of the little tyke. "Who's this? Let me know if this fella is giving you any lip."

Burton raised his arms like it was a stick-up, playing along, backing away from Finn. Then he waved at Finn before he jumped into his roadster, not bothering to give me a backward glance.

"Thanks, Finn." I smiled to myself, glad there was at least one friend on my side. "Where's Golliwog?"

"Beats me," he said with a shrug.

Even my feline friend had abandoned me, probably going on her daily search for scraps.

Frankly, I had no desire to see Eva and that clingy Sheriff Sanders smooching in the parlor to remind me of my miserable love life. So I headed toward Star Drugstore and my pal Amanda, who could cheer me up with a kind word and a fresh piece of pie or cake.

I dashed down the street, keeping my eyes glued to the rutted sidewalk, dodging shoppers and young couples and children playing hopscotch. I was so upset about Burton, I didn't even notice the Ford slowly driving down the street until I was almost to Star Drugstore. Was it my overactive imagination or was the car actually following me?

When I stopped to stare, the car sped away so fast I couldn't get a good look at the driver or the plates. Did they see me talking to Burton outside the *Gazette* building? Apparently the gangsters were up to their old tricks again.

Luckily I ducked into Star Drugs before the car could turn around. The diner was getting crowded but Amanda waved me over, motioning toward my favorite circular booth in the back, large and comfy enough for some privacy.

"What a nice surprise!" She gave me a quick hug and sat down. "Why the long face?"

"How much time do you have?"

"It can't be that bad. Can it?"

With a sad sigh, I told her my sob story over a big piece of German chocolate cake: Burton's rejection, my overpriced dress, the whole song and dance. Afterwards, we shared the latest gossip, keeping it to a whisper.

After I got an earful of broken hearts and shaky engagements and cheating boyfriends, I was definitely feeling better. Good to know I wasn't the only gal in town with a lackluster love life. OK, so I was as guilty as Mrs. Harper for enjoying good Galveston gossip. By the time I left an hour later, I had a spring in my step.

My confidence restored, I decided to walk the whole way home, wanting fresh air and exercise and a chance to clear my head. To be safe, I raced down the streets, looking out for any suspicious cars or characters. Half a block from the boarding house, I got a glimpse of Sheriff Sanders' squad car and saw him and Eva holding hands on the front porch swing. Oh, brother. How could I stomach their romance *and* avoid any nosy questions about Burton?

"Evening, Jazz," Eva said with a lilt in her voice. No wonder she was smiling. At least she had a sweetheart who'd asked her to a fancy ball. "How was your day?"

"Fine." I eyed Sanders suspiciously, who grinned from ear to ear. "How was yours?"

"Very nice, thank you. Say, when do you want to go shopping for a ball gown?" Her blue eyes danced in the fading sunlight.

"Whenever you want." I pasted on a smile, determined not to spoil her happy mood.

"Tomorrow? There's not much time left," Eva said. "Maybe we can meet at Eiband's?"

"Sure," I agreed. I didn't have the heart to tell her about my shopping spree today. My new gown might even fit Eva, and match her pretty blue eyes—if we could ever pay it off.

Inside the hall, I'd walked over to the stairway when I heard a familiar voice in the parlor. "What took you so long?"

Burton stood poised in the doorway, holding his hat, his cold mask gone, replaced by an expression of sincerity.

"You're right, Jazz. We need to talk."

CHAPTER THIRTY-ONE

My heart skipped a beat. "What are you doing here? I thought we weren't speaking."

Did Burton want to break up with me, in front of Eva and her new beau? I crossed my arms and took a step away, for protection. Honestly, I was all balled up, not ready to face him, yet needing some clarity. I had to admit, it was an opportune time to talk, to get answers to a few nagging questions. Were we destined to become sweethearts or just remain friends?

"True. But after I dropped off your statement at the station, Sanders and I had a little talk." Burton jingled some change in his pockets. "He convinced me to come here and even offered me a ride. I assumed if you saw my car out front, you might run the other way or hide in the parlor."

Flustered, I wanted to say a few choice words when I noticed it was totally silent outside. How could we carry on a decent conversation with those lovebirds eavesdropping on the porch?

Gesturing toward the front door, I whispered, "Let's take a walk around the block. I think we need some privacy."

Burton nodded and opened the screen door, his jaw set. As we walked outside, I waved to Eva and the sheriff who smiled in approval, no doubt hoping we'd smooth things over.

I tried to find the right words to explain my reaction without giving away Sammy's secret. Did Burton really need to know the truth, especially if we were about to break up? But we weren't going steady or engaged or officially dating—so what was there to break?

We walked apart for a few minutes until I couldn't stand the tension. "I'm sorry I got upset yesterday, at the funeral. Guess I'm overly protective of Sammy."

"I noticed." His stony mask was back in place. "What's with you two anyway?"

We'd had this discussion before, but I had to give him the same reply. "He's a close friend. I don't like to see him humiliated."

"Humiliated? All I wanted to do was talk to him, ask a few questions."

"How do you think it looked? You might as well have accused him of murder and handcuffed him, too!"

"You're all wet. I don't care how it *looked*. He knew the victim and I wanted answers."

I avoided his gaze, his frustration on display. Somewhere in the distance, a dog howled, setting off a chorus of barking and baying.

"So what about that goon who accused you of killing Parker? Did he say anything?"

"That palooka? He wouldn't talk. And we didn't have anything to charge him with, so we had to let him go." He let out a burst of air. "Waste of time."

"What about Sammy?" I asked innocently. "What did he say?"

"Not much. He said Parker was well-liked by the gang and knew their situation, so he helped keep their bets in check." Burton turned to me. "Why? Did Sammy say anything to you?"

I paused, then realized I wasn't breaching any confidences. After all, didn't Burton have a right to know?

"Sammy told me the guy admitted he was paid to plant your hat at the murder scene, but he didn't mention who hired him. Too bad the cops showed up before he could spill the beans. Sammy got the idea he was a goon-for-hire, freelancing for different gangs."

"Damn, that might have closed our case." Burton stomped his foot on the street, mumbling under his breath. "I wish Sammy had told me that while the jerk was still in custody so we'd have a reason to hold him. At least book him for tampering with a crime scene."

"Think about it." I grabbed his arm, trying to calm him down. "If you suddenly arrested him right after talking to Sammy, who do you think would get blamed?"

"So it's better if I get framed for murder?" Burton scowled. "What a pal. Thanks, Sammy."

I sucked in my breath. "Sammy was just saving his skin. You'd do the same thing if you were in his place." Why did I open my big, fat mouth? To distract him I added, "Say, did you notice the flashy cuff links that wiseguy wore? What's his name?"

"Harry Brogan. I assume it's an alias. He probably changes it with every job." His eyes narrowed. "What about the cuff links?"

"They appeared to be real gold. Either this guy has expensive taste or he's well-paid for his skills." I added, "They looked similar to the one I saw on your desk."

"Very observant."

"So were they the same cuff links? If so, how did they end up on his shirt?"

"That's a good question. The cuff link disappeared from my desk later that day."

I stopped walking. "Disappeared? You mean it was stolen?"

Burton nodded. "It's no longer in evidence. Probably some light-fingered con-artist swiped it while we were doing paperwork. Or some cop, hard up for cash."

"Maybe the cop owed some money to his bookie. Or to the mob," I suggested.

"I wouldn't be surprised. Half those cops are on the take."

An old truck barreled down the street with a fluffy dog in the back, barking at us as it passed. Poor puppy. Didn't the driver realize how dangerous that was for his pet?

Distracted, I racked my brain, trying to think of a way to bring up the dance.

"Speaking of cops, I didn't mean to put you on the spot today. I assumed you wanted to go to the policemen's ball, and I presumed, well, hoped...you'd invite me. Clearly I was wrong."

I didn't dare look at him, afraid I'd get too emotional. Was it too much of a commitment to attend the policemen's ball together? Maybe to him our relationship was just a lark, a fun pastime. Was he worried our names would be linked in the society pages, and attractive shop girls and teachers and nurses wouldn't get a crack at the handsome bachelor?

"I can't figure you out, Jasmine." Burton stared at me, frowning, as if I were a complicated crossword puzzle. "You treat me like a yo-yo, pulling me close then pushing me away."

"A yo-yo? That's not true..." I began, then considered my actions. "I didn't mean to give you mixed signals. I thought we had something special, whatever you call this relationship."

"What do *you* want to call it?" He studied me, wary. "Are we dating? Going steady? Friends?"

"I'm not seeing anyone else. Are you?" I felt my face flush. "The policemen's ball is this Saturday and you haven't mentioned it once." When he didn't reply, I asked, "Are you having second thoughts about this whole...thing?"

Thing? Boy, was I articulate tonight.

"Believe me, it has nothing to do with you." Burton moved closer, a hint of moonlight shadowing his face. "I know all you gals like fancy parties and dances. But think about it from my standpoint. Why spend an evening with a bunch of good-old-boys who can't stand me and vice-versa? Ever since I moved to Galveston, they've been trying to interfere with my job, sabotage my leads, ruin my raids. Worse, they try to take credit for all my busts."

My heart sank. "I had no idea. Why didn't you tell me?"

"I didn't want to burden you with my problems." Burton glanced up at the deepening sky as if looking for an aurora borealis. "Sorry to disappoint you, but spending an evening with these local yokels seems more like torture than fun to me."

"No wonder. I never considered your side of the story, James. All I could think about was the gorgeous gown, the ballroom, the band, the excitement," I admitted, feeling guilty for focusing on my own selfish desires. "Don't let those cops shut you out. Play their game. You don't have to prove anything."

"Still, I've made a promise. And yes, I do have something to prove, to myself."

I had to respect him for his dedication, his sense of purpose. But in this case, Sammy's life might be at stake. How could I change his mind? Did I even have a right to try to sway him?

"I know how you feel. Journalists are trained to be objective, detached, and heaven forbid we actually get involved or care about the people and subjects we cover. We must remain neutral, unemotional, impersonal.

"People are guarded around you, afraid to speak up. Or they may say too much and regret it later. In all honesty, I'm not sure being a society reporter is my cup of tea." I took a deep breath, worried that I'd revealed too much. "Frankly, I'm tired of feeling like a spy, an intruder who forces her way inside the forbidden palace. With you, I'd be an invited guest, not a gatecrasher."

Burton gave me a slight smile. "I thought the society set loved to see their names in the papers. Since I moved to Galveston, I've felt like an outsider who isn't allowed into an exclusive club I don't even want to join. When I show up, the party's over—literally."

"Guess my job doesn't seem so bad in comparison."

Sure, I had a position many gals would envy, but I wanted to get down in the mud with the real journalists, do some actual reporting, investigating corruption and crime—like my heroine, *New York World* reporter Nellie Bly.

The question was: Did I have the moxie to handle hard news?

"I wish I could work without these palookas interfering in my business," Burton added. "No matter what the gangs think, I still have pride in my job."

I leaned against his shoulder, feeling his warmth under the suit jacket. "Of course. But your job is so dangerous, I can't help but worry about you."

Why did I always fall for difficult men? OK, so I'd only had two real beaux, but each one was difficult in their own way.

"Glad to know you care."

Now I had to ask the question, though I'd guessed the answer: "Are you planning to raid the booze drop that night? Is that it?"

He nodded. "Don't tell Sheriff Sanders and for God's sake, don't tell your Aunt Eva."

My stomach knotted. "What about the temporary truce with Johnny Jack?"

"No one asked for my permission." Burton straightened his shoulders, standing tall. "What kind of Prohibition agent would I be if I stood by and let it happen, even for one night? I'd be a joke, a laughingstock, that's what."

I stared at his profile under the streetlamps. "Will the cops back you up even after Sanders agreed to stay away?"

"I don't know for sure. I won't find out until that night."

"By then it may be too late." I tried to think fast. "Why not get to know the cops on a personal level? At a party, they'll let their guard down, say things they wouldn't normally reveal. Show them you're a regular Joe who knows how to have fun."

"Tempting." His eyes began to show some spark again. "I still want to find out why they raided the Rusty Bucket."

"Same here. What are they hiding that's so incriminating?"

"We won't know until I start digging." He exhaled, defeated. "If you insist, I suppose we can go for a short while."

I felt like jumping for joy. "We'll have at least a couple of hours to dance before the actual booze drop. If we leave early, you'll still have plenty of time."

"Maybe it's not such a bad idea. I may get these cops to talk, and while I'm at it, try to recruit them for the drop."

"You sound like a reporter." I smiled. "Does that mean we're on for Saturday?"

"You twisted my arm. Sure you don't mind leaving early?"

"Fine with me." I beamed. "I can catch a ride home with Nathan. Mrs. Harper assumed we'd go, so she asked me to write a piece for the paper. Nathan will be there to take photos."

"So you had an ulterior motive after all." If he only knew. "OK, then, it's a date."

"Swell!" I reached up and hugged his neck, pulling him down to my level. "Since that's settled, I have a confession to make: I already bought my dress." I failed to mention that I needed to break my beautiful gown out of Eiband's pricey prison.

"You don't say." Burton gave me a grin that was worth the wait. "Gotta admit, Jazz, you sure have a lot of nerve."

I returned the smile, finally able to breathe. "I wouldn't be dating a Prohibition agent if I didn't."

CHAPTER THIRTY-TWO

I noticed the sky had deepened and a faded moon started to rise. The air felt crisp, a slight breeze cooling off the summer heat. As we walked along, our fingers brushed once or twice, but we didn't hold hands. Our feelings were still too raw—and Burton was too much of a gentleman—to make that leap.

"So when do I get a glimpse of your dress?" he teased me.

"It's a surprise. You'll have to wait until Saturday. I'll give you a hint: it's peacock blue."

Without warning, he pulled me to him and kissed me so hard, my head was spinning. Oh, my. Maybe he wasn't such a proper gentleman after all.

Too bad the boarding house was only a few houses away, since we didn't want an audience. "Now I'm glad we're going to the policemen's ball." He squeezed my hand.

"You said it." I couldn't wait to tell Eva!

By the time we returned, Eva and Sanders were standing on the porch, saying their goodbyes. Thankfully, they didn't kiss in front of us—too sappy for my taste.

"Good night, Sheriff." I shook his hand warmly. Still I couldn't bring myself to call him Walt, not yet—it seemed too familiar, too "welcome to our family" friendly.

Burton gave me a flirtatious wink, saying, "See you soon."

Once inside the parlor, Eva turned to me, her face flushed with excitement, saying, "What happened? Did you kiss and make up?"

Was she razzing me? "How could we sneak a kiss with you two watchdogs spying on us?"

"We could barely see you. Tell me, did he invite you to the ball?"

"Finally, after much prodding." I smiled, suspecting she had intervened. "Did you put the sheriff up to it? Was this all your big idea?" Her pale face turned crimson.

"So what if I did? Walt and I were only trying to help speed things along. We both need to shop for our frocks and hats and gloves. The men need to place their orders for our corsages. The ball is only two days away!"

I hung my head. "You might as well know the truth. I already bought my gown today from Eiband's. It's a gorgeous shade of peacock blue."

"You did? Where is it? I'd love to see it!"

"Eiband's is holding it for ransom. I put it on lay-away." I made a face. "I doubt I'll get it out in time, unless I ask Sammy for help."

Eva nodded in understanding. "We're both in the same boat. I've been eyeing a few dresses at Eiband's myself and they're all out of my price range. And I have too much pride to ask Walt for a hand-out." She plopped down on the settee with a sigh. "I hate to ask Sammy for a loan, but do you think he'll help us both out?"

"Help with what?" Amanda popped in and I could smell Star Drugstore's greasy griddle ten yards away.

"Good news. Burton asked me to the ball!" I smiled, elated.

"How exciting!" She clapped her hands. "I almost wish I was dating a copper—if they were sheiks like Burton. Sad to say, most of them look like Mutt and Jeff." She glanced at Eva and let the sentence drop. Sure, Sanders was no Romeo but to Eva, maybe he was a cuddly Teddy bear.

I interrupted her before Amanda hurt Eva's feelings. "The trouble is, Eva and I can't figure out how to pay for new ball gowns."

"Can't you wear something from last year?" Amanda suggested. "No one will notice."

"Last year?" My mouth dropped open. Usually I was the practical one, not Amanda. As a society reporter, I knew how critical women could be, no matter what their social status. Even policemen's wives recognized an old hand-me-down or last year's cast-off. Fact is: Old gowns are old news.

"I already put a gown on lay-away, but I'm in hock up to my neck." I turned to Eva "Don't worry, we'll figure something out. Even if I have to beg Sammy for spare change."

"Sammy will be glad to help out." Amanda smiled. "I love men with big hearts and big wallets."

Thursday

The next day at work, Mrs. Harper called me over. "Are you excited about the ball?"

"And how! In fact, I have my gown all picked out." I failed to mention that it was gathering dust in Eiband's basement.

"Good. I'll expect you to give a first-hand account of all the festivities." Naturally there was a catch. Would she pay for my new dress too?

Around noon, Nathan came by my desk. "Ready for lunch?"

"Sure, I've got lots to tell you." I gathered my hat and purse, ignoring Mack who lowered his newspaper as we passed. After our lunch, I made it a point to avoid him, and he gladly did the same. In addition to his precious hat rack, he was the only reporter allowed to smoke cigars at work. Must be nice to look down on us peons.

Outside on the sidewalk, Nathan said, "Is it true? So you're going to the policemen's ball with Burton?"

"I can't wait. Aren't you going as my photographer?"

He groaned. "As long as I don't have to dance with the policemen's wives. If they look anything like their husbands, I'll shoot myself—if they don't shoot me first."

"Nathan, be nice," I scolded, stifling a smile.

"What happened? How'd you convince Mr. Hard-boiled to go?"

I summarized our conversation, leaving out the few mushy parts. As I talked, a brainstorm began to take shape. "Say, I have an idea. What are you doing after the ball?"

"I assume I'm working. Why, what did you have in mind?"

"I promise, it'll be a lot more exciting than developing photos."

"You're going to ditch Burton?" His face lit up. "A bonfire on the beach? Skinny-dipping in the ocean?"

"Nathan!" I rolled my eyes at him, wishing he had a girlfriend. Too bad Holly, his bathing beauty flame, still lived in Houston.

I took a deep breath and edged closer. "Why don't we crash the Downtown Gang's booze drop on the beach?"

CHAPTER THIRTY-THREE

"A booze drop?" Nathan's mouth flew open. "Are you daffy? We'll be sunk!"

"Why not? We've done it before," I reminded him as we walked toward the sandwich vendor on the corner. "We might have saved Sammy's life that night on the docks."

"How could I forget? We almost lost our lives, too, in the bargain." He frowned. "But where would we hide? Not a lot of barrels or warehouses on the beach. We'd be like tin ducks at a carnival, waiting to get popped off."

"What about sand dunes?"

"In your prom dress?" Nathan snorted. "Some date you'll turn out to be, following your agent beau to his booze drop by the ocean. How romantic."

"I'm not worried about romance. We've got to be there to help Burton and Sammy." I swallowed hard. "The Cuban rum-runners are supposed to show up on West Beach after dark."

"The Cubans? Jazz, that's nuts." Nathan stopped in his tracks. "They have short fuses and long memories. Remember that time Johnny Jack stiffed the Cubans with soap coupons? What if he tries to pull another clever stunt and they start shooting? The Cubans won't care how many people get hurt—or killed. They'll just take off in the middle of the night and keep going."

"You said it." I heaved a sigh. "I think that's why Johnny Jack is forcing Sammy to lead the whole operation. The Cubans have no idea that Sammy represents the Downtown Gang. I hope."

He whistled. "Your pal Sammy? He got a promotion?"

"More like a death sentence." I took a deep breath, fidgeting with my bead necklace. "Either way, Sammy can't trust Johnny Jack *or* the Cuban rum-runners."

He leveled his eyes at me. "Whose side are you on? Sammy's or Agent Burton's?"

"Both. I'm hoping Burton may change his mind, but I want to be there, just in case. Any ideas?" Who was I kidding? Burton was determined to stop that booze drop if it killed him.

"Are you sure?" Nathan looked skeptical. "We may end up in quicksand—if the gangsters don't find us first."

"They'll be so busy with their booze, they won't know we're there."

"The question is, do *we* want to take that risk?"

After ordering sandwiches and soda pop from the street vendor, we settled down in our usual spot at the city park. Golliwog must have seen us because she soon made an appearance, circling my ankles, soft as fuzzy slippers. I tossed her my crusts and bits of ham, watching as she gobbled up the scraps.

"You've never been to a booze drop on the beach, have you?"

"Not the sort of event we society reporters cover."

"Exactly. These goons go out waist-deep in murky water and hand-carry the boxes of booze back to shore. It's dangerous and dirty work." Nathan gave me a warning look. "No telling what can happen in the dark, especially if the men *and* their guns are loaded."

My heart raced as I imagined the scenario. "So I'm supposed to sit by and do nothing? Wait for Sammy or Burton, or both, to get killed—or shoot each other?"

"What can we do, seriously? Is it better to watch them get shot in person?"

I tried to appeal to his sense of justice, as well as his vanity. "You're such a good crack shot I thought you could bring your gun...in case the situation gets out of control."

"Jazz, I *guarantee* it will get out of control. What do you expect? I'll bring my gun, but I can't compete with rum-runners and hit men. Let's just hope the Coast Guard shows up in time." Nathan scratched his head as if solving a math problem. "Say, if we pull it off, I might get some amazing shots of the whole scene."

"Photos? No, you can't take any photos! They may see us."

"Don't worry, I'll be careful. If I'm going to die, at least I want some great photos as part of my legacy."

Back at the office, I resumed proofing and typing up my boss's gossipy tidbits, wishing my biggest problems involved planning a wedding or charity event. Why did I feel the need to interfere in Sammy and Burton's troubles? Nathan was right: What could we really accomplish?

By the time I finished, it was after five and I'd planned to meet Eva at Eiband's after work. As I was getting ready to leave, I saw Nathan talking to Mack and a few other reporters. When I passed by their desk, Nathan tugged on my arm. "How about a ride home?"

"Would you mind taking me to Eiband's instead?" When he looked puzzled, I told him, "Eva wants me to help her pick out a dress. Mine is trapped inside, begging for freedom."

Perhaps I should take Amanda's advice and wear a boring bridesmaid's dress from last year, a sweet schoolmarm-ish frock Burton hadn't seen yet. But who wants to be boring?

In the car, I asked Nathan, "So what was that all about? You and the guys seemed to be in a deep discussion. Some hot scoop?"

"You could say that. We're planning our Friday night poker game at Mack's place."

"Good luck. Let me know what happens."

After Nathan dropped me off at Eiband's, I was once again swept into a fairy tale of French perfumes in crystal bottles, glittering cut-steel beaded purses, enameled tango vanity cases, embroidered piano shawls, lacy chemises and bias-cut silk gowns. So many exquisite creations from Europe!

A few flappers milled around the gowns, holding up the dresses and prancing in front of full-length mirrors. Were they also going to the policemen's ball? I spotted Eva admiring a fetching Paris evening gown with rosettes at the neckline and big bows at the sides, all in a rosy peach hue, perfect for Eva's porcelain complexion.

Taking one look at the price tag, I gasped and tried to steer Eva toward more affordable American designers, names no one recognized. Did it really matter? After all, this was the policemen's ball, not the presidential inauguration.

Apparently it mattered to Eva. I ooohed and aaahed as she modeled a number of gorgeous designer gowns—a lilac chiffon with a pleated skirt, a ruffled floral frock, a chemise with a Peter Pan collar, an icy blue silk gown with a handkerchief hem.

Still, she kept returning to her favorite, the peach Paris gown. No, it wasn't a Chanel or a Lanvin or a Poiret but it was perfect for Eva, the way it flattered her creamy skin and auburn highlights in her newly-hennaed hair.

"Why don't you show me the beautiful gown you put on lay-away?" she prodded. "Try it on for me, will you? I'd like to see it once before the ball."

Reluctantly I approached the same sales clerk, whose eyes lit up when she saw me, probably hoping I'd inherited a small fortune that day. After I tried on the teal-blue stunner, Eva's face shone as brightly as mine. The gown managed to cling to my figure without being too tight or tarty.

I certainly didn't want to look like a flashy flapper or a frivolous floozy in front of the police chief and city dignitaries, especially if my photo happened to appear in the *Gazette*. Wouldn't that pushy sales clerk be surprised if Burton and I showed up in the society pages?

"Oh, Jazz, that dress is made for you! It's the bee's knees! I can see why you splurged." Then she turned to the clerk and announced triumphantly, "We'll take them both."

Was she off her rocker? "Aunt Eva, wait." I pulled her aside, my face flushed. "I haven't had a chance to talk to Sammy. I have no way to pay for it, unless I take out a loan." A loan that would haunt me till I retired, poor but dressed to the nines.

"Who needs a loan when you have real gold jewelry? We must learn to be independent and resourceful, not rely on men to fulfill our dreams and desires."

She pulled out a wad of cash and I noticed that one of her gold bangles, passed down from her mother, was gone. My heart dropped, realizing she had to hock a family heirloom to pay for our dresses in cash. "Are you sure?" I asked, overcome by her generosity.

How could I ever pay her back? Somehow Sheriff Sanders had put a spark back into Eva's life. I hadn't seen her so happy since she got engaged, before her fiancé died in the war.

"We only live once." She smiled, placing a stack of bills in the clerk's eager, outstretched hand. "I'd rather have real memories than a fantasy that never comes true."

"Thanks, Eva." I gave her a quick hug. "I owe you."

"You don't owe me a thing." Her blue eyes sparkled. "But I may want to borrow your lovely dress one day."

"Anytime," I agreed, squeezing her arm.

Now I couldn't wait to go to the policemen's ball with Burton. If only we could skip the fireworks afterwards.

CHAPTER THIRTY-FOUR

A doorman held open the exit as Eva and I left Eiband's, floating on air, carrying our beautiful ball gowns tucked in oversized cream boxes tied with silky red ribbons.

"We can't take the trolley now, not with our nice gowns. Besides, it's getting dark," Eva said. "Let's get a taxi!"

Aunt Eva was getting all hoity-toity on me, buying fancy French gowns, dyeing her hair with henna and hailing a taxi. What was next? How would we ever return to normal life after all this luxury? Just as we stood on the corner, looking for a cab, I saw Nathan driving by in his Model-T and flagged him down.

"Boy, am I glad to see you!" I told him when he stopped. "Your timing is perfect. Can you give us a ride home, please?"

"Sure, but I'm on my way to take photos of a robbery. It was a bar off Market Street and luckily the victim is still alive. Thought you'd want to come along, ask a few questions."

"Would I!" I held my breath. "Anyone we know?"

I helped Eva get in the back, trying to squeeze in his tiny Tin Lizzie with our big boxes.

"It's not Sammy, if that's what you mean. A bar called the Stallion. Mack is already there waiting, so let's hurry. I was on my way out the door when he called."

Feeling guilty, I glanced at Eva's stern expression. I hated to abandon her after such an enjoyable—and expensive—shopping spree. "Is it OK if I miss supper?"

"Why do *you* have to go? It's too dangerous!" She scolded, her mouth tight. "Don't you want to show Amanda your new gown?"

"Yes, of course, after supper. Don't worry, I'll be surrounded by cops," I reassured her.

Nathan parked in front of the boarding house and helped Eva get out, practically shoving her out the door. I rushed up the walk, juggling both boxes, and placed them on the hall tree.

"Thanks again, Eva, for everything. See you later!" I didn't mean to be abrupt, but duty called.

In the car, Nathan raced down the street, tires screeching as he rounded the corner while I held onto the straps. "Hold your horses, Nathan! Tell me what happened."

He shrugged. "Mack told me some barkeep got robbed, but he's still alive. Passed out cold. You can't say the same for his slot machine. Some goon smashed it with a baseball bat."

"A baseball bat? Why beat a slot machine to death?" I stifled a smile, relieved no one was hurt. "Do they think they're the same guys who murdered Parker?"

"Makes sense." Nathan nodded. "But that's for you and Mack to figure out."

He stopped in front of the Black Stallion, an English-style pub and grill. A small group had already gathered outside, roughly half the crowd at Parker's murder scene. Blood and guts sold more papers than a mere robbery.

Inside, a few cops and reporters stood gawking at a middle-aged man lying on a faded rag rug on the floor, his wrists and ankles bound by rope, a wadded newspaper stuffed in his mouth.

Luckily, he only appeared to be unconscious, not seriously hurt. The dark, wood-paneled bar sported the usual British theme: posters of beefeaters and Buckingham Palace, faded photos of King George V and Queen Mary, adorned with the British flag in various sizes.

I spied Sheriff Sanders talking to the ruddy-faced cop I'd seen at the station, motioning toward the victim. Pete and Chuck, our cub reporters, stood by Mack with their pencils and pads, raising their brows when we walked in. Wasn't I invited to this shindig?

Parts of a slot machine, along with tokens and crumpled up newspapers, littered the worn, wooden floor. What was the significance? Was this a warning to the reporters? An old baseball bat, splintered in two pieces, lay under the bar.

Mack glared at me and called out to Nathan, "Hey, what took you so long? Try to get some decent shots before the medics take him away, will ya, sport?"

Nathan sprang into action, snapping different angles, shoving the men aside. Meanwhile I glanced around, looking for anything amiss, clues of a break-in. A couple of overturned bar stools and several broken glasses indicated a struggle. Still, nothing like the chaotic murder scene at The Rusty Bucket.

"What happened?" I asked Pete and Chuck, avoiding Mack. "Why all the newspapers?"

"Looks like some joker kept stuffing the machine with papers so the coins wouldn't drop," Pete said. "It's an old trick. These types of models are easy to jam. Then the culprit comes back later to cash in."

"Any idea who did it?" I asked. "Not the owner?"

"I doubt he jammed his own slots or he'd be dead by now," Chuck added. "The gangs don't mess around when someone cuts into their take."

I nodded, recalling the horror stories from Sammy about greedy gamblers. "What's his name?"

"Ted Blake. From the looks of this place, I take it he's more into horse-racing than slots."

I noticed Blake was coming to, struggling against the ropes, rocking back and forth, groaning and trying to speak. The reporters either didn't care or didn't see him moving, but just stood there, making small talk about other cases.

Exasperated, I tugged on Nathan's sleeve. "Are you done yet? This poor guy needs some air or he'll suffocate!"

Without waiting for permission from the cops, I knelt by the victim and removed the newspaper from his mouth. He coughed and managed to gasp, "Thanks, doll."

"Are you hurt?" I asked but he shook his head. "Who did this to you?" I hoped he'd reveal some secret the other reporters wouldn't overhear. "Did you recognize anyone?"

"Two guys attacked me, but their faces were covered." Blake tried to sit up, clearly dazed. "Can you untie me, please?" He must have assumed I was some floozy or gangster's moll who wouldn't blab to the press or police.

I noticed the deep grooves in his skin, his swollen hands, but there were no major cuts or abrasions. The rope scratched my fingers as I struggled to loosen it, but those thick knots wouldn't budge. "What happened?"

"They ransacked the place and took all my cash right before they knocked me out. I don't remember much." He attempted to stand, but then looked over my shoulder, eyes wide, whispering, "Parker!"

I glanced toward the doorway, and saw Chad Parker there, looking upset, perhaps reminded of his father's death. If Blake *was* robbed by the same men who killed Charlie Parker, he may have felt guilty for surviving the attack.

When the reporters realized that Blake was able to speak, they crowded around, badgering him with questions. "Does anyone have a knife to cut his ropes?" I asked the group.

"Wait till I finish taking photos!" Nathan walked around with his camera, taking shots of Blake struggling with the ropes. Finally Pete and a dark, diminutive guy in a cap helped Blake to his feet while the reporters continued belting him with questions.

Blake clammed up, glancing around the bar, clearly nervous. Was he afraid the robbers might return and finish the job? Or was he worried what Johnny Jack might do if he talked?

"How many men?" Mack persisted. "Surely you can count. Did you see their faces?"

Mack could be as intimidating as any gangster. Finally Blake spoke up. "Two guys. Both big and tall. They wore cowboy hats and bandanas so I didn't get a good look at their faces. One pointed a gun at me and forced me to empty my cash register. The other robber beat my slot machine with that baseball bat."

He pointed, hand shaking, his voice raspy. "They got angry when they saw all those newspapers. Accused me of stiffing my own customers. Hell, I didn't even know they were in there!"

"Did you recognize their voices, their clothes, anything? Could they be disgruntled customers, gamblers who lost a wad on your slots or games?" Pete asked while Mack nodded in approval.

"Who knows? They might be." Blake shrugged. "The guys sure seemed familiar with the place 'cause they knew where I kept everything. Even took my pistol."

"That narrows it down," Mack said, taking notes. He leaned over, whispering to a goon in a fedora and I wondered if he was pumping him for information. Was I seeing things or did Mack slip him some dough? Could he be an informant or a bookie? You never knew with Mack.

The interviews seemed to be over, so I approached Chad, who leaned against the doorway, arms crossed, watching the scene.

"Remember me? You met my friend Amanda at the Oasis the other night."

"Jazz?" His face broke into a smile. "I sure do. How's Amanda doing? Too bad you two had to take off so fast."

"She's fine. Maybe we'll see you at the Oasis again soon?"

"Maybe. So tell me, what are you doing here?"

"I'm a new reporter, learning the ropes." I let out a sigh. "But to these fellas, I may as well be invisible."

"A reporter, huh?" Chad gave me the once-over, apparently deciding I was harmless. "Then, maybe you can help me. I suspect the same guys who killed my dad robbed this place."

"You don't say. Because of the baseball bat?"

"It's too much of a coincidence." His eyes narrowed. "I need to talk to this Blake fella and find out what he knows. Why'd they spare *his* life and not my dad's? How'd he manage to scare them off? I just want to find out who killed my father—and why."

CHAPTER THIRTY-FIVE

From his bitter tone, it was clear that Chad wished Blake had been murdered instead.

"Was Blake a friend of your dad's?" I asked, taken aback.

"I wouldn't call them friends." He scowled. "More like rivals."

"Is that why you were at the Oasis, to get information?"

"Yeah, but no one there knew anything. Your pal Sammy hardly talked to me. I'm reaching a dead end." His face twisted, clearly upset, when he realized his choice of words.

"I'm so sorry." Then seizing my chance, I started firing off questions: "Did you see that guy get shot at the funeral? Tony Torino? I was scared to death!"

"Luckily, I was a few yards away but I didn't see the killer. I was distracted by the drive-by shooting."

Yikes! "Good thing no one else got hurt. So how well did Torino know your dad? Did they ever do business together?"

"That asshole? I've seen him in my dad's bar, but I assumed he was a bootlegger. Turns out he's some big-shot bookie in Houston." Chad frowned, crossing his arms. "Why the third-degree? You should be asking Blake questions about his robbery, not me."

I got the message. "Sorry. Goes with the territory."

"No problem." His voice softened. "Say, let me know if the paper boys find out anything. Tell Amanda I said hello." With that, he turned away and walked out the door.

Poor kid. I really didn't blame him for being bitter or confused. I knew how it felt to lose a father at such a young age. He'd be grieving for the rest of his life.

The small group filtered out onto the street, jabbering and comparing notes. An ambulance arrived for the victim, despite his protests. "All I got was a bump on the head," he complained as they led him outside, refusing to be moved on a stretcher. "I don't need a doctor. I'm A-OK, I swear."

After most of the newshawks left, I finally had a chance to snoop. While Nathan packed up his equipment, I wandered through the bar, looking at the memorabilia and old photos covering the walls and shelves. Every juice joint sported a different theme: Sammy displayed nautical items from his days as a sailor, some dives displayed wild animal heads and taxidermy, while the high-class speaks favored a more upscale atmosphere with chandeliers and stained glass. The Turf Club adopted a sleek, "men's club" theme with a boxing ring on the top floor.

By the bar stood several trophies and bronzes of horses and dogs, next to photos of various sports teams and racehorses. At least the barkeep seemed to be an animal lover or avid gambler—probably both. A rusty horseshoe hung upside down on a nail, as if placed haphazardly. Wasn't that a sign of bad luck? I noticed a faint outline of a horseshoe facing upwards and wondered if it had been knocked off during the scuffle, or used to strike the victim?

Looking around, I almost tripped over the rag rug and uncovered two tokens on the floor, marked JP—exactly like the ones found with Parker and Torino. They must have fallen out of Blake's pockets or maybe the robbers dropped them during the attack. Sure, it could all be coincidental and I was jumping to conclusions.

In a flash, I slipped the tokens in my clutch bag, hoping no one noticed. Still, I suspected there had to be a connection between the three victims—but what?

Nathan sidled up, handing me his flash to carry to his car. "Ready to go? I'll drop you off before I develop these photos."

"We're not far from the Oasis. Want to stop by and have a drink? Soda pop, since you're still on duty," I teased him. I hadn't seen Sammy since my talk with Burton, and I needed to warn him that he still planned to raid the booze drop Saturday night.

"Sounds good to me," Nathan agreed. "As long as the big Bruno will let me in the door."

At the Oasis, Dino ignored Nathan, telling me, "It's not a good time to be here. Sammy's setting up a card game."

"Just cards? I'll make it quick. Promise." I rushed downstairs and waved to Frank behind the bar. Nathan took a seat on a barstool and I heard him order two orange Nehi's for us. Careful fella.

I found Sammy in the back, moving tables and chairs, grunting and groaning under the strain. "Jazz, what are you doing here?" He looked up, surprised. "You kids better scram. I've got a poker game in an hour."

"Hello to you, too." I patted his shoulder. "I assume you heard about the barkeep down the street. Fred Blake?"

"Sure, but I hated to go down there with all those hounds sniffing around. Blake wasn't badly hurt, was he?"

"Just hit on the head, nothing serious. Sadly, his slot machine died a painful death. You think the Beach Gang did it to eliminate the competition? As a warning to Nounes?"

"I wouldn't be surprised." Sammy shrugged, sitting down. "No great loss. The barkeeps hate these new slots. Hate paying extra to Johnny Jack, but he's forcing us to install them to line his pockets. Not only does he raise his rent and expect us to pay him part of our profits, he also controls our slots."

"That's not fair."

"Johnny Jack doesn't play fair." Sammy wiped his perspiring forehead with his sleeve. "And it doesn't help that the guys on his turf are getting attacked—two men in one week."

"Do you think Parker and Blake tried to defy him somehow and got punished?"

"That's possible." He nodded. "Between you and me, I think Johnny Jack is losing control over the whole operation. The Downtown Gang is ready to mutiny."

"Mutiny?" My ears perked up. "What will they do?"

"Who knows? But if Johnny Jack doesn't lay off, the guys will stop taking his orders."

I took a deep breath, not wanting to voice my fears. How long would Sammy keep performing for his ruthless mob boss like an organ grinder's monkey?

I pulled out the tokens and handed them to Sammy. "By the way, look what I found at the Black Stallion. They're just like the ones Parker and Torino had on them when they were killed. Any idea how they're connected?"

"Good question." He studied the tokens, flipping them over as if he'd never seen them before.

"Let me know if you hear anything, OK?"

Sammy nodded, but I could tell he didn't mean it. To change the subject, I told him, "Guess what? Burton finally invited me to the policemen's ball." I smiled. "Aunt Eva is going, too, with Sheriff Sanders. She even sprung for both our dresses at Eiband's."

"No shit? I thought she was such a tightwad."

Sammy wasn't known to mince words. "Eva has to be careful with money to cover expenses. But she seems lighter now, brighter. Believe it or not, Sanders is helping her come out of her shell."

"Good for her." He stared hard at me. "Just my luck that you two are seeing lawmen. Well, I hope Burton knows this booze drop is no picnic on the beach. As long as he stays out of my way, no one will get hurt. I hope."

What did that mean? "Sammy, I've tried to change his mind, but I can't guarantee you Burton won't intervene. He's as stubborn as you are. What time is the drop?"

"How can I predict exactly when these Cubans will show up? All I know is it'll be dark, usually after ten o'clock or later. They flash their lights, give us some kind of signal." He cocked his head toward the table, with eight chairs in place. "That's why I'm hosting this poker game with my crew, to figure out a plan so nothing goes wrong. We need a foolproof strategy."

My stomach knotted, realizing the drop was taking place in only two nights. I hated to see Burton and Sammy face off, risk their lives—and for what? Some stupid Cuban rum. So suckers could drink their fool heads off?

And thanks to me, I even got Nathan involved, so now all my favorite men would be in danger. Couldn't they come to an agreement, perhaps a truce? Frankly, I hoped for a miracle—even a mild hurricane would do, not a disaster like the 1900 Storm.

"Can you keep it peaceful, leave the guns at home?" I pleaded. "I'd hate for anything to happen to you—or Burton." I knew it was futile. Asking gang members to give up their guns was like expecting children to forsake candy on Halloween.

"Jazz, you know I can't control these men, especially not the Cubans. They shoot first, ask questions later. I wish Burton would wise up and let us do our jobs."

"That's what Burton is trying to do. His job."

"The difference is, the government won't kill Burton for not making an appearance." Sammy scowled. "Me? I'd rather take my chances with the Cubans than Johnny Jack. If I don't show up or if my guys think I'm cooperating with Burton or the cops in any way, I'm a dead man. If Burton keeps his nose out of my business, then everyone is safe."

"I can't make any promises." I heaved a sigh. "All I can do is try to stall him for a while."

"Thanks." He attempted a smile and stood up. "Try not to worry. Once I prove myself to Johnny Jack, I'm off the hook. Collections is a piece of cake compared to leading a booze drop."

"Just be careful, Sammy. Watch your step." Who was worse: dirty cops or gangsters or rum-runners?

"I'll try. Hard to do when you don't know who to trust."

Now I was really worried. My heart heavy, I went to sit by Nathan at the bar, taking a few sips of my orange Nehi, but it tasted flat, dull. The fizz had gone out my drink and my day. Even Doria, the Oasis' mascot, failed to cheer me up.

By now, it was nearly eight o'clock and Frank tapped his watch face. "Hey, you two, we've got plans tonight. Best if you're not seen here when our *guests* arrive."

Guests? Didn't he mean goons?

"OK, we're going," Nathan said, pulling out his wallet.

"It's on me, sport." Frank held up his hand. "Now shake a leg. Or all the legs you need."

Boy, even Frank sounded testy tonight. No wonder. Booze drops made everyone jumpy.

"What's the rush?" Nathan whispered, as we climbed the stairs.

"I'll tell you later." I waved to Dino, who looked relieved that we were leaving.

The door opened and I ran right into Chad Parker, natty in his crisp khaki pants and striped shirt. He stared at me, blinking in surprise. "You again. What are you doing here? Is Amanda with you?" He glanced at Nathan, curious. "Working on a new story?"

"Just visiting friends. I can ask you the same question. What are you doing here?"

"I might as well tell you." Chad shrugged. "Your friend Sammy invited me tonight. Told me he needed an eighth man for a special card game."

"A card game? Is that all?" I wondered what else was cooking.

Chad clearly he had no idea what Sammy had in mind. Was he grooming him to take his father's place? Or did Johnny Jack need a new errand boy?

"Please be careful," I warned him. "There's a dark cloud hanging over Market Street."

CHAPTER THIRTY-SIX

"What was that all about?" Nathan asked after we got into his Model T. "Why did Chad get an invite but not me?"

"Trust me, you don't want to be part of this poker game. Sammy's planning the booze drop Saturday, and he needs Chad to participate. Why, I don't know."

"In that case, count me out. I play for cash, not rum. Talk about high-stakes poker!"

"I'll say." Now I had to worry about Sammy, Burton, Nathan *and* Chad. "Are you still on for your game at Mack's tomorrow? Keep an eye on him, see if he tries to cheat."

"Will do, boss. Gotta go develop these photos." He let me out in front of the boarding house, beeping his horn as he drove off.

Inside the hallway, I apologized to Eva for coming in late, then carried my new gown up the stairs. I couldn't wait to show it off to Amanda, wishing she could attend the policemen's ball as well. But she was too smitten with Sammy to date a cop or anyone else.

When I walked by her room, she grabbed my box and pulled out my gown, holding it up to admire. "Oh my goodness! Look at that number. Why, you'll be the belle of the ball!"

"Thanks! I can't wait to wear it Saturday." I blushed, delighted. "You should see Eva in her gown. I really wish you could come."

"Sounds like fun, but I hate to be a fifth wheel. By the way, where were you? It's a school night."

"There was a robbery on Market Street, but don't worry—it wasn't Sammy. Nathan and I stopped by the Oasis afterwards. Say, guess who showed up at both places? Your new pal, Chad Parker."

"Cutie pie Chad? What was he doing at the Oasis?"

I didn't have the heart to tell her the truth, so I ad-libbed a bit. "I think Sammy's taking him under his wing, watching out for him."

Frankly, I hoped Sammy and his gang wouldn't try to convince Chad to follow in his father's footsteps. If he got caught helping the Downtown Gang at the booze drop, he'd be spending time behind bars, not in a college classroom.

Friday

Thank goodness Friday was payday since I was one-hundred-percent broke. I almost snatched my check out of Mr. Thomas' hand, not waiting for permission to rush down to Lone Star Bank. I wanted to pay Eva back for my gorgeous new gown—if she'd even accept.

As I passed Eiband's, I smiled to myself, glad I didn't have to deal with that pushy blonde clerk. At the bank, I cashed my whole check, determined to give Eva a few extra dollars.

After a quick bite, I returned to the *Gazette* and stopped to talk to Nathan about his crime scene photos. "See anything unusual? Did anyone or anything seem out of place or suspicious?"

Before he could reply, Mack sidled up, avoiding my gaze. "I'd also like to take a look when they're ready. See if I missed something." Then he turned to me, brows raised. "By the way, I saw you talking to that Parker kid. What did he have to say?"

Why didn't you interrogate him yourself? I wanted to retort.

"Nothing much. He just wondered if the robbery was connected to his dad's murder."

Frankly, I wanted to protect Chad from news vultures like Mack and not force him to rehash his father's violent death.

Mack nodded. "I'd be wondering that too. But from the looks of it, the baseball bat gave out before they could complete the job."

"True, seems Blake got lucky. Say, who was that guy next to you? A source?" To be honest, I suspected he was a bookie, but decided to hold my tongue.

"Who?" Mack's face flooded with color.

Who knew Mack could act? "The weasely guy with the fedora."

"I asked him a few questions, that's it. Why? What did you think, that I was playing the ponies?"

Why was he so defensive? "So what'd you find out?"

"Not that it's any of your business, but he mentioned that Blake co-owned a prize horse that they'd raced last week over in Louisiana. Word is, the jockey was supposed to throw the race, and ended up winning instead. Afterwards, both the horse and jockey disappeared, taking all the prize money with them."

"Disappeared? You mean...they were killed?" I hated to think that such an intelligent, proud animal would be punished along with its jockey for no good reason.

"Who knows?" Mack shrugged. "But I've heard rumors."

"I'd hate to be in their shoes. Or should I say, horseshoes," Nathan cracked.

"That's not funny," I groaned. "An innocent horse and jockey might be dead just because they won a stupid race and took the cash—money that they both deserved."

"Who said they're dead? That's crazy to kill a winning combination," Nathan said. "What if he's on the run? Say, the jockey changed his name and left town to escape the mob?"

"I hope so." I turned to Mack. "Who are they? Do you know their names?"

"Why? What difference does it make to you?"

I tried to seem nonchalant. "Just curious. I can ask Sammy if he's heard anything."

"OK, kid." He nodded. "The jockey is a little shrimp named Paco Torres, and the racehorse was called Queen of Sheba. A fine Arabian mare." He paused a beat. "So I hear."

I recalled the JP tokens and wondered if the robbery was connected to the horse race. Did the bronze horse at the bar represent Blake's pride and joy? Was the horseshoe deliberately placed upside-down as a threat? Were the robbers looking for the prize money?

"What if the jockey fled to Mexico with his horse?" I suggested. "I just hope they're safe."

"It's possible." Mack shrugged. "They could be across the border by now. Personally, I'd rather take my chances with a few Mexican banditos than a mob of angry Texas gangsters."

Then he slapped Nathan on the back and leaned forward, saying, "Don't forget. My place. Eight o'clock sharp. Good thing it's payday 'cause I'm gonna clean out all you saps."

"Oh yeah?" Nathan thrust out his chin, challenging Mack. "We'll see who wins tonight. Prepare to fork over all your jack, old man."

"Old man?" Mack flared up, rearing his torso like a bucking bronco. "I'll have you know I killed more enemy soldiers than anyone in my battalion during the Great War. Won quite a few medals, too." Then he grabbed his right leg, wincing. "Got a bit more metal than I bargained for." Shoulders slumped, he limped back to his desk, weary as a wounded warrior.

I'd never noticed a limp before. Was he faking it for sympathy?

"Go easy on him tonight." I nudged Nathan. "But not too easy."

CHAPTER THIRTY-SEVEN

That evening, Eva and I modeled our new gowns for Amanda, twirling around in circles, until we were quite dizzy, and giddy with excitement. I enjoyed seeing Eva relax and pamper herself, instead of the boarders, for a change. Two older widows came down to watch the spectacle in the parlor, while we posed and preened, pretending we were Paris fashion models.

Naturally I felt a pang of guilt for showing off in front of Amanda, but after all, it was also her idea. Instead of going to the policemen's ball, she'd spend the night worrying about Sammy and the booze drop.

After the impromptu fashion show, Amanda and I went upstairs, whispering while I changed back into my everyday clothes.

"Jazz, I don't expect miracles, but you've got to find a way to distract Agent Burton at the ball. Long enough to let Sammy get the booze and get out safely. With you in that dazzling dress, he'll be like putty in your hands."

"I think you overestimate my powers of persuasion." I let out a sigh. "Even if I could stall Burton, Sammy can't predict or plan what's going to happen. Too many variables. The Cubans call the shots, literally."

Amanda fidgeted with her long locks, her pretty features creased with worry. "Well, I have a good mind to show up at the booze drop myself!" she declared. "Maybe I can distract those goons long enough for Sammy to load up, and the Cubans to ship out."

I stifled a smile, imagining the chaos if a beautiful blonde showed up suddenly on the beach, willing to do whatever it took to help Sammy, including stripping off to her knickers.

The hallway creaked and a light knock sounded before Eva swung open my bedroom door. "James Burton is here! He's waiting in the parlor. My, I hope nothing's wrong. He looks so serious."

My heart skipped a beat. What was Burton doing here now? Had he changed his mind? After all the anticipation and excitement, it would break my heart if he had to cancel our plans.

Anxious, I flew down the stairs and rushed into the parlor. "James, what is it? What are you doing here?" One look at his somber expression told me something was wrong.

"Sorry to drop in unannounced, but I've got some news. Can we take a short walk?"

I nodded and waved to Amanda and Eva who stood on the porch. Once out of earshot, I wanted to know: "What's the matter? We're still going tomorrow night, right?"

I didn't want to sound like a spoiled debutante, but I was so looking forward to the ball! Tell the truth, I was curious about the police and couldn't wait to eavesdrop. Didn't cops talk shop like everyone else at these hoity-toity events? Were they really crooks or did a couple of rotten apples spoil the bunch?

"Sam Maceo allowed our men to search the Hollywood grounds. Evidently they found the bullet that we suspect hit my Stetson."

"You don't say. I'm surprised he let the cops onto his property."

"Maceo was very cooperative. If anything, he doesn't want to damage the club's excellent reputation." He cleared his throat. "We just got the forensics on the bullet."

"What did they find out?"

"The bullet was a .38, probably shot from a high-caliber rifle, the kind used by an experienced sharpshooter or marksman." Burton fingered his hat, his face tense.

I tensed up. "You mean a hit man."

"Most likely, considering I was the target."

"Can you trust him or the cops? How do you know it's not some random bullet?" Then I remembered Big Sam's offer to help that night, almost a week ago. Seems he was sincere.

"Believe me, I was skeptical too until the lab did the forensics on the bullet lodged in Torino's forehead. Since the MO was similar, they compared the two bullets to see if they could be a match."

"What's the verdict?" I held my breath.

"Turns out the bullets were a perfect match, probably fired from the same gun. But we can't be sure unless we find the murder weapon. Chances are, it's still in the possession of the sharpshooter. Whoever he was, this guy doesn't usually miss his target."

I was floored. "It was the same gunman? You think he deliberately missed you, and shot your hat instead?"

"Looks that way." Burton nodded.

"Thank God he missed. Still, it doesn't make sense. If he's a hired hit man, why go to such great lengths to avoid his mark?"

"That's what I'd like to know." Burton's face darkened in the shadows. "Obviously the sniper knows how to hit a moving target, especially if he served in the Great War."

"Perhaps the gunman changed his mind or chickened out, or maybe it was just a warning shot." I frowned, mulling it over.

"From my experience, hit men don't usually chicken out. They see their target as part of a mission, just a job to do."

"Are you sure the shootings are related?" I wondered, thinking out loud. "What's strange is he took shots on rival gangs' turfs: the Hollywood on the Beach Gang's turf, and the funeral home on the Downtown Gang's turf."

"Maybe he's a lone wolf, acting on his own."

I thought of the goon-for-hire with the gold cuff links. "What if the marksman freelances for both gangs? Say he's trying to throw off the cops?"

"You may be right. Whatever the scenario, the shooter is still out there." Burton rocked back on his heels, avoiding my gaze. "Deliberate or not, I'm afraid he may show up at the ball and try to finish the job."

"In front of a whole crowd of cops?"

"Why not? He shot at a funeral full of gangsters. Clearly he likes public settings. These hit men thrive on danger. The more difficult the shot, the bigger the challenge. Even if he's not there tomorrow night, someone else may take his place."

Frankly, I was torn. "Is it really safer if you stayed home, waiting for him to come after you? If we go to the ball, at least you'll be surrounded by a room full of armed officers."

"I'm not afraid for myself, Jasmine. I'm worried about you."

"They're not after me." I squinted at him under the tall Victorian lamps, trying to lighten the mood. "Hey, are you trying to weasel your way out of taking me to the most coveted event in town? Nice try, buster."

Was I doing the right thing by insisting Burton take me to the ball, exposing him to more danger? Maybe I was being selfish, swept up in this silly Cinderella fantasy without considering the risks— though I never cared for sappy fairy tales at all.

Then a disturbing thought crossed my mind. Burton had complained about the cops more than once: their mutual dislike, distrust, even hatred of the lone agent.

My heart sank at the possibility. What if the hit man wasn't a gangster at all? What if the shooter was actually a cop?

CHAPTER THIRTY-EIGHT

How could I voice my fears to Burton after talking him into going to the ball? Would he be walking into an ambush—or worse, attending his own funeral?

I walked ahead, mulling over the different scenarios. Obviously the cops had something to hide, the way they cleared out the Rusty Bucket. Who knew if the bullets really were a match? Maybe the cop bribed someone in forensics, who made up the results to fool the force into believing there was a lone gunman?

Burton noticed my sunny mood darken. "What's wrong, Jazz?"

"I'm having second thoughts," I admitted, trying to work up my nerve. "What if the hit man *is* there, waiting to catch you alone? What if they gang up on you?"

"They? What do you mean?"

"I was just thinking... All this talk about the rivalry between you and the local cops." I ran my fingers through my hair, curly from the heat and humidity. "You know, what you said about not trusting the cops? Do you think it's possible...that a dirty cop is the shooter?"

Damn, I didn't mean to blurt it out.

"It all makes sense. Maybe there were two different snipers with two different guns. What if a cop shot at you Saturday, and a Beach Gang thug took out Torino during the funeral?" I searched his face for a reaction, but he stood there, studying me, speechless. "That explains why the shootings occurred on both gang's turfs. There may be a copycat gunman who stole the gun. After all, the methods *and* the cars were similar—driving by in a nondescript Ford."

Finally Burton's eyes met mine. "I'd considered that possibility. All the more reason to show up at the ball Saturday, if you're sure."

"I can help watch your back, and tell you if I see anyone or anything suspicious."

He took my hands. "Jazz, I don't want you putting yourself in any danger. Still, I doubt the gunman will make his move during the ball. Maybe afterwards, during the booze drop."

"You're right. He may volunteer to help just to get you alone. Think about it. He could shoot you in the dark and no one would know. He'll get away with murder—yours." Panicky, I grabbed his hand, pleading, "Do you have to go through with it? Sanders gave you a way out. Why don't we just go to the ball? Do you always have to be a hero?"

"A hero?" Burton caught up with me, taking me in his arms. "This is my job. If I back down every time I get threatened, then I may as well give up."

"Can you blame me for being upset?" My eyes welled with tears.

"Actually, it's nice to know you care."

I nuzzled in his embrace and he gave me a kiss on the neck, his lips warm and soft. Why did we have to be standing in the middle of the street, right under the street lamps, with all the neighbors watching from their front porch swings?

"Tell me, James, what do *you* want to do?"

Such a different scenario from my high school dances, when our biggest worries were finding the perfect gown as well as getting a corsage and boutonniere to match, not to mention transportation.

"I'd love to take you to the ball," Burton told me sincerely. "I'm just warning you, there might be fireworks later."

Saturday

Saturday promised to be cool and clear, rare for a usually hot summer day. After finishing the weekly chores, Eva and I began pampering ourselves for the big night ahead: moisturizing our skin, applying face masques, painting our nails, washing and styling our hair, the works.

Amanda showed up after her lunch shift reeking of bacon and grease, just in time to shower and help us get dressed. She'd worked as a beautician and knew all sorts of tricks to keep hair styled and smooth in this humid climate. If only I had a sleek, chic bob like Louise Brooks!

Though it was still light outside, I wanted to be ready in case Burton showed up early. The ball was being held at the Galveston Harbor Yacht Club and I hoped for a sparkling view of the setting sun over the bay. To be honest, I also wanted a good look at all the cops as they entered the ballroom, wondering if Burton had assembled his team for the night. Should I tell him that Sammy was leading the booze drop?

Amanda and I chatted while I sat at my vanity applying my face paint, my Cleopatra perfume lamp scenting the room with jasmine and rose. I knew she was worried about Sammy, still hoping I'd persuade Burton not to show up.

"I've changed my mind. I want to go to the ball, after all—as Nathan's date," she announced. "Afterwards, we can all follow Burton to the beach."

"Amanda, I'd love for you to go. But a booze drop isn't a luau where anyone can attend. These men are armed and dangerous."

"I know." She shrugged. "I just want to help. You two aren't exactly experienced gunslingers either. So what if I show up?"

I felt a pang of doubt. She was right: How could our presence help Sammy or Burton? "If you distract Sammy, he'll lose his concentration and that may be fatal. He can't control these bootleggers or his gang. Who knows what could happen?"

"I guess you're right." She remained silent while putting the finishing touches on my newly-marcelled hair. For once, my hair behaved and didn't fly off in all directions.

To top off my new wavy 'do, I added a beaded headband ringed with the eyes of peacock feathers, complementing my teal-blue gown. Amanda helped me slip the silky frock over my head—snug but not tight—and I added long sparkly teal and crystal chandelier earrings.

"Wow, that dress is the leopard's spots on you!" Amanda raved. "Fits you like a glove."

"Thanks. You don't think it's too risqué for the policemen's ball? I suspect the wives are on the conservative *ruffles and lace* side."

"Why don't you just put on an old burlap sack and tie it with a curtain sash?" she teased me. "Remember, you're getting dolled up for Burton, not those dowdy dowagers."

"Nothing wrong with dressing to the nines and painting the town red." I carefully sat down on the bed, adding: "I just wish the evening wouldn't end with a showdown between the cops and the Cubans, with my big brother and Burton in the middle."

"You said it." Amanda clutched a pillow, embroidered with a Scottie dog. "I feel better knowing you two will be there to watch Sammy's back. Oh, and of course, Burton."

I'd just brushed my skin all over with fine shimmering dusting powder when I heard the doorbell ring. Hardly anyone used the doorbell in Galveston—they just knocked and walked inside. Except on weekends, when gangsters and gamblers took over the town.

I flushed, getting excited. "Maybe it's James! Amanda, please be a peach and go see who it is, will you?"

I took a quick look in the mirror before I followed her downstairs and peeked around the corner. Amanda opened the front door and Sheriff Sanders stepped into the living room. Was I seeing an optical illusion? He actually looked rather handsome in his fancy black tuxedo, the dark fabric slimming down his considerable weight.

Eva floated out of her room, her hands outstretched toward Sanders, exclaiming with delight: "Why, sheriff, I didn't know you cleaned up so well. If I'd known you looked this good in a tuxedo, I'd make you wear one all the time."

"Honey pie, you're a sight for sore eyes!" He gave a wolf-whistle so loud that Eva turned scarlet. "Turn around so I can get a good look at you."

"Thank you, Walt," she purred, giving a slight twirl.

"This is for you." He beamed, holding out a pretty orchid. "But I don't know where to pin it. I'd hate to mess up your pretty new dress." Fumbling like a prom date, he attempted to attach it to her gown, sticking her once or twice, while she tried not to wince in pain.

Peering out from the staircase, Amanda and I traded grins as we watched them bumble like high school kids on a first date. Finally we came out of hiding, all smiles.

"You look gorgeous, Eva. That gown is the cat's meow," I said as she smiled with pride.

"Has the party started without me?" I heard Burton's voice on the porch. "Is that Sheriff Sanders? I hardly recognized you out of uniform. Who's this attractive young gal on your arm—Eva? You're a lucky man, Walter!"

Boy, Burton could turn on the charm when he wanted. Tonight he looked especially handsome in a snazzy black tuxedo with satin lapels, his thick blond hair a nice contrast. I couldn't help but notice how tanned and fit he looked, and the way he filled out his jacket.

"Speak of the devil," Sanders joked. "Say, you two, how about a ride to the dance?"

Burton looked uncomfortable for a moment. "Thanks, but we're taking the scenic route." Then he gave me a sly wink, as if I knew what he meant.

"All right, then, we'll see you there." The sheriff looked disappointed. I suspected he realized Burton still planned to raid the booze drop later tonight.

"See you at the ball. Can't wait to watch you cut a rug," I added.

"Have fun, everyone!" Amanda said, flashing a smile of approval before going upstairs.

After they left, Burton gave me the once-over from head to toe, slipping his arm around my waist to give me a tight squeeze. "I'm not sure I should let you out in public looking this way," he whispered. "This orchid is for you, beautiful."

"Why, thank you, kind sir. You look like Christmas in July."

I held still while he carefully attached my corsage, noticing his intent gaze. Seemed he had past experience at fancy balls.

He touched the peacock feathers on my headband, then ran his finger along my neck. "Do you care if I ruffle your feathers?"

"Not at all." I smiled. "But don't forget, I'm ticklish."

"I'll keep that in mind." Burton gave me a sly grin. "I'm tempted to stay here and skip the ball. It may not be safe for you to be around that pack of wolves they call cops."

"Flattery will only get you so far." I batted my lashes. "The corsage is the cherry on top."

He escorted me to his roadster and held open the door, lifting my gown off the street while I got in. As we drove off, he turned onto Broadway, heading in the opposite direction of the wharf.

"Where are we going?" I asked him, surprised. "I thought we planned to go straight to the Yacht Club."

Had he changed his mind about the dance?

"We're taking a little detour," he announced. "First stop, the police station. While the cops are away, it's time to play detective."

CHAPTER THIRTY-NINE

"The police station?" I held my breath. "Will anyone be there? What if we get caught?"

"Caught doing what?" Agent Burton gave me a sideways glance. "I need to know what these jokers are doing behind my back. Come on, don't look so scared. This should be right up your alley."

"You mean snooping?" I swept my palms across my dress. "I'm not exactly dressed for the occasion. I wanted to go dancing tonight, not get arrested for breaking and entering."

"I have every right to be there." He frowned. "If anyone asks, I'll just say I forgot my badge or something. In those glad rags, you can distract the hell out of the sergeant on duty."

"Gee, thanks. Now I'm just your sidekick?" Was all of my primping and preening just so I could be his cover, an accomplice? This wasn't the romantic evening I'd envisioned, though I admit, the idea of foraging through the police station appealed to my Nosy Nellie side.

The lone cop on duty did a double-take when we showed up in our finery. "You and Cinderella took a wrong turn. Hurry, Prince Charming, you don't want to be late to the ball."

"Go jump in the lake." Burton grinned. "Just need my watch. Must have left it in my desk."

The guard eyed me. "Sorry, doll. Cops only. No visitors allowed after hours. Even if she does look like a million bucks."

"I'm taking my gal inside with me. I don't trust her alone with the likes of you." Burton took my arm, ignoring his warning look.

His gal? I admit, I kind of liked the sound of that now.

Inside the station, I whispered, "What do you want me to do?"

"Act as a look-out while I search these desks, starting with Chief Johnson's office."

"The chief of police? Don't you trust him?"

"Everyone's got skeletons in their closet." Burton shrugged and held out his hand. "Speaking of skeletons, wish I had the keys to these old desks. The drawers are locked. Got a bobby pin?"

I pulled one out and placed it in his outstretched palm, then patted my hair in place. "I doubt they want anyone snooping in their personal effects."

"I'm not just anyone," he reminded me. "It's my duty as a Federal agent. I need to know what these local yokels have been up to. Why did they clear out the Rusty Bucket?"

I watched as he tugged at a couple of desk drawers, rifling through the stack of paper on top, reminding me of Sammy's messy desk and office. Every two minutes I'd look at my watch and stand by the door, waiting to see if the sergeant was getting bored or suspicious. So far, the coast was clear.

While Burton poked around the station, I meandered around the office, noting the photos of cops with their wives and children, appearing sincere and earnest, not like the smart-alecks I'd encountered. I heard Burton say, "What have we here?" and he rushed over, clutching a small black ledger—not unlike Horace Andrews' bank book. Uh oh—not a good sign.

Excited, Burton stood by the window and flipped through the pages, eyes squinting in the fading sunlight. I tiptoed over to him. "Any luck? Anything incriminating?"

His eyes lit up. "I found a bunch of betting sheets and gaming tokens along with this ledger in Deputy Connors's desk. Apparently it's a record of bets, along with a list of names and numbers. They must be wagers placed on various sports events, probably boxing matches, baseball games and horse races."

"No kidding?" I sucked in my breath. "Do you recognize any names or is it all in code?"

"Names and initials. Wish I could borrow this list without anyone noticing."

"Why not take it now and return it later tonight?" I suggested. "A different cop may be on duty by then. This is big news."

"I've got other plans, remember? Nice try, though." He ran his fingers down the page, brows furrowed "I bet they'd raise hell if they knew this was missing. Once I figure out this code, I'm sure a few folks won't be too pleased."

I looked over his shoulder. "You think this was all from Parker's bar? Which tokens did you find?"

Burton led me to Connors' roll-top desk and opened the drawer. "Come take a look. Why?"

"Parker and Torino had the same tokens on them when they were killed," I told him, scanning the scattered tokens. Sure enough, a few Jefferson Race Park tokens stood out from the group. "Just like these. Should we take a couple?"

"I doubt they'd notice a few missing tokens, but Chief Johnson will sure as hell miss this book. Besides, I don't trust that guard. If the chief finds out it's gone, I'll be the first one he'll suspect."

"True. OK, I'll keep an eye open while you give it a closer look."

By chance, I happened on Sheriff Sanders' desk, wondering if Burton planned to search it as well. Why not do it for Eva's sake? Curious, I scoured the surface, looking for tell-tale clues, incriminating photos or signs of a wife hidden away, perhaps out of state. So far, he seemed to be on the up and up. I gave his roll-top desk drawer a good tug, but it also was locked.

Burton edged closer. "Find anything interesting? I see you left your post."

"I hate to be so suspicious, but can you open this drawer?"

"Isn't this Sanders' desk? You want to spy on Eva's beau?"

"Better to find out now whether he's a good guy or not."

"Gotta admit, since he made that deal with Johnny Jack, I've had my doubts. Got another bobby pin?" I hated to mess up Eva's handiwork, but it was for her own sake. He fiddled with the lock a minute, then yanked out the drawer. "OK, you asked for it."

"Boy, are you good. Were you ever a cat burglar?"

"You're a riot." Burton grinned. "I've got lots of skills you haven't seen, yet. Let's hurry before the guard catches us snooping."

Carefully, I pushed aside a few papers, sifting through assorted coins, keys, marbles, packs of gum until something glittering caught my eye. Eureka!

I felt like a pan-handler striking gold. Was it a wedding ring? Don't be so skeptical of Sanders, I admonished myself. At his age, it was possible he'd been married and divorced once or twice by now.

"What is it?" Burton leaned over, curious.

"Maybe a gold ring." Hands trembling, I reached in the back of the drawer and pulled out not one, but two familiar gold cuff links.

I inhaled, trying to understand the significance: Did they belong to him or someone else? I held them up to show Burton, the gold glittering in the fading sunlight.

What in hell were they doing hidden in Sanders' desk?

CHAPTER FORTY

"Recognize these cuff links?" I handed them to Burton for inspection. "They look like the one missing from your desk—and the ones worn by that joker who planted your hat at Parker's murder scene. Question is, why does the sheriff have them hidden away? If they're not his, why didn't he turn them over as evidence, or to lost and found?"

"Good question." Burton's eyes narrowed. "Cops can't afford such expensive cuff links on their salary—if they're honest."

"I doubt it's a coincidence." I thought it over. "I wonder if it's some secret society where the members get gold cuff links, perhaps as a reward?"

"A reward for a job well done." Burton nodded. "Sounds like Johnny Jack. He's such a big spender, showing off his money to judge and jury alike."

"Say, why don't you wear the cuff links tonight and see how Sanders reacts? They'll look perfect with your snazzy black tux."

Burton shook his head. "Too dangerous. We don't know who else has the same cuff links. I need to keep this quiet, avoid causing a ruckus in front of the force. As the only Fed agent in town, you could say I'm outnumbered."

I hoped to God—and for Eva's sake—that the cuff links didn't involve or incriminate Sanders in any way. After all, he was at numerous crime scenes and may have forgotten that he pocketed them afterwards. I hated to think about the other option—that he was involved in any of these crimes, or murders. How could I face Eva and Sanders tonight with these nagging doubts and suspicions?

When we heard footsteps plodding down the hall, I carefully stuck the cuff links back in place and shut the desk drawer.

Without warning Burton grabbed me around the waist and pulled me to him, pressing his lips to mine. I felt a flush of fever, my whole body tingling. Jeepers!

"Whoa! Excuse me." The sergeant stuck his head in the door and grinned. "Now I know what took so long. Did you ever find your watch?"

"Yes, everything's fine." Burton sounded calm and cool, unlike me, who was shaking all over. I'd never make it as a jewel thief. "We're just leaving. Thanks, pal."

We dashed out in a hurry and I sheepishly waved to the guard, who grinned at me like a happy hyena. "Some fellas have all the fun," he griped, raising his brows.

"Close call," I whispered, my face still flaming. "Hope he didn't suspect anything."

"All he suspects is that we want to be alone. Can he blame me?"

I smiled in response, glad he couldn't see me blush in the dark.

As we drove off toward the Yacht Club, Burton said, "Sorry for smudging your lipstick. Gotta admit, I enjoyed fooling the sergeant. That impromptu kiss worked like a charm."

"I'll say." I gave him a Cheshire-cat smile. "Don't worry, I came prepared in case you want to smudge my lipstick again." I pulled out my teal tango compact, squinting in the tiny mirror, trying to apply sunburst pink lipstick without smearing. "Do you think the sergeant saw me poking around in Sanders' desk?"

"If he did, I think he got so rattled, he forgot all about it. You left the cuff links there?"

"Of course. I don't have any place to hide them." I indicated my form-fitting dress and Mandalian mesh bag.

"I noticed." Burton gave me a devilish grin.

"What about the ledger? You still have it on you?"

He patted his pants pocket. "I had to hide it before the guard caught me red-handed."

"Red-handed to go with my red face. How will you put it back?"

"I haven't thought that far ahead. Maybe I'll stop by Sunday? Can't wait to check it out, see what these crooks have been up to."

"You and me both. Let me know if you find any familiar names on the list."

At the Yacht Club, I admired the spectacular view, the sun casting shades of gold and rose over the harbor, silhouetting the sailboats and yachts moored at the docks. Must be nice to own a boat. Valets rushed over to open our doors and I shivered with excitement as I stepped inside. Since I didn't have any millionaire friends, I'd never before entered this exclusive world. Of course, I doubted most of the cops had ever been inside its doors either.

In contrast to the mob joints, the Yacht Club seemed sparse yet sleek with its sophisticated décor and the expected maritime accoutrements. The floor to ceiling windows provided a spectacular view of Galveston Bay. A few heads turned when we entered and I admit, I was proud to be wearing my elegant new teal gown, on the arm of my tall, handsome date.

Boy, were we wrong about the cops' so-called dowdy wives: All the women were decked out in the latest fashions: beaded silk gowns, bias-cut frocks, sleek chemises, lacy ruffled dresses. Were their fellas on the take or did they save their cash or splurge, like we did?

A five-piece band, complete with a pianist, saxophonist, drummer, trombone and trumpet player performed some jazzy tunes. Everyone perked up when a robust woman in a Grecian-style gown graced the stage, belting out a few fun Cole Porter tunes.

Normally, I preferred instrumental jazz but this gal's voice was so smooth and sultry, we stopped to watch her animated performance. I couldn't help but wonder: How would these good-old-boys react if she was a Negro dancer and singer like Josephine Baker? Would they even allow her inside the club? Not that they could afford the popular Paris sensation!

"We'll be lucky to find a table in this crowd," Burton said. "Let's take a look around."

"Do you see Eva and Sanders?" I asked Burton as we made our way into the glittering ballroom. "Honestly, I'd be too uncomfortable to sit at their table."

"I'll say. I don't want Sanders trying to detain me tonight. How could he make a deal with Johnny Jack and expect me to fall in line?"

To tell the truth, I had mixed feelings: I didn't know whether to defend Sanders or agree with Burton. "He did it for you," I reminded him, parroting Eva.

"Are you sure? Maybe he did it for himself, to make points with Nounes. I doubt his trade-off had anything to do with me."

"For Eva's sake, I hope you're wrong." I took his hand and stood up. "Now enough cop talk. Let's dance."

I led him to the dance floor where breathless couples danced cheek to cheek, their bodies pressed together in improvisational tangos and rumbas. After all, most of the couples were married—or were they? Anything goes!

While we danced the foxtrot, I scanned the crowd, looking for a familiar face or two. I couldn't find Eva and Sanders or Nathan, surprised he hadn't made an appearance yet. I couldn't wait to find out about his poker game went with Mack and the newsmen.

At the head table, I saw Mayor Hodgkins and his wife, making small talk with a couple of councilmen I recognized from the papers. My stomach knotted, thinking of the risks we'd just taken at the station. "Did you see the mayor?" I pointed him out. "Say, I'm having second thoughts about keeping the ledger. Maybe you should turn it over to him? Too incriminating."

"I'd better examine it first. For all we know, his name is also on the list." He frowned. "I don't know who to trust with this ledger."

"You said it." With so many cops and politicians mingling with criminals, you never knew who was on the level in Galveston.

Out of the corner of my eye, I spotted Sheriff Sanders in deep discussion with Paul Johnson, the chief of police, both looking agitated. Jeepers, I hoped the guard on duty hadn't shown up and told them about our surprise visit. And where in the world was Eva?

"I wonder what that's all about?" I whispered to Burton.

"Good question. Mind if we take a break?"

"Not at all. I'll go look for Eva."

I felt a slight squeeze on my arm, and turned around to see Eva smiling at me, a vision in her pale peach gown and a tiara of peach rosebuds across her dark hair, that I'd helped secure with bobby pins. With a pang of guilt, I gave her a hug, careful not to muss her dress.

"You look like the sunset in that sumptuous gown." I leaned over to whisper, "It was worth every cent."

"I'll say! I'm over the moon. We're having so much fun." She flashed a radiant smile, a hint of sparkle on her cheeks. "We haven't stopped dancing since we got here, until now. How about you?"

"Let's just say we took the scenic route." I noticed that Burton had joined the sheriff and police chief, and now they all appeared to be arguing. I tilted my head. "Any idea what they're talking about?"

Eva nodded, and rolled her eyes. "I have an idea. Walt said the police chief is feeling threatened by his presence at the station. He thinks Walt is trying to undermine his power."

She leaned against me, lowering her voice. "Between us, I think they're both intimidated by your Burton—not only because he's a Federal agent, but he's almost half their age with twice their energy."

"That makes sense," I nodded. "Is this Sanders' jurisdiction?"

"Yes, but he's over all of Galveston County, not just the city. He was supposed to be here on a special assignment, but the police chief thinks he's overstayed his welcome."

I raised my brows. "Reminds me of gang leaders battling over their turf."

"I guess that's true." She nodded. "No wonder Sammy always seems on edge."

My stomach did flip-flops when she mentioned Sammy. Glancing at my watch, I imagined he was en route to the booze drop.

"Why don't we get some hors d'oeuvres?" I suggested to Eva— anything to quell my nerves. Negro waiters in black suits and bow ties floated around the room with canapés on silver trays. In lieu of a sit-down dinner, the police had opted for several snacks and appetizers: smoked salmon on crackers with caviar, tuna and chicken finger sandwiches, bites of cheese and ham.

I made a beeline for the dessert trays covered with mini fruit tarts, tiny apple turnovers, chocolate balls, ginger snaps and macaroons. A Mexican waiter approached us with a smile, holding a tray of fluted glasses, fizzing with tiny bubbles.

"Champagne?" I exchanged surprised glances with Eva and took a sip. Would a roomful of cops be so blatant? Everyone knew the cops drank behind closed doors, but they didn't usually advertise it in public. A tad disappointed, I sighed, "No, just ginger ale."

Eva and I held up our glasses, drinking pretend Champagne, nibbling on delicious treats, admiring the ladies gowns. While enjoying the view of the spectacular sunset, we made small talk as if attending fancy balls at the exclusive Yacht Club was the most natural thing in the world.

"Let's go powder our noses," Eva said. "I want to look around."

We took our time passing through the crowd, giving us a chance to appreciate the panoramic views of the bay. I smiled at the cops' wives and girlfriends, holding tight to their fellas' arms. No doubt they lost sleep at night, worried about their husbands and sweethearts. Though Agent Burton and I weren't going steady or engaged, I sympathized with their situation.

The restroom was located near the back, close to the kitchen, with a separate powder room where a Negro woman passed out hand towels. I forced a smile at the flappers who watched me reapply my Prairie Fire lipstick, their chatter subsided.

After retouching my face paint, I heard loud voices out the window and took a peek: The sky darkened to a deep coral, and the dimming sunlight bounced off the bay like a chandelier, illuminating two silhouettes. The men stood by the harbor, clearly making a deal, one in a tux, the other in a striped suit.

A flash of light caught my eye and I froze when I recognized the goon with the gold cuff links. The Irish gangster handed over a small wooden crate—of booze, no doubt—to a man in a tuxedo I assumed was a cop. Since I'd already seen a few flasks in the crowd, the crate of booze didn't surprise me at all. Was this an under-the-table transaction or a pay-off for getting the jerk out of jail?

The cop pried open the crate with a pocketknife, pulling out a bottle and studying the label. Unfortunately since his back was turned, I couldn't make out his face. As he lifted the bottle to sample, I did a double-take when I saw that he also wore gold cuff links.

Were they identical to the ones in Sheriff Sanders' desk drawer? I dropped the curtain shade, alarmed. Had the guys seen me spying out the window?

CHAPTER FORTY-ONE

"What is it, Jazz?" Eva asked, concerned. "Something wrong?"

"Nothing. I thought I recognized someone." I turned away so she wouldn't see my worried expression. Frankly, the gold cuff links threw me off: What was the connection? Surely they didn't all shop at the same jewelry store! What kind of *secret* society flaunted their membership—and gold cuff links—in public?

Eva and I returned to stand by the dance floor, making small talk, when Burton appeared and whisked me away. "I was looking all over for you. Where were you?"

"Powdering my nose." I took his arm, grateful.

"I'll save you a seat at our table!" Eva called out. I forced a weak smile, hoping I didn't have to face her questionable beau just yet.

Pulling me close for a tango, Burton asked, "You seem jittery. Is everything jake?"

"I hope so." I stood on tiptoe and whispered in his ear, "You'll never believe who I saw outside the bathroom window. That guy with the gold cuff links who planted your hat at Parker's murder scene. He handed a crate of liquor over to a cop."

"Brogan's here?" He scanned the room. "Where? Which cop?"

"They were outside, by the bay. But I didn't see the cop's face 'cause his back was turned, just his profile."

"That goon has some nerve, showing up here. I wonder who he works for? Let me know if you recognize anyone, OK?" He picked up the pace, twirling me in circles like a gypsy, his head whipping around. Dancing with Burton was easy, effortless and I only wished we didn't have to worry about cops and robbers and bootleggers.

Still, as he constantly reminded me, enforcing Prohibition was his job—after all, that's how we met, while he was raiding Sammy's bar. What a far cry from the glitzy ballroom tonight. Still, were they so different, Sammy and Burton, both stubborn, proud men, determined to do their best?

"Say, did you look over the ledger yet? Any familiar names?"

He nodded. "Quite a few, in fact. If this information got out, a lot of important people could lose their jobs."

I eyed him. "Really? Who? I won't tell anyone, promise."

He pressed his lips to my ear. "Hate to tell you that both the deputy chief and Sanders names are on the list, along with half the cops on the force."

My heart skipped a few beats. "What are you going to do?"

"I may have a word with your aunt's suitor." Burton glanced across the room, at the crowd of cops and politicians. "If anyone finds out I have this book, I'm in danger."

I stole a few guilty glances at Eva, dancing the Charleston with Sanders like they were America's sweethearts, Douglas Fairbanks and Mary Pickford. How could I be so suspicious of Eva's new beau? Anyone who made her this happy was A-OK in my book—even if he was a bit on the shady side.

No one was perfect, especially not the holier-than-thou hypocrites who pretended to be angels, showing up in church every Sunday morning after a night of drinking and debauchery. I'd seen enough headlines and heard enough gossip about the high-and-mighty who'd taken a tumble or two down the rabbit hole.

Unfortunately my boss thought it was her appointed duty to gloss over such misbehavior, rather than risk offending polite society. Even Mr. Thomas tended to agree with her, particularly if the guilty parties held powerful positions.

A ruddy-faced cop tapped Burton on the shoulder, and I held my breath, noticing his bright gold cuff links. He seemed familiar. Was he the cop who'd met the goon outside? Did he see me spying or had he overheard us talking?

"Looking good. Mind if I cut in?"

With a start, I recognized him from the police station and later the Rusty Bucket raid. I stepped back, glancing at Burton in panic, saying, "Thanks, but no, thanks."

"Sorry, I don't like to share," Burton said, adding with a smirk, "Where's your wife?"

"Can't fault a fella for trying." The roly-poly cop shrugged and walked off, grumbling.

"Who was that?" I wondered, rattled. "When I was at the station, he asked if I was your gal. Then I saw him clearing out the Rusty Bucket with his cop buddies."

"I hope you told him you're taken." Burton scowled. "His name's Stan Smith, a desk sergeant in Homicide. He thinks he's a big wheel 'cause he helps Deputy Chief Connors." He shot Smith an irritated look. "Smith must fancy himself a Casanova, trying to cut in on my date. He needs to pay more attention to his wife."

I sensed the friction between the men was more about testing Burton than my irresistible charms. "I wonder if he's the cop I saw outside. Did you see his gold cuff links?"

"I couldn't miss them. They look like the ones in Sanders' desk."

Before I could reply, we heard angry voices across the room and all heads turned toward the scuffle by the dance floor. The band members slowly stopped playing while everyone watched Sheriff Sanders shove the police chief into the gathering crowd. In turn, the chief took a swing at Sanders, who ducked and tried to throw a punch back. The men bounced and jabbed around the dance floor like two heavyweights who'd met their match.

"What's going on?" I nudged Burton as the crowd gasped and gaped at the lawmen.

"I'd better put a stop to this fiasco before they make total fools of themselves."

"It's too late for that. Good luck."

A line of cops formed behind the two officers, cheering them on, calling out their names and waving their fists. Were they placing bets on this fight too?

Luckily Burton managed to elbow his way into the crowd and stood between both men, arms outstretched, like a referee in a boxing ring.

CHAPTER FORTY-TWO

A flash burst in my face and I waved it away, blinking at the powder residue floating in the air. "Nathan, you scared me! It's about time you got here."

"I wanted to wait till you two lovebirds stopped making goo-goo eyes at each other," Nathan teased me.

"Lovebirds? You're all wet!" I blushed. Did we look that sappy?

"Say, what's the ruckus between the sheriff and police chief? This bash is getting more exciting by the minute. Sure you wanna leave early?"

"Typical power struggle. According to Eva, the sheriff wore out his welcome a while ago."

Transfixed, we watched the two middle-aged lawmen, still fighting like ruffians in a schoolyard. We moved closer to the crowd and I stood by Eva, who stared at the spectacle with a horrified expression, exclaiming, "Why can't anyone stop them?"

"They seem determined to duke it out." I motioned toward the group of cheering men. "Seems the cops are taking sides."

"Well, this isn't the time or place to settle a score," Eva huffed. "They're making fools of themselves. Law officers ought to know better than to brawl in public like common drunkards at a bar."

Nathan piped up. "Leave it to me, ladies."

Fearless, Nathan circled the officers, snapping photos of the fight and the crowd of onlookers. He edged closer to the police chief and sheriff who froze in place, blinking at the flashing bulb. Then Police Chief Johnson came alive, taking a swing at Nathan, reaching for his camera. "Get that thing out of here!"

Nathan ducked out of his way, taunting him. "Say cheese!"

Burton stepped between the men, motioning for them to get closer, his arms across their shoulders like a football huddle. Instantly the chief and sheriff stood tall, patted each other's backs and shook hands as if they were old pals. Then Burton posed between the men, both facing the camera with pasted-on smiles, stiff as totem poles.

"Thanks, fellas. That's all I need for now." Nathan took a few shots of the men, then scurried away.

"Wait a minute, you scoundrel. Who are you and what are you gonna do with those photos?" Chief Johnson headed toward Nathan, his beet-red face flushed with fury. "Give me that camera and get out!" He tried to grab his equipment but Nathan eluded his grasp.

As Johnson reached for the camera, I caught a flash of light: The police chief also wore a pair of gold cuff links, with a diamond in the center. Coincidence?

"I'll have you fired so fast you won't know what hit you," the chief shouted as Nathan rushed away. "You and your editor too!"

Fortunately, Burton and the sheriff managed to grab his arms, holding him back, while the crowd tittered, enjoying the ruckus.

"Thank you, Nathan," Eva stopped him as he darted by. "Your quick thinking worked like a charm."

"Maybe too well. Now the chief is after me. Gotta run!"

I followed Nathan as he raced toward the back exit. "You're not leaving, are you? What about our plans?"

"Time to make myself scarce. I'll meet you by my car—if the police chief doesn't find me first."

"Don't worry, he just needs to cool down. That was some fancy footwork." I smiled at his flushed face. "See you soon."

Eva left to console Sanders while I saw Burton, standing by the chief's side like a body guard. Chief Johnson scanned the room, sputtering and flustered, no doubt looking for Nathan.

When the band started up again, the cops left to find their dates and wives. Burton and Sanders finally released the chief, who returned to sit by the mayor at the head table, his face twisted in fury, mopping his sweaty brow.

I tapped Burton on the shoulder. "Remember me, your date for the evening? How about a dance, handsome?"

Burton's face lit up. "Anytime, doll face. Sorry I had to leave a classy dame like you alone with these hooligans."

"Thanks to you, the sheriff and the police chief managed not to kill each other."

"I give your pal Nathan all the credit. He's the one who really broke up the fight."

"I'll say. He's fast on his feet, all right. Did you see the chief try to deck him?"

Burton grinned. "Gotta hand it to these two old coots. Still some fuel left in the tank."

I returned his smile, hoping he'd changed his mind. "Nothing like a fistfight to liven up a party. So what set it off?"

"Me." He grew solemn. "The chief heard that Sanders gave Johnny Jack a free pass, and he was furious. He told me he still expects me to raid the booze drop tonight."

"I agree with Sanders. Why can't we stay here, have some fun for a change?"

His back stiffened. "I wish we could stay here, too. It'd be so easy to forget the whole thing, to pretend it's not going to happen."

"One booze drop isn't going to make a difference. Prohibition won't stop people from drinking, no matter how hard you try. What's the use?" I had no right to advise Burton or criticize his job, but it was my desperation talking.

"Jazz, you know I agree with you in many ways. But I need to at least try to stop the bootleggers before they hurt anyone."

"But Cuban rum won't kill you like bathtub booze. It's the real McCoy," I pointed out.

"Tell that to the poor saps who wind up blind or dead from drinking bad booze. I can't allow some rum-runners in and shut the door on the rest."

"I've heard your soap-box lectures before." I turned away, tired of his Dudley Do-Righteousness.

Irritated, I rushed outside to find Nathan by his car, staring out at the bay. "What took you so long?"

"Burton's got a thick skull," I griped, watching a seagull glide over the bay and land on a small yacht knocking against a sailboat, a schooner in the distance. "Nice view."

"Wish I had this view every day. In case you haven't noticed, it's getting dark. You still want to follow Burton to the drop?" He waited for my reaction. "I'm willing to stay here if you are. Not a bad gig."

"Of course I still want to go. Not only for Burton, but for Sammy's sake." I tugged on his arm. "Hope you brought me a change of clothes."

"Don't worry, I know the drill."

As I turned to go inside, I saw Burton heading out the back exit with Sanders in tow, heading toward the bay.

"When did those two get so chummy?" Nathan frowned.

"I have an idea," I whispered, my stomach in knots. "Wait here for me while I find out. Please no photos!"

Knowing Nathan, he wouldn't stay put for long. I crept toward the lawmen, wondering where I could hide.

Was Burton really going to confront Sheriff Sanders now, with his shady cop pals just a few yards away?

CHAPTER FORTY-THREE

Fortunately I managed to duck behind the majestic white columns facing the bay, wide enough to provide ample cover. Like a kid playing hide-and-seek, I tiptoed between columns, edging closer to Burton and Sanders as they walked to the docks.

Burton pulled the ledger out of his pants pocket, and waved it in front of Sanders' face. "What do you know about this ledger?" he demanded, opening his jacket slightly, just enough to reveal his gun holster, flashing in the fading sunlight.

"Nothing. Where'd you get it?" Sanders looked blank.

"Don't play dumb. You know exactly what's inside this ledger. What I want to know is, why is *your* name in here?"

Even in the dusk, I saw Sanders face fall. "My name? They must have planted it there."

"Says you. Who's they? Maybe I'll give it to the police chief and see what he has to say." Burton raised his voice, but the waves and seagulls muted his words.

"Please, don't do anything stupid." Sanders blanched as he tried to grab the ledger. But Burton was almost a head taller, and had no problem keeping it out of his reach.

"Tell me the truth. Is that why the cops cleared out the Rusty Bucket, because of this ledger? What else were they looking for? Were they following your orders, trying to cover your tracks?"

Sanders glanced over both shoulders, looking guilty as hell. "Sure it's safe to talk here?"

"Would you rather talk to a county judge? Level with me, Sanders. Now—we don't have much time."

A few seagulls cried in the distance and I crept closer, straining to hear his explanation.

"OK, but keep this between us or both our lives are on the line." Sanders paused, looking around. "Fact is, I'm working undercover. Lots of corruption in Galveston, as you know."

Undercover? I perked up, hopeful. That explained some of Sanders' conflicting actions. Was Eva privy to his secret?

Burton looked unfazed. "Oh yeah? How can I believe you?"

"Don't you get it? To find the source, I need to pal around with these bums." He shrugged. "You gotta have faith in the system."

"Who hired you?"

"The Texas Rangers." One look at Sanders' solemn expression and I knew he was telling the truth.

"The Rangers?" Burton worked his jaw, eyes blazing. "Is that why you made that crooked deal with Johnny Jack?"

"Yeah, I tried to get in their good graces." He faced Burton, like a dare. "I wanted to protect you, get you off the hook. We're both outsiders, brought in to make sense of this crazy town. That ledger is just the ammunition I need to ID the dirty cops on the force."

"Who do you suspect?"

"Deputy Chief Connors. He's the troublemaker." Sanders leaned forward and I edged closer to hear. "Don't let him near your raid tonight. Trust me, he and his men will try to sabotage you."

"Figured as much. First, answer a few questions. Who ordered that wiseguy to plant my hat at Parker's bar?"

"Johnny Jack, who else? I knew you weren't guilty, but I had to make it look real. You know how it works. I gotta play along for a while, gain these cops' trust."

Burton folded his arms across his chest. "What about those gold cuff links hidden in your desk drawer?"

"You went through my desk?" Bristling, Sanders puffed out his barrel chest, his eyes bulging, and took a menacing step toward Burton. "What right do you have?"

"I'm trying to uphold the law, like you." Burton glared at him. "You didn't answer my question."

"I found them on Fred Blake, after the Black Stallion robbery."

"How do I know they're not a gift from your good buddy, Johnny Jack?"

"They're evidence, I swear. You don't see me wearing them, do you?" He drew back his jacket sleeve to show his shirt cuffs. "Johnny Jack has a list of cops and goons who do favors for him. The gold cuff links are their reward for a job well done."

"What job did Blake do for Nounes?"

"That's what I intend to find out," Sanders snorted. "It makes me sick to my stomach to see these cops flaunting their flashy cuff links like a badge of honor."

"The wrong badge."

Sanders nodded, holding out his palm, wiggling his fingers. "The dirty cops are probably named in that little black book. If you hand it over, it'll make both our jobs a lot easier. Can I have it now?"

A couple wandered out toward the docks, laughing and whispering, clearly zozzled from too much booze. The men clammed up, waiting until the two walked down to the docks.

With a shrug, Burton slapped the ledger onto Sanders' outstretched palm. "It's not my area anyway. Don't make me regret this, Sanders."

"Don't worry, I won't. Swear to God." Sanders crossed his heart and turned to go. Holding my breath, I inched around the column as he passed, hoping he wouldn't notice me.

Luckily he was too distracted, flipping through the ledger before he walked inside. Burton stood facing the bay, watching the seagulls fly over, then headed back inside.

I sucked in my breath, not sure what to believe. Was Sanders telling the truth? What did he plan to do with the ledger? Guess we'd find out soon enough.

I walked toward Burton, reaching for his arm, pretending I'd just left the building. "There you are! I've been looking all over for you. What are you doing out here?"

"I've got some news. Don't know if it's good or bad." He paused, his face sullen. "I gave Sanders the ledger."

"I know. I heard the whole conversation."

Burton stared at me without blinking. "You what? How? Where were you?"

"I hid behind those columns," I said, pointing. "I got worried."

"Hope I did the right thing." His face clouded. "I didn't have time to examine all the entries, but I do remember the big shots' names. I'll be interested to see what he does with this information."

"You and me both. Let's hope Sanders is on the up and up."

My heart heavy, I prayed Sanders was telling the truth: Was he really working undercover, trying to investigate the corrupt local force? Or was it just a convenient cover story, fabricated to throw Burton off his trail? Did he lie about the gold cuff links as well?

Was Sanders actually in cahoots with Johnny Jack? What if he gave him *permission* for the drop in exchange for a cut of the take?

Silently we headed inside the club and as we entered, strains of "Rhapsody in Blue" filled the room.

"I love that song! Care to dance?" Playfully I tugged on Burton's hand, pulling him onto the ballroom floor.

"Yes, ma'am!" His face lifted and he thrust his shoulders back, leading me in a slow, graceful waltz. For a while, I forgot everything but the music, the swirl of color and elegant surroundings as we whirled around the ballroom. When the band changed its tempo, we swayed to the rhythm, watching the giddy couples glide by.

"Do you realize we haven't sat down since we arrived?" He grinned. "I need a break."

"What about paying attention to your date?"

"Sorry, Jazz. You know I've been preoccupied lately."

"I'll say. You've been too busy trying to keep the peace. I just wish we could dance all night," I said, wrapping my arms around his slim waist. "I wish you didn't have to go...to work."

Burton clutched me tight, pressing against me for a proper tango, literally taking my breath away. "I'd like to stay here, like this, but you know I have to go soon. It's getting dark."

I didn't answer, only kept dancing, wishing the moment would never end. Finally I took a deep breath, squeezing his hands, wanting to shake some sense into him. "James, what can I say to change your mind? Would it make a difference if I told you Sammy was leading the whole booze drop?"

"Your good pal Sammy? I'm not surprised. After that stunt Johnny Jack pulled on the Cubans, he wouldn't dare show his face again." Burton raised his brows. "Since the Cubans won't do business with Nounes, how'd Sammy convince them to meet?"

"As far as I know, he told them he belongs to a Houston gang. At least he has eight men to back him up." I stopped dancing and eyed him. "How many men do you have?"

Burton shrugged, acting nonchalant, but I saw a flicker of panic cross his face. "Depends who shows up. You saw the fight. The guys are divided, right down the middle."

"Tell them to be careful. Tell them to watch your back." My eyes started to tear up and I buried my face in his shoulder, hoping no one noticed. "It's just one more stupid booze drop. Sure it's worth the risk?"

"Jasmine, I made a pledge to uphold the law, even if I don't agree with Prohibition. I have to try to stop these rum-runners, even if I'm not successful." Burton stroked my hair. "Why are you so upset over this one drop?"

"I care about both of you, and I don't want to see you get hurt." In the background, the band played: "*Yes, sir, that's my baby.*"

"Thanks, Jazz. But I knew the dangers when I took this job."

My throat felt dry, raw. Finally I couldn't keep my secret any longer: "You want to know the truth? Because you're my guy and Sammy is my brother."

CHAPTER FORTY-FOUR

Agent Burton stopped dancing and studied me for what seemed like ages but was probably only a minute or two, his face solemn.

"That explains a lot. I should have guessed you and Sammy are related." He stared across the harbor, deep in thought, watching a tugboat chug along the bay. "Now I know why you're always so worried about him. It all makes sense. I only wish you hadn't waited so long to tell me the truth."

"I was afraid of your reaction," I admitted. "Technically, he's breaking the law."

"What did you think I'd do? Use it as leverage? Blackmail you both?" Burton frowned. "Jasmine, don't you trust me by now?"

"Yes, but I didn't want your cop buddies to know. Sammy is none of their business."

"Agreed. I like Sammy. He's a bit rough around the edges, but he's always been a stand-up guy." Burton squinted, pushing my hair off my forehead. "Now that you mention it, there is a slight family resemblance, especially around the eyes. Isn't he quite a bit older?"

"By ten years." I nodded. "Actually he's my half-brother, on my dad's side. Long story."

"I'd like to hear it, but not now. I've got somewhere to be."

I faced him, almost pleading. "I wish you'd reconsider. What if the raid gets out of control? I don't want you or Sammy to get hurt."

"Jazz, I can't back down now. Besides, I'm not going after Sammy." His expression softened. "You know I'm not a violent person. All I want to do is scare off these rum-runners. They need to know they're not welcome here."

"Why don't you call the Coast Guard? Warn them the Cubans are coming tonight."

"I already did that, but there's no guarantee they'll show up. For all I know, Sheriff Sanders told them to take the night off."

My heart sank. "So you're going. You won't change your mind."

"I promise you, I'll be careful. Don't worry, I won't let anyone hurt Sammy." His eyes held mine as he stroked my cheek. "Thanks for telling me. Your secret is safe." Then he turned and gave a signal to a few men who, on cue, followed him out the door like wind-up toy soldiers.

What did I expect? That he'd drop everything and run into my arms like a love-struck hero in a romantic melodrama?

I made my way over to Eva, pulling her away from Sheriff Sanders who was scanning the room, probably wondering where Burton and his men went.

"Did Agent Burton leave already?" Eva asked.

"Yes and nothing I said would stop him."

"What do you mean? You didn't mention Sammy, did you?" Her eyes widened in alarm.

"I felt I had no choice. He promised Sammy wouldn't get hurt."

"Jasmine, are you sure that was smart? What if Walt finds out we're related?"

"I know you're related." Walt crept up behind us, slipping an arm around Eva's waist. "You're sisters, right?" His mood was jovial, as if throwing punches at the police chief in public was only sport. Frankly, I suspected he was relieved to get his hands on the ledger.

"Right." Eva linked her arm through mine, giving him a tight smile. "Sisters."

"Say, where's that tall Fed fella of yours?" Sanders asked me, eyes narrowed. "If I were him, I wouldn't leave you alone with this pack of wild dogs."

I avoided his gaze. "Guess he went out for some fresh air. I'd better go look for him."

After Sanders turned away, Eva said in a low voice, "Why don't you stick around, enjoy yourself? Show Burton you don't need him to have a good time. It'll take your mind off...things. "

"I'm too worried to have any fun. Besides, Nathan offered to take me home."

"Is that all? You two aren't going to do anything stupid, are you?" Her wary look spoke volumes.

Did I give it away? "Applesauce! Since I've lost my dance partner, I'm ready to leave." I patted her arm. "You two enjoy the evening. Get your money's worth out of that gorgeous gown!"

"I intend to." She beamed at Sanders, who seemed oblivious to my doubts. For her sake, I hoped he wouldn't let us down.

As I pushed through the crowd toward the exit, Sergeant Smith roughly grabbed my hand, saying, "Can I have this dance?"

"What do you want?" I struggled against his grip, but his hands tightened around my wrist. "Let go of me!"

"Where's your date? Did your agent boyfriend desert you?" He kept moving toward me, backing me in a corner.

"Leave me alone!" Shaking, I scanned the crowd of cops, looking for help, yet no one seemed to notice this masher was assaulting me.

"Give your fella a message from Deputy Chief Connors." Smith squeezed my arm so hard it left red marks.

"Get your paws off of me!" I twisted away from him and tried to scream but no sound came out. As I struggled, the band broke into a loud rendition of "Ain't we got fun?" Yeah, right—if you call being manhandled tons of fun.

"Stand still, bitch. You don't want me ripping off your pretty new frock, do you?"

He yanked me by my neck, forcing his mouth on my ear, pushing so hard, I could smell the smoke and whiskey on his breath. Repulsed, I squirmed and tried to shove him away, but he clutched my throat tighter. "Tell your Fed friend to quit snooping around and stay out of our business. Or you'll both be sorry."

I managed to dig my fingernails into his beefy arm, pressing harder until he released me with a yelp. "Go to hell!" I hissed. "He's not afraid of a dumb palooka like you."

Why did this keep happening to me? Maybe Sammy was right: As long as I kept seeing Agent Burton, I was in danger. By now, Burton had already left for the booze drop so it was too late to pass on Sergeant Smith's warning.

Still shaking, I ducked into the nearby bathroom to hide. Once inside, I saw two attractive flappers getting dolled up in front of the vanity, a bleached blonde and brunette. Where had I seen them before—at the Oasis or the Hollywood? Was I hearing things or did I hear them mention "Cuban rum" and "West Beach" and "raid"? They clammed up when they saw me, putting their fingers to their lips, like they had some big secret.

"Having fun, ladies?" I forced a smile, pretending like nothing was wrong.

"And how!" the striking brunette said, waving as they left.

I sank into the chaise longue in the powder room and took a few deep breaths to calm down. My head was throbbing and I pressed on my temples to stop the pounding pain. How could I admit to Nathan that I was getting the jitters? Would it really make any difference if we even showed up? Still, staying home and worrying all night would accomplish nothing.

I stole a quick look at the vanity mirror lit up like a marquee, straightened my headband and applied fresh lipstick. As quietly as possible, I crept out of the bathroom, and made my way to the exit. Outside, a lone valet with a top hat and tails stood in front of the Yacht Club and I reached out to steady myself, stumbling a bit for effect. Could I pull it off?

"Excuse me, where'd you park the deputy chief's car?" I smiled, slurring my words. "I think I need to lie down. Got a bad headache."

"The black Cadillac? Want me to bring it around, miss?"

"No, that's OK, I just need to take a nap. Can you show me where it's parked? Please?"

"Sure thing. Got a hold of some hooch?" The valet winked and led me out to the lot, where a gleaming black Caddy was parked to one side, separate from the lowly jalopies.

"I'll say! Thanks," I told the valet with a grateful grin, pretending to open the door. "You're a peach!"

"Anytime, doll." He waved as he returned to the entrance. Seems I'd picked up a few acting lessons from Amanda, after all.

When the valet was out of view, I raced over to Nathan's Model T, but he was gone. I rummaged through his glove compartment and found what I wanted. Leave it to Nathan to always be prepared in case of an emergency.

I entered the ballroom through the side door, and noticed Nathan taking photos of a few tipsy older couples, arms around each other's waists, leaning on each other for support.

"Excuse me Nathan." He looked startled when I tapped his elbow. "I need your help." I faked a smile. "Sorry to interrupt, folks."

"You took so long, I thought you'd changed your mind?"

"I have a small job for you. Outside. Can you wrap it up?"

"Just give me a minute." Nathan took a few more posed shots, then waved to the group, as we left. "Thanks, kids. Look for your photos in the society pages!"

"How exciting!" the women squealed.

"Nathan," I scolded, grabbing his arm. "We can't guarantee their pictures will be in the paper."

"You never know. So what's this hush-hush job you want me to do? Take photos of the mayor cheating on his wife? Police Chief Johnson wearing a wig and frock?"

"You're a card." I cupped the pocketknife, motioning for him to follow me outside through the back exit.

His mouth popped open. "Where'd you get that?"

"Guess. Don't you recognize it?"

"Jazz, what's this all about?"

"Can you keep a secret?" In the parking lot, I said, "I need you to slash the deputy chief's tires. Make sure he can't leave this place."

"What in hell?" He stared at me in shock. "Deputy Connors?"

I nodded, finger to my lips. "I'll explain later. Any idea what Sergeant Smith's car looks like?"

"You're in luck. I happened to see the sergeant drive up in his new Ford roadster."

We stopped by Nathan's Model T and dropped off the camera equipment. "I'll keep a look-out while you..."

He cut me off with a frown. "Do you really expect me to slash two top cop's car tires outside a ballroom full of boozed-up lawmen? I swear, Jazz, you'd better have a damn good explanation."

CHAPTER FORTY-FIVE

"How about the fact that they both are dirty cops?" I told Nathan. "They're in cahoots with the Downtown Gang and probably the Beach Gang too."

"Sure about that?" He looked skeptical as we wove our way through the rows of cars.

"Dead sure. I heard the deputy chief is on the take and plans to block Burton's raid tonight. Remember when the police cleared out the Rusty Bucket? Burton found a ledger in Connors' desk, listing names of dirty cops and their bets. I suspect he uses it as leverage to blackmail all the men."

"A ledger, huh? No wonder they were in such a rush to clean out the place. I won't ask how you stumbled on that incriminating piece of evidence."

When I found the deputy chief's Cadillac, he let out a low whistle. "Nice wheels. Now we know why he can afford a new Cadillac on a cop's piddly salary."

In one quick motion, Nathan gripped the pocketknife and pulled out the blade while I scanned the parking lot, making sure we weren't being watched. Taking a deep breath, he squatted by the car and jammed his knife into each tire.

"Thanks, Nathan." Frankly, I enjoyed hearing the air hiss out of all four tires, watching the Cadillac sink to the ground. "Let him try to stop Burton now. Where's the sergeant's Ford?"

"Damn, they all look alike in the dark. We'd better go. *Now*. I see some cops heading this way—without their wives."

"You're right. Let's hit the road. Think we missed them?" Why wait for the valet to point me out to the deputy chief?

Nathan helped me inside his car, holding onto my hem. "Naw. When I was taking pics, I overheard Burton and some cops talking. Reminded me of a football team but with tuxes and top hats on."

"Did they mention the booze drop?"

He nodded. "I happened to hear them say they're meeting at Rum Row on West Beach."

"Really? That's near the Hollywood, by the Beach Gang's turf. Boy, Johnny Jack sure likes to live dangerously."

"So do you." He grinned, his eyes tracing the length of my gown. "Good luck taking that fancy frock off without my help."

He handed me a shirt and pants, raising his brows as he watched me struggle with my gown. "We've got to stop meeting like this. You can't seem to keep your clothes on whenever we're alone."

"Nate! Go jump in the lake." I rolled my eyes.

"How about the ocean? Will that do?"

I was too worried about Burton and Sammy to be amused. "Just keep your eyes on the road and let me fiddle with my frock. Did you see where they went?"

"Hard to miss a caravan of police cars, even at night. Gotta keep a safe distance or they may see me trailing behind and get suspicious." While he drove, I tried taking off my dress without tearing the silk but I couldn't manage in his tiny Model T.

"Is Rum Row the usual drop-off point?"

He nodded. "All the schooners from Cuba, Jamaica and the Bahamas like to drop anchor there, about thirty miles off shore."

"That's a long haul for some rum. Must be worth a mint."

"Rum brings up to fifty bucks a case and these schooners can carry thousands of cases in one trip. Depends on how much Johnny Jack is willing to shell out. Let's hope they don't play games. If Sammy comes back empty-handed, then..."

"Don't say it. I know." I squeezed his arm to shut him up.

"So how do you know Deputy Connors is involved?"

"I overheard Sanders talking to Burton, warning him that Deputy Connors might sabotage his raid." I took a deep breath. "Did I mention that his pal Smith threatened me after Burton left?"

His head snapped sideways. "What did Smith do? Are you OK?"

I held up my manicured hands. "These small fingers may look fragile, but my nails are as strong as an eagle's talons."

"Good for you." Nathan grinned. "Serves that bully right." He slowed down as a huge crane flew low in front of us, its wings flapping furiously against the strong Gulf breeze. "Boy, am I glad we slit Deputy Connors' tires now. You said he had the ledger in his desk? How'd Burton get his hands on it?" he asked.

"Promise not to tell Mack or the newsboys?" I filled him in, adding, "Talk about a close call. I only hope the cop on duty doesn't tell the police chief or the deputy we were both there."

"You searched the police station? I knew Burton had some balls, but I didn't know they were solid steel." He gave me a sheepish smile. "Excuse my French."

"Don't tell a soul, OK?" I pleaded, not mentioning that Burton already gave Sanders the ledger. For all we knew, Sanders was protecting both the dirty cops and the crooks. I stared out the window, watching the clouds float across the sky, temporarily obscuring the moon like sheer organza.

Beach Boulevard snaked along the ocean, the half-moon providing some light as Nathan trailed a good thirty yards behind a couple of cop cars. I assumed Burton's roadster was already parked, but where? Far beyond the Seawall, West Beach was an undeveloped section of the beach—miles away from the hustle and bustle of Downtown, Murdoch's, the Hotel Galvez and Crystal Palace—and a natural drop-off spot.

One by one, the cop cars cut their headlights and started turning down the road, lining up behind big boulders and sand dunes. The Gulf of Mexico roared in the background, drowning out the engines.

Sammy's crew was probably parked on the other side, closest to the ocean, but the clouds had passed over the moon again and at the moment, it was too dark to see clearly.

Nathan dimmed his lights and waited to ease his car down the beach, positioning it several yards away by a huge sand dune, near an abandoned fishing boat. Thankfully the sand was damp and solid enough to park without the tires sinking.

From our vantage point we watched the cops—when had they changed into street clothes?—position themselves behind the large dunes and boulders. On the jetties, I noticed a lone figure standing at the end of the concrete boulders, left-over slabs from the Seawall's construction, no doubt acting as a look-out. Sammy?

The moon illuminated a half-circle of old Fords parked on the beach, reminding me of Wild West wagons forming a barricade in old cowboy movies. Where was Sammy's snazzy new roadster? Somehow I doubted he'd risk ruining his precious auto during a booze drop on the beach.

Puffy clouds passed over the moon, carving out a sliver of light with stars providing a few bright spots. Nathan was so engrossed, he didn't pay any attention to me while I managed to peel off my snug gown and pull on his old jeans and shirt without too much fuss.

I saw a few men outlined against the sky, sitting on rocks around a campfire. A flame leapt up and I took a good look: Hard to miss Sammy, standing in the center of the group, talking to his team, as if giving them a pep talk before a big game.

Crouching down in the front seat, I counted the number of cops compared to Sammy's gang: His men outnumbered Burton's crew two to one, roughly six men versus three.

I didn't know whether to be relieved or afraid—frankly, I was glad for Sammy, worried about Burton. Which team was I on anyway? Couldn't I root for both? Seems Nathan's nifty knife skills had worked—Deputy Connors was nowhere in sight.

"I hope Burton has enough back-up in case things get out of hand," I told Nathan, praying that the men on both teams would follow orders and not act on their own.

The waves crashed and foamed on the shore, muffling the men's voices. Once or twice, some headlights flashed on and I tried to make out the figures. Where was Burton?

"Should we stay here?" I whispered. "Or try to move closer?"

"Let's stay put for awhile, in case this whole operation is a bust. Who knows? Some snitch may have tipped off the Cubans or the Downtown Gang that the cops were coming."

After half an hour, my legs felt cramped, my muscles tense, my back aching. I wanted to stretch but was there was no room to move. The salty sea air whipped through the car, blowing my hair into my face and eyes. "This could be a long night," I sighed, hoping the Cubans had hit a snag or changed their minds.

"Give it a few more minutes," Nathan said. "The men are getting restless. Looks like the Downtown Gang is playing cards around the fire."

"Better than taking potshots at cops. Think the gang knows they're here?"

"If they do, they sure are playing it cool. I wonder if Sammy has a game plan?"

"His goal is to get a hold of that rum and get away. No one wants a bloodbath."

"Wouldn't it be easier if they shared?" Nathan cracked. "Split it in half?"

"Tell that to Johnny Jack."

Hidden behind the dune, we watched Sammy pace back and forth across the sand, between the shore and the campfire, in the restless way he paced at the Oasis. Silhouetted against the night sky, he somehow seemed bigger, braver, larger than life. He looked out at the ocean, staring at the cavernous sky. Did he miss being a sailor?

I knew that one day he'd want to leave Galveston, the Oasis, that his life here was too small, insignificant—that one bar, one dream couldn't contain him for long. Whatever he wanted, I hoped he lived long enough to accomplish his goals.

When the clouds swept by the moon, I saw that the cops still laid in wait, holding a rifle in their hands, ready to do battle with an unseen enemy. Why so many guns? Didn't Burton tell me that he only wanted to stop the Cubans from coming ashore—not shoot anyone? Was he just placating me?

I wanted to reach out to both Burton and Sammy, warn them, but what could I do, stuck in Nathan's car? As the minutes dragged on, I noticed a tall, lean figure moving stealthily among the dunes, talking to his men, gesturing and pointing.

Finally, I caught a glimpse of Agent Burton's face in the moonlight, surprised at his calm demeanor. Was he giving last-minute instructions or was it a change of plans?

Almost an hour had passed since we'd arrived and no boats were in sight. To be honest, I didn't have the stamina or patience to wait much longer. "Looks pretty peaceful to me," I nudged Nathan. "Ready to call it quits?"

"Are you chickening out?" he teased me. "As I recall, this was all your big idea."

"Don't remind me." I sunk down in my seat and tried to make conversation. "Say, what happened at Mack's poker game last night?"

"He won the whole shebang," Nathan admitted. "He must be picking up some tips from his card shark friends, damn it. Lost a big wad to that old coot."

"So why is he acting so strange? What's wrong?"

"Plenty. Promise not to say anything to Mack or Sammy or anyone else? Especially not to the news staff or your big-mouth boss." Nathan gave me a warning look.

"Me? My lips are sealed. Come on, you can tell me."

"OK, but it ain't pretty." He let out a deep breath. "Turns out Mack was playing cards with his *sources* a week ago and they caught a poor sap cheating. Big-time."

"You mean his gangster buddies? What happened?"

"Unfortunately for Mack, he witnessed the poor guy being tortured and the goons say he'll be next if he ever spills the beans—in print or otherwise."

"Torture?" My jaw dropped open, like a mechanical bank. "Oh my God. No wonder Mack is terrified. Who was the victim? Is he still alive? Which gang?"

"Who knows? That's all Mack said." Nathan eyed me. "No more questions. It's for our own protection."

"Jeepers!" I shivered, the muggy night suddenly turning cold. "Poor guy. Poor Mack. I've heard enough, thanks."

Glancing around West Beach, I noticed a faint spark of light in the distance, blinking once, twice, then it went dark. Was it the Cubans' signal?

Then I saw the lone figure on the jetty race down to the beach, waving his arms, rushing over to say a few words to Sammy. When he turned around, the moonlight caught his profile: Chad Parker.

CHAPTER FORTY-SIX

Immediately Sammy's crew sprang into action, carrying lanterns toward the shore. A few fellas in thigh-high wading boots began dragging out rowboats into the ocean with the help of two baby grands on either side. Then two men jumped into each boat, rowing furiously against the breakers.

I watched as the beam of light grew closer, heart hammering, wondering why the cops hadn't reacted yet. Still, they waited on the beach, not making a move, not making a sound.

"What's the hold up?" I wondered. Frankly I wanted this whole business to be over with before the Cubans got onshore. If tempers flared or a fight broke out, we'd all be sitting ducks.

"They're more interested in confiscating the cargo than making arrests now," Nathan told me. "Without the booze, they could be simple fishermen in row boats."

"Right. Evidence." I was so nervous, I couldn't think straight. "What's next?"

"Depends on the Cubans. If they don't meet the men halfway, it may take a while."

I settled in for a long wait, trying to get comfortable in Nathan's cramped Model T.

"You're armed, right? Just in case?"

"Armed but not very dangerous. I doubt my pistol is any match against their firepower."

"Better than nothing." I shifted in my seat, staring out into the bay, but couldn't make out anything. "I'm getting the heebie jeebies. It's so quiet out here. Too quiet." The men must have rowed quite a distance in a short period of time. "I can't see any boats, can you?"

"The men don't want to advertise their positions. They only use lights as needed."

"Makes sense." I nodded, wondering what Burton was planning. Why didn't he react? Was he waiting for the Coast Guard to show up? I felt like running over and tapping his shoulder to alert him.

Suddenly a flash of headlights lit up the desolate road, driving right toward us. A snazzy hay-burner turned toward the Downtown Gang's camp and parked halfway on the road, as if planning a quick get-away. Nathan and I traded nervous looks when we saw two guys walk out, one tall, one very short, like a child.

Sammy faced them, holding a lantern in one hand, the other grasping a gun. He raised the lantern to the men's faces and with a start, I recognized Fred Blake from the Black Stallion, standing next to a small Mexican, smaller than Buzz—no doubt Paco, the jockey.

"I've got to hear this." I cracked open the door, glad for the distraction.

"Jazz, be careful!" Nathan tried to pull me back but I waved him away. Slowly I crept toward the campfire on my hands and knees. Lying flat on my stomach, I hid behind a small sand dune nearby and positioned myself where I could see and hear everything. I was too excited to be nervous, my heart banging against my chest.

Nathan settled in next to me, our elbows touching, eyes wide as mine as we watched the scene unfold. Sammy gestured toward the ocean, arguing with the late arrivals. Luckily the wind carried their voices across the beach and I could hear Blake say, "Thought you could use a translator. Paco here speaks fluent Spanish."

"Paco? Who in hell is this Paco?" Sammy snapped, raising his gun. "If I'd needed a translator, I'd ask."

Blake held up his hands in mock-surrender. "Hey buddy, calm down. We're just here to help. He's my jockey, straight from Mexico. If anyone can understand the Cubans, he can."

"Your jockey? I thought he was supposed to be dead." Sammy scowled, the lantern's light flickering across the men's faces.

"Surprise. He knew he'd be horse meat after the race so he skipped town," Blake cracked. "Wouldn't you?"

Sammy glared at the two men, crossing his arms. "You have some balls bringing this midget here tonight, without my say-so. Who in hell do you think you are?"

"Relax, I'm not trying to cut in on your action. Just figured you could use an extra set of eyes. And guns."

Frowning, Sammy motioned for them to join the campfire, walking behind the two men like a jailer. I didn't blame him for being so careful: Blake and his jockey could stab him in the back, literally.

"What's he doing here?" an angry voice cried out.

I heard the men arguing, and craned my neck for a better look.

Chad Parker charged at Blake, pulling a pistol out of his pocket, waving it around. "Don't trust him! He killed my father."

"What?" Blake backed off, hands up. "Now why in the hell would I kill Charlie? He was a simple barkeep, like me. A friend."

"Oh yeah? That's how you treat your friends? Beat them to death with a baseball bat?" Chad yelled, facing off against Blake and Paco, raising his pistol. A couple of goons stepped back, not wanting to interfere with their private feud.

"Don't blame me, kid. Your dad was in debt up to his eyeballs."

"Because of you and Torino." Chad aimed his gun at Blake's chest. "Admit it, my dad figured out you goddamned cheats were fixing the horse races. Changing the odds, fudging the numbers, paying off jockeys. So you and Torino shut him up before he could tell your clients all about your little scam."

Blake blanched. "You got no proof. Torino got whacked, remember?"

"I bet that was your doing, too. Just so happens my father's gun was missing after he was murdered." Chad spat in Blake's face. "Don't forget, I've been running numbers for my dad since I was a kid. He told me everything before you beat him to a pulp."

The jockey stood behind Blake, crying out in Spanish, waving his hands in crazy circles. "No fue mi culpa!" Not my fault?

"Shut up!" Blake yelled at the jockey. "You're part of it, too."

"I heard your horse and jockey just won the last race. So where's the prize money?" Chad moved closer to Blake. "Bet your clients can't wait to get a piece of your winnings."

"It's all gone." Blake shrugged. "We were robbed, remember?"

"You liar. Why weren't *you* killed, like my old man?" Chad snapped. "How did you manage to survive that attack? If you ask me, the whole thing was staged, faked to fool everyone."

"Faked? Says you!" Blake backed away as the gang circled him, swearing and grumbling under their breaths.

Chad turned to Sammy's men, waving his gun. "Do you believe his story? I don't. You're a cold-blooded killer, you son-of-a-bitch!"

"Give me the gun, Chad." Sammy stood in front of Chad, gripping his shoulders. "We've got too much at stake. If you shoot now, you'll alert the Cubans *and* the cops."

"You're not my father. Thanks to this asshole, my father is dead." His face twisted, Chad cocked the gun and pressed it to Blake's temple.

"We all heard the story," Sammy said, calmly, reaching for Chad's gun. "Let *us* take care of Blake."

Chad slowly lowered his gun, his face inches from Blake's, his voice hoarse. "I should make you suffer the way my dad did. Beat you to death until you're all broken up into little pieces. Blowing out your brains out is too easy."

CHAPTER FORTY-SEVEN

"That's enough, Chad. We've got it covered," Sammy said. "Go home. Get some rest."

"How can I rest while Blake is still alive?" Chad sputtered, breathing hard. "I'd better keep an eye on that bastard myself."

"We won't let them out of our sight." Sammy called Blake over, gesturing toward the Gulf. "We'll need help off-loading our crates. Go out by the shore and wait for the boats to come back."

"We didn't agree to go fishing," Blake griped. "I just wanted to bring some fire power, along with my translator."

"Get to work!" Sammy snapped. "You're lucky to be alive, both of you jerks. Get a move on."

Heads down, the two men rushed to shore, looking over their shoulders, eyeing Chad and Sammy. Nathan and I exchanged nervous looks. All these fireworks and the Cubans hadn't even shown up yet.

I followed Sammy's gaze and in the distance, I heard a small powerboat heading toward us. When a light flashed twice, he called out to his men: "That's our signal. Hurry. Line up."

Squinting, I saw a small boat slow to a stop, idling about twenty yards offshore. A stocky man handed over a couple of bulky sacks to two guys standing waist-deep in water. I shuddered, amazed at both their bravado and recklessness. After all, real sharks had been spotted in these waters—not just sharks toting guns.

The group formed a chain and handed over each bag to the next guy, assembly-line, and finally deposited the cases along the shore. Sammy motioned for two of his remaining men to pull up their vehicles. By now, they'd placed lanterns along the shoreline, the area lit up like a beach party.

As I edged closer, I could see the cases wrapped in burlap sacks and tied together, I assumed for easier handling. "Hurry, bring your trucks around so we can get these loaded. Keep going," Sammy said, sounding breathless. So far, the cops hadn't made a move.

Did he even realize Burton and his men waited on the other side of the dunes, watching the entire exchange? If Sammy thought I'd managed to charm Burton into staying late at the ball, he was sadly mistaken. I only wished my powers of persuasion worked that well.

Sammy's crew continued to stack the crates on shore, moving faster now, like a human conveyor belt. Despite the fact he was breaking the law, I felt a surge of pride in my big brother, impressed by the efficient way he'd planned this whole operation.

Yes, it was wrong and illegal and risky, but unlike many barkeeps, he was buying real rum, risking his life in the process—not doctoring up some cheap industrial crap and endangering lives.

I doubted Burton condoned his actions, but Johnny Jack had given him no other choice. If there was such a thing as a responsible criminal, then Sammy fit that bill.

While some men stacked the crates of rum, the others loaded up their trucks and cars as fast as they could, only stopping to move the rest of the vehicles in place.

"Get your car over here!" Sammy commanded, pointing to Blake's fancy Studebaker. "We need all the transports we can get."

Grumbling, Blake broke away from the group, trudging across the sand to his car. Without warning, a gunshot sliced the air, shattering the silence.

Out of the darkness, Burton appeared, one hand raised high holding his gun, the other flashing a badge on his lapel. My heart seized, recalling the first night I'd seen him in action at the Oasis.

Now here we were, weeks later, replaying the same scenario: Burton and Sammy were facing off, under different circumstances but still on opposite sides of the law.

"Cuidado! Federales!" The jockey started waving his arms and yelling in Spanish at the power boats, probably warning the men to stay offshore. The gunshot served as enough warning, for Sammy's gang wasted no time running to their cars. I watched them start their engines and roar away into the darkness. Why didn't the cops try to follow them? Why didn't they go after the rum-runners? Where in the world was the Coast Guard?

Blake darted toward Burton, his arm outstretched, pointing a pistol straight at Burton's head. "Drop it, Fed."

"You're making a big mistake," Burton said, edging toward Blake, without flinching. "Sure you want to shoot down a Treasury agent, in front of all these cops? All these witnesses?"

"Hell, they'll back me up." Blake laughed in his face, and cocked his pistol. "Want me to prove it?"

I wanted to run out from behind the sand dune and yell, anything to distract the men, but I remained frozen, afraid that any sudden movement could cause Blake to fire—if not at Burton, then at me. "Nathan, get your gun ready to shoot." I nudged him.

"Now? What do you think they'd do to us? Shoot first, ask questions later."

"We can't sit by and do nothing." Surely Sammy would intervene? Burton steadied his gun and aimed at Blake while the men gathered behind them, watching and waiting.

I glanced over at Sammy, wondering what he'd do. If he helped Burton, his men might gang up and shoot him *and* Sammy themselves. Damned if he did...

And I wasn't any help, hiding here behind a sand dune like a bug-eyed Betty, afraid to make a move. Why did I bother to come?

"Hand me the gun," I hissed to Nathan. "If you won't shoot Blake, I will!"

"Right. And when was the last time you handled a gun? Never?"

From a distance, a gunshot rang out and Blake's pistol flew through the air. Blake jerked up, looking around, yelling, "What in hell? Who did that?" Dropping to his knees, he scrambled on the sand for his pistol and then aimed it at Burton.

Chad stepped out of the shadows, brandishing his gun. "Put that down. I'm warning you."

Who knew Chad was such a crack shot?

"What do you think you're doing, you punk kid? Trying to impress daddy? Well, daddy's long gone." Blake stood up shakily, moving toward Chad with his pistol.

A second shot fired and I saw an explosion of red.

Blake screamed, grabbing his hand, and dropped on the sand. "You little bastard, you shot my hand off!" He curled up in a ball, rolling from side to side, moaning and cursing.

Chad stood over Blake as he writhed in pain, a satisfied smile spreading. "That was the whole idea. Let's hope you don't hurt anyone else with your one good hand."

"Ay Dios mio!" the jockey cried out, jumping around Blake. "Perdio su mano y se va morir!"

Sweat dripped down Blake's face and he clutched his wrist, gritting his teeth. "Goddamn it, somebody help me!"

Crawling closer, I snuck a peek and cringed, feeling faint. Dots swirled before my face and I squeezed my eyes shut, feeling ill.

Part of a hand lay on the beach, most of its fingers blown away by the blast. Whether or not Blake was a killer, I couldn't stand to watch anyone suffer. Doubling over, I clutched my gut, ready to upchuck. In place of his hand, all that remained was a bloody stump.

CHAPTER FORTY-EIGHT

"This man needs a medic!" Burton called out, kneeling by Blake. "Any war veterans with medical training?"

A few fellas gathered around Blake, not moving, while the wounded gangster moaned in pain, clutching his wrist, cradling what was left of his hand.

"Here, this might help." Sammy glanced at Burton, then used his gun handle to bust the wood crate, opened a bottle of rum and handed it to Blake. "Drink this," he commanded, holding the bottle over Blake's mouth, letting the liquid spill down his throat and neck.

"Thank God for booze," Blake said, guzzling the rum. Wobbly, he attempted to stand up with Paco's help. Suddenly his whole body slumped and his eyes glazed over, no doubt going into shock.

The tiny jockey tore off part of his shirt and wrapped Blake's hand with a make-shift bandage, yelling, "Se va morir!"

"Would someone shut him up?" a stocky man muttered. "I'll be glad to do it myself."

"Like hell you will." Burton stepped forward, asking the jockey, "Can you speak English?"

"Poquito, sí," the Mexican man, nodded. "Yes, yes. I will tell all. Whatever you want."

"Good. You'll have plenty of time to talk later." Burton pointed to one of the cops, an older man I didn't recognize, saying, "Take Blake to the hospital. Now."

I knew Burton wasn't just being kind, he wanted to make sure Blake was in good enough shape to interrogate later.

"Why bother? Let him suffer the way my old man did," Chad sputtered in disgust.

The cops and the jockey helped Blake into his snazzy car, loaded down with liquor. They laid Blake in the back seat, his legs out the window, jogging a sad memory of Horace Andrews.

As the cop raced off, I wondered: Did it occur to Burton that one of his men had just confiscated a car load of illegal rum? Obviously Burton trusted him—but who knew where the rum might end up? The second cop returned holding the jockey's arm and shoved him at Burton.

Paco stared at the sand where Blake had been shot, his dark eyes despondent, clasping his tiny hands. Then he looked up at the sky, perhaps hoping to find heaven, crossing his heart and speaking Spanish, no doubt praying for his and Blake's life, if not his soul.

Burton turned toward the few men in Sammy's gang. "Now that your vehicles are all ready and loaded, I'd like you gentlemen to follow me to the police station. This is a raid by order of the Galveston Prohibition Squad."

He said it with such authority, such force, that I was impressed. Trouble was, his polite, commanding tone had little effect on a group of thugs. Sammy stood his ground, watching both groups circling each other like two packs of stray dogs.

My heart seized: This was the moment I'd dreaded for so long. Alone, both men could be civil, tolerant—at times, they even got along well. But in public? Both Sammy and Burton had to save face, put on a good front to earn their men's respect.

I wanted to jump in the middle, act as referee, say, "Aren't you both against poisonous hooch—not real Cuban rum?"

In the distance, I heard a speedboat roar across the ocean, near the rowboats. Sammy's men stopped in place, glancing at each other with question marks. The Coast Guard? Then a loud foghorn blasted out: "Back away from the cargo! Leave it alone, coppers."

Johnny Jack arrived in his speedboat, the Cherokee, just in time to rescue his precious crates of rum. Loud popping noises shattered the night and a shower of bullets sprayed the beach, followed by screams and yelps as the men scattered like sand crabs among the dunes. Cursing and yelling, they raced toward their vehicles and started the engines, driving off into the dark without looking back.

Instinctively, Sammy and Burton and the few remaining men ducked, flattening out onto the beach like sand dollars. Typical reckless Johnny Jack, acting on impulse without any regard for his men's safety. He probably hijacked his own boats, taking the rum for his private stash.

I screamed so loudly I was sure I'd blown our cover. Fortunately the waves and wind and gunfire drowned out my cries. I covered my face, peering through my fingers, afraid to look: Was anyone hit?

Nathan and I traded frightened looks. Thank God no one appeared to be hurt.

Then I heard pounding on the sand and a small figure appeared to be running right by our sand dune. The jockey? With all the commotion, no one seemed to be paying attention to Paco—all except one man gaining speed on the little guy.

I crawled across the sand and managed to position myself in his way, reaching out and grabbing his ankles when he tried to run past. He fell flat on his face and I had to squeeze my eyes shut as he kicked sand in my face. "Ay Dios mio!" he said, cursing "Oh my God" in Spanish. Still, I held tight onto his scrawny legs, no mean feat since he was kicking and rolling around in the sand.

Finally I sat on his back, knocking the wind out of his bony chest. "Tell us the truth, Paco. Were you part of this scheme? Did you help Blake kill Parker?" I demanded, pinning his arms down.

"No, no. Not me. Blake and Torino." Paco struggled against my grip, knocking me off my perch. He tried to stand up, then stopped moving, staring at Nathan's pistol, aimed at the jockey's head.

"Did you help Blake kill Parker?" I repeated. Dark eyes wide with fright, the jockey sunk to his knees in the sand, trembling, muttering in Spanish.

"Don't make me hurt you," Nathan threatened, fingering his gun. "Cut the crap. I know you speak English."

"No, no, Mister Blake and Torino killed Parker."

"So who killed Torino—was it you?" I asked, grabbing his shoulders. He wouldn't answer, shaking his head no. "Come on, Paco. The police won't let you off so easy."

"Listen to the woman." A shadow crossed Paco's face and Chad appeared, placing his boot on the little man's knees. "Talk, Paco. You saw what I did to Blake."

"No, Chad. You know me long time. I like mister Parker. Blake and Torino beat your father, not me. Then Blake shot Torino to shut him up. They threatened to kill my horse, Queen of Sheba, if I squealed." In the moonlight, I could see the jockey's black eyes well with tears. "I love my Sheba, so I keep her safe, away from bad men like Torino and Blake."

"Where's Sheba now?" Chad's face brightened. "I've always wanted a racehorse, especially a fine Arabian filly like Sheba." He turned to us, steadying his gun. "You two, turn Paco over to me."

"What are you going to do to him after you find Sheba? Shoot off his kneecaps?" I got up and faced Chad, my hands balled into fists, standing by Nathan. I wasn't that brave, just upset, emotional.

"Hell, no. I want to keep Paco safe and healthy, so he can keep winning races with Sheba. I need him to tell the authorities exactly how Blake killed my dad and Torino. He was just a pawn, a patsy." Chad helped Paco to his feet, draping his arm around the petite man's shoulders. "We're going to be partners, aren't we, pal?"

"Sí, partners. Amigos." Paco nodded. As they walked off, Paco looked back at us, eyes big as the moon, clearly afraid of Chad.

"Think we can trust him?" Nathan said, putting away his pistol.

"Who? Chad or Paco?"

"Both. Should we go after them, make sure nothing happens?"

"Chad isn't that stupid. He knows what's at stake. Besides, Sheba won't be able to win any races without her best jockey."

CHAPTER FORTY-NINE

After the ruckus died down, I looked over at the shore, but no one seemed to notice, or care, that Chad and Paco had disappeared. Thank goodness they were too distracted by Johnny Jack to pay attention to our scuffle. I hoped Chad would keep his word and come to realize that Paco had been a victim, just like his father.

Burton calmly assessed the area, checking his men, calculating his next move. They seemed nonplussed, almost as if they'd expected Johnny Jack's sudden appearance.

A few men still stood on shore, staring into the Gulf for signs of Johnny Jack, but his launch had already vanished. Sammy backed away, toward the cars, no doubt looking for an escape route.

With only a skeleton crew and a handful of vehicles left, the men appeared to be on equal ground—depending on who carried the most weapons.

"Not so fast, Sammy," Burton said, patting his gun. "You're coming downtown with me. Tell your crew to put their hands up."

"You can't make me do anything. Look around. You're outnumbered." Sammy faced Burton, balling his fists.

"Wanna bet?" Burton drew his gun, aiming it at Sammy.

My heart stopped. I'd never seen Burton actually pointing a gun at Sammy, not even during the raid. What happened to his promise, that he'd "watch out for Sammy"? Was he just "humoring me," as Sammy would say? Or were they showing off in front of their men?

"You wouldn't dare." Sammy lifted his chin in defiance.

Despite their show of bravado, I knew both men had too much respect for each other to engage in gunfire, or even a fistfight. Like Zorro, I wanted to swoop down with Nathan and rescue Sammy, and drive off where Burton and Johnny Jack couldn't find him.

"You're right. Violence never solves anything." Burton nodded, motioning to the remaining cops with his gun. "Put this man in my car. We're going to take a long drive."

A long drive? What did he mean by that? I froze, shocked by his statement. Surely Burton didn't mean to hurt Sammy, especially after I'd confided in him. Both cops flanked Sammy and one of the men cuffed Sammy's wrists.

"Sammy, tell your men to follow the squad cars downtown," Burton ordered. "Or we can cuff your men and take them in our cars if you want. Your choice."

Head low, Sammy nodded, his eyes on fire. "Do what he says," he ordered his gang. "Don't worry, Johnny Jack will spring us from jail in no time."

Slowly the men from both camps drove their cars onto Beach Boulevard, with Sammy and Burton lagging behind. My whole body tensed as Burton marched Sammy toward his roadster.

If Sammy hadn't been handcuffed, I bet he'd use some of his boxing skills on Burton's face. Shame to ruin such a handsome face.

What did I expect? A slap on the wrist and a scolding? Brother or not, Sammy had publicly engaged in an illegal booze drop—in front of a Prohibition agent. Still, I couldn't help but be upset. I was losing my trust in Burton—and fast.

"Let's follow them!" I told Nathan, tugging on his arm. "Hurry, catch up!" Without thinking, I raced after them toward the car, but my feet kept slipping and sliding in the sand. "I've got to convince Burton to release Sammy."

"I doubt he'll listen to you now. How could he treat your friends that way?" I could tell Nathan was as disappointed—no, disgusted—as I was by Burton's use of force.

Out of breath, we jumped into Nathan's Model T, the car sputtering along as we tried to chase down Burton's roadster.

Desperate to catch up, I yelled to Nathan: "Get their attention! Flash your headlights!" Finally Burton's car slowed down and when Nathan stopped, I jumped out of the Model T and ran behind the roadster, waving my arms like a whirligig.

Burton jerked to a stop. "Jasmine? What in hell are you doing here?" He and Sammy spoke almost in unison, staring at me in disbelief as they both got out of the car. I was relieved to see he'd at least managed to remove Sammy's handcuffs.

Breathing hard, I admitted, "We've been here the whole time, hiding, behind a sand dune. Nathan and I saw everything."

"Everything? Are you nuts? You followed us here after the dance?" Burton frowned.

"What do you think?" I walked toward Burton, my hands flying. "Where are you taking Sammy? He's not causing any trouble. Why can't you give him a warning and let him go?"

"You know it's not that simple, Jasmine. Just calm down and let me do my job." Burton glanced at Sammy's stony expression. "You shouldn't be here. You both could've gotten killed in the crossfire."

"What were you thinking?" Sammy scowled. "This is too dangerous for you kids. Go home and stay there. Nathan, you know better than to indulge her."

"Indulge me?" I flared up. "I was worried to death about you, both of you. Good thing Johnny Jack is such a lousy shot—you were right in the line of fire."

"Johnny Jack was probably shooting blanks. That's a game he likes to play—scare everyone to death so they keep their distance. He's cares more about rescuing his precious rum than killing anyone." Sammy gritted his teeth, eyes flashing.

"Looks like he got away—again. So why don't you go after Johnny Jack and the dirty cops and leave Sammy alone?" I yelled at Burton, the wind whipping my hair across my face.

"Let me handle everything. As you can see, Sammy is cooperating, so you've got nothing to worry about." Burton rested his arm on the open car door, standing halfway outside, one foot on the running board. "Say, Jazz, I had a swell time at the ball and I've enjoyed this chitchat, but now I've got to do my job. See you soon?"

"When hell freezes over," I fumed, turning on my heel. "Sammy, be careful. Nathan, let's get out of here."

Burton's face fell and he slammed the door so hard the car shook. I watched the tail lights fade into oblivion, my heart breaking. My fears had come true: I trusted Burton and he'd betrayed me.

Instead of helping Sammy or even Paco, I'd made things worse. I felt as useless as Blake's blasted hand.

CHAPTER FIFTY

Shaken, Nathan and I took our time getting home, and by the time I crawled into bed, it was two a.m. and everyone was asleep. All night I tossed and turned, worrying about Sammy and Burton, doubting my instincts: Was I such a poor judge of character? Was Burton duplicitous or overly ambitious?

The next morning, I got up bright and early, before anyone was awake, determined to confront Burton at the police station and beg for Sammy's release.

At the station, I barged in, looking for Sammy. Unfortunately, the same guard was on duty. Didn't he ever get a day off? "I'm here to see Sammy Cook. Agent Burton brought him in last night," I told him without any further explanation.

"Hello, Cinderella," he razzed me. "How was the ball?"

"Swell. Except for the fact that my friend got arrested."

"Friend? Sorry to tell you, the jails are empty for once. Burton never came by last night, except with you. I was here, remember?"

"Are you pulling my leg? I swear I saw Burton arrest Sammy last night." I didn't offer any more details.

"It's Sunday. No one else is here." The guard cocked his head, no doubt wondering if I was a ditzy dame or just looney. "Take a look around, toots. See for yourself."

"I'll do that." I stomped off, wandering around the station, peeking in all the jail cells. By damn, he was right—not a soul in sight, not even a plastered sot on the floor.

My heart lurched and I began to worry: What happened to Burton and Sammy? Did Johnny Jack's goons catch up with them? Did his car get hijacked, along with the rum, by the Beach Gang?

I stopped by Sanders' desk, and gave the drawer a quick tug: it opened without a hitch. Did we forget to lock it last night? I glanced inside and bit my lip: The gold cuff links were gone.

"Is that you, Jasmine?" a familiar voice called out, but not the one I wanted to hear.

Yikes! Did Sanders see me poking around his desk?

"Hello, Sheriff Sanders. Looks like you and Eva had a ball last night," I teased, trying to steer him *and* the conversation away from his desk. What I really wanted to ask him was: Are you on the level or are you as dishonest as your cop buddies? Are you going to break Eva's heart?

"I'll say. I didn't know Eva was such a lively stepper. She wore me out!" He gave me the once-over. "So what brings you here, little lady? Looking for your beau? I figured you two would be sleeping late after last night."

"Yes, actually..." I racked my brain for an excuse. "I left something in his car. A compact. Any idea where he is?"

"I assume he's at home, but I'll tell him you stopped by. Tell Eva I'll be seeing her soon at the boarding house."

Whew! As I turned to go, I heard a commotion at the front desk and headed toward the entrance. A woman's voice called out, "Who's in charge? I want to press charges against one of your officers."

With a start, I remembered the young brunette at once: She was Deputy Chief Connors' date for the evening, but she looked decidedly different from the night before. A few bruises and a swollen black eye marred her pretty features, scratches and cuts covered her pale thin arms.

With her pale porcelain skin and wavy dark hair, she reminded me of Holly, Miss Houston, the bathing beauty who'd spent several days in the hospital after her worthless gangster beau beat her to a pulp. Thank goodness Nathan had whisked her away to her home in Houston to recover.

"Didn't I see you at the ball last night? What happened to you?" I blurted out, barely recognizing the brunette beauty. Her eyes had lost any sparkle, and she seemed to have aged by ten years overnight.

Her face reddened and she looked away, then stared at me in surprise. "You were with that good-looking agent, the Fed."

"What can I do for you, miss?" The guard sounded weary, as if he'd seen and heard it all before.

She blinked back tears. "I'm Florence Bellows, and I want to file charges against Deputy Chief Connors. He did this to me. I need to file a restraining order."

"Aren't you Paul's gal?" the cop said. "Now why would you want to do that to poor old Paul? You know we can't file a restraining order against our good pal. Why don't you go home and get some rest? Maybe you'll feel better tomorrow."

"I got plenty of rest in the hospital! I had to have stitches 'cause of that lousy bastard. I can't go home—not after last night. I don't feel safe there." She started crying, trembling all over.

Sheriff Sanders came over and put his arm around her shoulders, leading her into the main room. "Tell me what happened, miss. Florence, is it?"

Naturally, I followed them, trying to eavesdrop but they didn't seem to notice.

"Call me Flo. Paul accused me of slitting his tires last night, can you believe?" She waved her manicured hand around, one hand on her hip. "He was upset that he couldn't make it to some damn booze drop. He cares more about his fancy Cadillac than he does about me. Now why on earth would I slit his stupid tires?"

"I'm so sorry," I told her, feeling more than a little guilty

"Why should you be sorry?" She looked confused. "You had nothing to do with it, sweetie. Paul has a bad temper and he took it out on me, that lousy son-of-a-bitch."

"Matter of fact, I've been conducting my own investigation into Connor and his shenanigans," Sanders told her. "Sorry to say, we can't charge him with assault and battery. Do you have anything else we can use? Anything more incriminating?"

What could be more obvious than a beautiful gal beat black and blue? How could we have faith in a system that allowed such abuse?

Flo perked up. "Sure do. Did you know he takes bribes from both gangs? They pay him off to look the other way. He worked with that barkeep, Fred Blake, who just got robbed at the Black Stallion."

"Yes, I was there at the crime scene. Blake looked like he'd been worked over pretty bad." Sheriff Sanders nodded."What about it?"

"Well, let me tell you, it wasn't a real robbery at all. It was fake. Me and his little Mexican jockey staged the whole thing ourselves. Paco knocked out Blake with a horseshoe—so hard, he passed out. Who knew the little fella had it in him? Matter of fact, I saw Blake at Big Red last night. Some wiseguy blew his hand off."

I shuddered, recalling Blake's bloody stump.

Sanders' eyes widened. "You positive, miss? Those are some mighty serious charges. Now why would Blake go and do a thing like that, fake a robbery?"

"So he doesn't have to give up that loot he won at the horse race in Louisiana." She smacked her bubble gum. "See, his jockey was supposed to throw the race, but the prize money was so good, Paco kept pushing that filly till she won. What a beauty that Sheba is, Blake's baby."

"Oh yeah? Got any proof?" By now, Sanders was so excited, he leaned forward, his eyes bright, like a dog begging for treats.

"Paul kept all the bets in some little black book. If you find that book, you'll have a whole pile of charges." She looked smug. "You may not be able to legally get him for beating the crap out of me, but you sure as hell can get him on lots of other crimes. Johnny Jack paid him to recruit other cops to be on his payroll. Imagine that—getting paid to do nothing."

"Don't worry, I'm aware of the book." Sanders patted her back. "Tell you what, Flo. Why don't you come into my office and tell me more about Deputy Connors and Fred Blake. Are you willing to go on record? Testify in court?"

"Sure, as long as I'm safe. I'll tell you whatever you want to know. Anything to get away from those no-good bums." Flo shivered, wrapping her arms around her torso like armor.

"I can guarantee your safety. The Rangers are transporting Deputy Connors to the Harris County jail today. Besides," Sanders snorted, "he couldn't go far in his Cadillac with flat tires."

I piped up. "Flo, you're welcome to stay at our boarding house for a few days, if you want. My aunt has a couple of extra rooms empty." Least I could do for the poor girl after her beating.

"I can personally vouch for Eva." Sanders beamed with pride. "She's some gal—in fact, she's my gal."

"Why, thank you, miss. I might take you up on your offer. For now, guess I'll stay with my mom and pops."

"I'm Jasmine, but I go by Jazz." I stuck out my hand. "I work as a reporter for the *Gazette*. Maybe I can interview you later for the paper? Of course you can remain anonymous, if you want."

"Sure, I'll be glad to bust their balls. Just say when." She touched her face, wincing. "Let me give you a tip, Jazz. All those baubles and perfumes the fellas bought me? Trust me, it ain't worth the pain."

"After you make your statement, I'll be glad to drive you to your folks' house. If you want, we can stop by your place on the way," Sanders suggested.

"Gee, thanks," she brightened. "I had no idea cops could be so nice. You, too, Jazz."

After we made arrangements to meet, I headed home on the trolley, puzzled and worried about both Sammy and Burton. Why would Burton go to so much trouble to arrest Sammy—but never bring him in? Surely nothing happened on the way? Wouldn't the cops know if it had?

Then it hit me: Johnny Jack's henchmen could have chased them off the road or tried to shoot them and steal the crates of rum. Maybe they didn't realize Sammy was inside the car, but wanted to target Agent Burton. What if they were hurt—or worse?

CHAPTER FIFTY-ONE

At the boarding house, I told Amanda and Eva the whole story, not leaving anything out.

"I had no idea all this was going on during the ball," Eva said, wringing her hands. "I thought Walt's feud was with Chief Johnson, not Connors. I wonder what else Walt is hiding from me?"

Amanda refused to believe anything was wrong. "Don't worry, you'll hear something soon," she reassured me. "Why don't you go to work today? It'll take your mind off last night."

"I doubt it. I don't feel like doing anything. I'm too upset."

All afternoon, I moped, waiting and wondering where in the world were Sammy and Burton. We even called the Oasis but Dino told us the same thing: Sammy wasn't there and never came home that night. "Call us if you hear from him," I made him promise.

"I know what'll cheer us up!" exclaimed Amanda. "Music!"

Sick with worry, I plopped down on the couch in the parlor, playing jazz records over and over, Amanda by my side, not saying a word. What else could I do?

After lunch, I decided to take a walk to calm down and clear my mind. "I'll wait here for any news," Amanda offered, always hopeful. But when the phone rang, I rushed to answer it, my heart thudding.

"It's for you, Jasmine! Long-distance!" the operator gasped, clearly surprised anyone would spend that much on a phone call, especially to talk to me. Was it my long-lost beau calling from Hollywood? An old friend from school? A prank?

The line was so full of static, I couldn't hear well. "Jasmine, it's me, Sammy. I just want you to know I'm safe."

"Sammy? Thank God! Where are you?" I practically shouted into the phone, releasing my pent-up anxiety. "I went by the police station today and you weren't there."

"We stopped by my place instead." A brief pause. "Now I'm in Houston."

"Houston?" Stunned, I stared at the candlestick receiver, picturing his face. "Why did he take you to Houston? Does he think you can't break out of jail there?" I couldn't help but be sarcastic.

"I'm not in jail. Believe it or not, Burton gave me a few cases of rum and let me go."

I was floored. "He let you go? Why? What happened?"

"You know why. He dropped me off at a friend's bar on the East side. Harrisburg, they call it." He paused, and I imagined him smoking his Camels. "We talked about it in advance. Burton knew I'm not safe in Galveston. He promised that if I gave him the goods on Johnny Jack, he'd help me escape." Sammy laughed into the phone. "I shoveled enough dirt to put Johnny Jack away for life."

I smiled so wide that my cheeks hurt, overwhelmed by the news and by Burton's change of heart. "Why didn't you tell me sooner? After the drop? I was worried sick."

"We had to make it look legit. Besides, your nosy pal Nathan was with you."

Good point. "Are you safe there? Where will you stay?"

"Safer than Galveston. My pal and I are going into business together. I'll help run his place while I get on my feet. Burton said as long as I stick with the real stuff, he'll leave me alone. Hey, that's my plan. First-class joint, top-shelf booze all the way."

I felt chills up and down my arms, despite the 95-degree weather. "Atta boy! What about the Oasis?"

"Frank and Dino will run it, but I hope you'll keep an eye on those two knuckleheads."

"At your service. " I suppressed a laugh. "When can Amanda and I come visit you?"

"Soon as I get all settled, I'll give you a call." He paused. "Let me tell Amanda myself."

"Of course. So where's Burton?"

"Burton stopped by the Texas Rangers' office today after he dropped me off. Told me he wanted to make sure Sheriff Sanders was legit. He should be on his way back to Galveston."

"I hope so," I grinned into the phone as if Sammy could see me. "I can't wait."

"Hey, tell Burton thanks for me. He's a good egg, after all."

"I'll be glad to. Take care of yourself, Sammy. Thanks for calling." I waved Amanda over. "Amanda is dying to talk to you."

"Sammy! Are you OK?" she squealed. "What happened?"

His news began to sink in and I felt both upset yet elated. No more weekly visits to the Oasis, no more big-brotherly advice and lectures. I knew Amanda would be depressed at first, but happy for Sammy in the long run. If moving to Houston meant he'd stay out of jail, and alive, then she'd want the best for him.

How could I have been so distrustful of Burton, so suspicious? Yes, they'd planned Sammy's escape in secret—behind my back— but it was for his safety. Besides, did it matter, now that he was safe?

When I told Eva the good news, she squealed almost as loudly as Amanda. I sank into the couch, smiling up at the water-damaged ceiling, seeing fluffy clouds instead of stains.

All afternoon, I sat in my happy stupor, daydreaming, wondering if Sammy would like Houston. I knew Amanda had mixed feelings about his announcement, but I consoled her saying, "He's only a train ride away. Maybe we can visit him in the fall, when it's cooler."

The next day at work, I was still floating on Cloud Ten. Even Mack and the staff noticed my elated mood. I couldn't wait to tell Nathan the good news, and found him by the darkroom.

"You'll never believe who called me from Houston on Sunday— Sammy!" I blurted out, not caring who heard. Then I whispered: "He told me Burton let him go and drove him to Houston that night. Finally he's safe, away from Johnny Jack."

"You're not bullshitting me?" Nathan looked shocked. "Gotta hand it to Burton. He sure had us fooled. Now Sammy can get out of gang life. What's he going to do there?"

"His friend owns a bar on the East side. I'll miss him, but now he can start over with a clean slate."

"Good for him," Nathan smiled. "Keep me posted."

I returned to my desk and started typing up my copy, still dazed.

"How was the policemen's ball?" Mrs. Harper asked when she arrived. "I heard there was some excitement."

"I'll say. Sheriff Sanders and Chief Johnson almost came to blows on the dance floor. Want me to write it up?"

Mrs. Harper's eyes twinkled. "We'd better leave that little tidbit out, though I know it's already the talk of the town. I wish I'd been there! Let's hope Nathan took some good shots of the whole event, especially the fight. Sadly, they'll never make the paper but we'll keep the photographs on hand, just in case."

Just in case someone wanted to blackmail the police force?

I didn't mind writing up my personal experiences at the ball, but what I really wanted to report was the behind-the-scenes action, as well as the public displays of machismo: the crooked cops, the bootlegger sneaking rum, the incriminating black ledger, the gold cuff links gang.

No doubt I'd have to bypass my boss and convince Mr. Thomas to give me a chance, even if it meant working with Mack and sacrificing my byline.

Lost in thought, I was pounding the keyboard when I heard a loud voice across the newsroom, speaking in a formal tone: "Is Miss Jasmine Cross here? I have some police business to discuss."

CHAPTER FIFTY-TWO

Agent Burton didn't need to use that old excuse. I practically flew across the newsroom, ignoring the stares and whistles of the staff, and threw my arms around Burton's neck. All I could manage to say was, "Thank you. For Sammy, for everything."

"Happy to help. Sammy deserves a second chance. Don't we all?" Burton smiled, glancing around the newsroom at the attentive audience. "Let's get some privacy, shall we?"

With a grin at the reporters, I followed him outside, floating out the door.

Standing on the sidewalk, I shielded my eyes from the sun, squinting up at his handsome face. "Sammy called and told me the good news yesterday. How can I ever thank you?"

Burton grinned. "I figured as much with that warm welcome. Let's hope he stays out of trouble in Houston."

"Don't worry, Sammy won't let us down. He's had a tough life, but he's got a heart of gold." I eyed him. "So when did you two hatch this secret escape plan?"

"A few days ago, before your big news. I've always liked the guy, even before I found out he was your brother."

"Thanks, James. He may not admit it, but he feels the same."

"All this time I thought you had a thing for Sammy, but you were just being an overprotective little sister."

"Can you blame me?" I looked around the bustling sidewalk. "Say, what does this remind you of?"

"The first time I asked you to lunch? If I recall, you turned me down. Flat."

"A raid isn't the most romantic way to meet a fella."

"Let me make it up to you. For now, how about a sandwich, so we can talk?"

"Sounds swell," I told him, squeezing his hand.

After we got our sandwiches and sodas—a Coca-Cola for him, a Moxie for me—we sat side by side at the city park. Finally I could ask him a barrage of questions between bites of ham and cheese: "Have you interviewed Blake yet? Did he confess to killing Charlie Parker?"

"In so many words. Paco confirmed that Blake and Torino were fixing the races, and they killed Parker so he wouldn't squeal. He's agreed to testify in exchange for a plea deal. Luckily we've got enough evidence to keep Blake behind bars for life."

"Good to hear." I nodded. "What about the hit on Torino? Who was the killer?"

"Apparently Blake arranged the drive-by shooting as a cover. What's stupid is he used Charlie Parker's gun to kill Torino, which we confiscated at the booze drop." Burton shifted on the bench. "Turns out Charlie's the one who fired at me that night at the Hollywood Dinner Club. If you recall, the two bullets were a match."

"Why in the world would Charlie Parker try to kill *you*?"

"It was Johnny Jack's idea, a way for Charlie to pay off his debts. But he wouldn't go through with it, and missed on purpose, trying to warn me." His smile was sad. "I knew he was a decent guy all along."

"In a way, he sacrificed his life to save yours." A pale gray dove landed on a nearby bench and I threw it some bread crumbs, watching it peck the ground. "What about Chad? Will you charge him with anything? I think losing his dad is punishment enough."

"Technically, he's guilty of assault with a deadly weapon, but we can call it self-defense since he's considered a juvenile. Besides, I hate to waste all that raw talent. With an aim like his, Chad should join the police force, preferably the Prohibition squad." Burton grinned. "He can shoot all the gangsters he wants—in the line of duty."

"Great! I hope he can go to college first." I recalled his exchange with Paco on the beach, and wondered if the jockey had kept his word about Blake's horse. True, Chad was pointing a gun at Paco at the time. "Say, what about the racehorse, Queen of Sheba?"

"Chad is now the proud owner of a fine Arabian filly. Blake lost Sheba when he committed two cold-blooded murders." Burton seemed pleased by the outcome. "He deserves a hobby, something to take his mind off his family's misfortune. Turns out Chad is a natural with horses. In fact, he invited us to watch Paco race Sheba in New Orleans next month. Feel free to bring Eva and Sanders along as chaperones."

"Peachy! I'm sure they'd love to go to New Orleans with us, but maybe in the winter. I hear it's like Galveston, but with swamps."

"Sounds good to me," Burton grinned.

"Sammy told me you stopped by the Texas Rangers. So Sanders is on the level?"

He nodded. "Not only is Sanders a straight-shooter, he helped us follow the trail of gold cuff links. Eva will be happy to know he's applying for Connors' job."

I felt like clapping. "Eva didn't doubt his integrity one bit. Do you think Chief Johnson and Sanders will ever get along? After that boxing match at the ball, I'm not so sure..."

"I heard it was all an act, to expose the dirty cops." Burton took a sip of his Coke. "At least I hope so. Sure seemed convincing."

"Speaking of dirty cops, I was there when Flo came by the station to press charges against Deputy Connors. What's the story?"

"His gold-digging girlfriend ratted him out, but good. We let Flo off easy, since she helped us with both Blake and Connors."

"Flo may be a gold digger, but she sounds like a goldmine of information." I raised my brows. "That gal gets around town."

"You said it." He winked. "Lucky for us."

We'd almost finished our sandwiches, enjoying the cool clear day, when Golliwog showed up, just in time to polish off our scraps.

For once, I felt a sense of calm, of order, the chaos of the last few weeks contained, wondering how long it would last.

"Thanks, James. You made my day. No, my month." I wrapped my arms around his neck and gave him a proper kiss—yes, in public. Never mind the old-fashioned rules at my University of Texas dorm: No ODA—overdisplay of affection.

"Thank *you*." Burton gave me a wicked smile, his slate-blue eyes sparkling in the sunlight. "How about celebrating at the Hollywood Dinner Club tonight? I'd say Sam Maceo still owes us a bottle of fancy French Champagne."

1920s JAZZ AGE SLANG

All wet - Wrong, incorrect ("You're all wet!" "That's nuts!")

And how! - I strongly agree!

Applesauce! – Nonsense, Horsefeathers (e.g. "That's ridiculous!")

Attaboy! - Well done! Bravo! Also: Attagirl!

Baby grand - A heavily-built man

Balled up - Confused, Unsure

Baloney - Nonsense, Hogwash, Bullshit

Bathtub Booze - Home-brewed liquor, Hooch (often in tubs)

Bearcat - A hot-blooded or fiery girl

"Beat it!" - Scram, Get lost

Bee's Knees - An extraordinary person, thing or idea

Berries - Attractive or pleasing; Swell ("It's the berries!")

Big Cheese - Big shot, an important or influential person

Blotto - Very drunk, Smashed

Blow - (a) A wild, crazy party (b) To leave

Bluenose - A prim, puritanical person; a prude, a killjoy

Bohunk - A racist name for Eastern Europeans, a dumb guy

Bootleg - Illegal liquor, Hooch, Booze

Breezer (1925) - A convertible car

Bruno - Tough Guy, Enforcer

Bug-eyed Betty - An unattractive girl or student

Bum's rush - Ejection by force from an establishment

Bump Off - To murder, to kill

Cake-eater - A lady's man, a gigolo; an effeminate male

Carry a Torch - To have a crush on someone

Cat's Meow/Whiskers - Splendid, Stylish, Swell

Cat's Pajamas - Terrific, Wonderful, Great

Clams - Money, Dollars, Bucks

Coffin varnish - Bootleg liquor, Hooch (often poisonous)

Copacetic - Excellent, all in order

Crush - An infatuation, attraction

Dame/Doll - A female, woman, girl

Dogs - Feet

Dolled up - Dressed up in "glad rags"

Don't know from nothing - Don't have any information

Don't take any wooden nickels - Don't do anything stupid

Dough - Money, Cash

Drugstore Cowboy - A guy who picks up girls in public places

Dry up - Shut up; Get lost
Ducky - Fine, very good (Also: Peachy)
Dumb Dora - An idiot, a dumbbell; a stupid female
Egg - Nice person, One who likes the big life
Fall Guy - Victim of a frame
Fella - Fellow, man, guy (very common in the 1920s)
Fire extinguisher - A chaperone, a fifth wheel
Flat Tire - A dull, boring date (Also: Pill, Pickle, Oilcan)
Frame - To give false evidence, to set up someone
Gams - A woman's legs
Gate Crasher - A party crasher, an uninvited guest
Giggle Water - Liquor, Hooch, Booze, Alcohol
Gin Joint/Gin Mill - A bar, a speakeasy
Glad rags - "Going out on the town" clothes, Fancy dress attire
Go chase yourself - "Get lost, beat it, scram"
Hard Boiled - A tough, strong guy (e.g. "He sure is hard-boiled!")
Hayburner - (a) A gas-guzzling car (b) A losing racehorse
Heebie-jeebies (1926) - The shakes, the jitters, (from a hit song)
High-hat - Snobby, snooty
Holding the bag - To be cheated or blamed for something
Hooch - Bootleg liquor, illegal alcohol
Hood - Hoodlum, Gangster, Thug
Hooey - Bullshit, Nonsense, Baloney (1925 to 1930)
Hoofer - Dancer, Chorus girl
Hotsy-Totsy - Attractive, Pleasing
Jack - Cash, Money
Jake - Great, Fine, OK (i.e. "Everything's jake.")
Jeepers creepers – Exclamation of surprise ("Jesus Christ!")
Joe Brooks - A well-groomed man, natty dresser, student
Juice Joint - A speakeasy, bar
Keen - Attractive or appealing
Killjoy - Dud, a dull, boring person, a party pooper, a spoilsport
Lollygagger - (a) A flirtatious male (b) A lazy or idle person
Lounge Lizard - A gigolo; a flirtatious, sexually-active male
Mick - A derogatory term for an Irishman
Milquetoast (1924): A very timid person; a hen-pecked male
    (from the comic book character Casper Milquetoast)
Mrs. Grundy - A prude or killjoy; a prim, prissy (older) woman
Moll - (Gun Moll) A gangster's girlfriend
Neck - Make-out, kiss with passion

"Oh yeah?" - Expression of doubt ("Is that so?")

On a toot – On a drinking binge, Bar-hopping

On the lam - Fleeing from police

On the level - Legitimate, Honest

On the trolley – In the know, Savvy ("You're on the trolley!")

On the up and up - Trustworthy, Honest

Ossified – Drunk, Plastered

Palooka - A derogatory term for a low-class or dumb person
   (Re: Comic strip character Joe Palooka, a poor immigrant)

Piker - (a) Cheapskate (b) Coward

Pitch a little woo - To flirt, try to charm and attract the opposite sex

Rag-a-muffin - An unkempt, dirty and disheveled person/child

Razz - To tease, to insult or make fun of

Rhatz! - "Too bad!" or "Darn it!"

Ritzy - Elegant, High-class, "Putting on the Ritz" (Re: Ritz Hotel)

Rotgut - Cheap hooch, inferior alcohol, poisonous bootleg liquor

Rummy - A drunken bum, an intoxicated man, a wino

Sap - A fool, an idiot; very common term in the 1920s

"Says you!" - A reaction of disbelief or doubt (also "Hogwash!")

Screaming meemies - The shakes, the jitters, to be afraid

Screwy - Crazy, Nuts ("You're screwy!")

Sheba - An attractive and sexy woman; girlfriend
   (popularized by the film "Queen of Sheba")

Sheik - A handsome man with sex appeal
    (from Rudolph Valentino's film "The Sheik")

Scram – "Get out," "Beat it," to leave immediately

Speakeasy - An illicit bar selling bootleg liquor

Spiffy - An elegant appearance, well-dressed, fine

Stuck On - Having a crush on, attracted to

Sugar Daddy - A rich, older gentleman (usually married)

Swanky - Elegant, Ritzy

Swell - Wonderful, Great, Fine, A-OK

Take for a Ride -To try to kill someone (bump them off)

Torpedo - A hired gun, a hit man

Upchuck - To vomit, especially after drinking too much

Wet Blanket - A dud, a dull date or person, a party pooper

Whoopee - (Make whoopee) To have fun/a good time, to party

"You don't say!" – i.e. "Is that so?" "Oh, really? I didn't know"

"You slay me!" -"You're hilarious!" or "That's funny!"

Zozzled - Drunk, intoxicated, (Also: Plastered, Smashed)

BIOGRAPHY

Ellen Mansoor Collier is a Houston-based freelance writer and editor whose articles, essays and short stories have been published in a variety of national magazines. Formerly she's worked as a magazine editor and writer, and in advertising/marketing and public relations.

Collier first became interested in Galveston's gangster era after a trip to Chicago, where she and Gary visited Al Capone's old haunts and headquarters during a "mobsters tour" and drank cocktails at the Green Mill lounge, a former speakeasy.

A flapper at heart, she's the owner of MODERENMILLIE on Etsy, specializing in Deco to retro vintage items.

Collier graduated from the University of Texas at Austin with a degree in Magazine Journalism, where she lived in a c. 1926 dorm her freshman year. In her free time, she worked as an editor on UTmost magazine and was active in Women in Communications (W.I.C.I.), serving as President her senior year.

FLAPPERS, FLASKS AND FOUL PLAY (2012) is the first novel in her "Jazz Age Mystery" series, followed by BATHING BEAUTIES, BOOZE AND BULLETS (2013), GOLD DIGGERS, GAMBLERS AND GUNS (2014) and VAMPS, VILLAINS AND VAUDEVILLE (2015).

DEDICATION

Thanks to Gary, my wonderful husband, who has helped and supported me from day one and read virtually every draft of this novel. To my mother, May Mansoor Munn, also a writer, who inspired me to write at a young age and to my late father, Isa Mansoor, who always encouraged me to do my best.

ACKNOWLEDGEMENTS

Many thanks to my editors, Noreen Marcus and Karen Muller, who read and meticulously edited various drafts. A special thank you to my beta readers, especially to author Leti Del Mar, whose encouragement and feedback kept me on the right track.

Thanks to *Texas Monthly* contributor Gary Cartwright, author of *Galveston: A History of the Island*, whose painstaking research made Galveston's past come alive.

For my cover art, I'm delighted to credit George Barbier, the fabulous French Deco artist (1882-1932). My talented brother, Jeff J. Mansoor, created the great graphics for the covers.

I'm especially grateful to the friends and family members who read drafts of my novel and offered suggestions and encouragement.

(Special thanks to Gary, Mom, Karen, Jeff and Amy!)